Triumph Over Fear

A tale of wilderness survival

By

Karen D. Nichols

Nichols' Books

In Black & White
Florence, OR

Cover design by Karen D. Nichols

This is a work of fiction.

Cover Design: Karen D. Nichols

ISBN 13: 978-1517133504
ISBN 10: 1517133505

Website: www.florenceartists.com

Email: **knichols222@q.com**
http://
noss?u   Web site:htttp://karendnichols.com   l-
keywo   Email:
                nicholskaren222.com

ACKNOWLEDGEMENTS

There were some very special people who helped me to complete this novel. Thank you: Coastal Writers for inspiration while helping me edit and revise the chapters. I took my story to Him, without whose inspiration this novel would still be knocking around in my head, to my dog, Buddy, who always sneaks his way into my novels, (maybe because he snoozes beside me when I write) who gives unabashed love, and especially for my dear husband, who put up with my frustrations, shared my dream, made sure I ate breakfast, lunch and dinner so I wouldn't starve to death at the computer, and for his invaluable input, insights, editing and loving consideration of time to let me create.

This is dedicated to all those who have lost their way. May they find the light that guides them on their journey.

Chapter 1
Where Am I?

Ever find yourself alone, in the middle of nowhere, miles to the nearest town, the only thing you know is that you are somewhere in the middle of Wyoming without a single man-made structure in sight?

I guess I should start at the beginning.

It all started the day Gabriella DiCarlo (that's me—Gabi) received her diploma from the University of Oregon.

I sat quietly applauding my classmates until my boyfriend, William Warren, (Wil for short) was announced and swaggered up to receive his diploma. If I hadn't been graduating, I'd have fallen asleep with some 4,000 robed graduates marching up the aisle. Since there were no Xaviers, Yardleys or Zieglers, Wil Warren lined up as the very last graduate to make his way up to the podium in a most unusual way.

Wil joined the line forming in the aisle by backing up to it. Once there, he faced the audience waving, blowing kisses and bowing while he continued to walk backwards. Once he received his diploma and shook hands, he fumbled with the back of his velcroed robe. Abruptly he turned with his back facing all the family and friends. His graduation robe's backside had been neatly clipped out to expose Wil's derrierre, clothed only in a pair of boxers covered with glitter-red hearts. That jump-started the ruckus.

It shattered a reserved graduating class into a chaos of applause, cheers, as well as flying mortarboards.

My mop of blond curls, freed from my graduation cap, blew and bounced in the breeze. "Free at last!" I shot an arm in the air.

I smiled at Papa as my locks swirled in a gust of wind. He ran a hand through his dark wavy hair. I had taken after Mom with her northern Italian light complexion and my Scottish grandmother. While my brother, Leonardo, was a mirror image of my dad.

Fighting his way through the crowds, Wil elbowed his way to me much like he rampaged on the football field, his carrot red hair bobbing above the throng, reminding me of a romantic slow motion movie scene.

All at once I spun deliriously in Wil's arms, feeling lighter than air facing nothing but our future.

A friend used my cell to take pictures of my diploma presentation, as well as Wil's, which captured every one of Wil's antics. Then my friend grabbed the phone and emailed all those photos to Wil's parents. I don't know if Wil wanted to share his gesture with them, but my friend emailed it off before I could stop him. Since it came from my email, I sure hoped they had good senses of humor. I hoped they knew their son well enough so that any future plans of ours might not be adversely affected by that email.

Papa planned my commencement party at our house just for a few neighbors, so Wil and I wouldn't be taking the same plane. We were meeting up in Wyoming to start our summer hike in the wilds of his beautiful state. We only had a few minutes together as his friends were whisking him to the airport to head back to his parent's ranch in Wyoming. Wil's family wanted him home to celebrate his graduation. As they couldn't attend, they planned a party at their ranch.

It had been a while since Wil and I had been apart. I began missing him as soon as he disappeared in the crowd.

Papa knew about the engagement before me, because Wil ask his permission. This, of course, endeared him to Papa. My brother Leonardo likes him too. With just Pop, Leo and me, enlarging the family would be nice.

When I joined Wil in Wyoming, I would be meeting his parents for the first time. The thought of which caused me a bit of consternation. What would his family say when we tell them we are engaged—too young, not established? They owned a large ranch. My papa merely owned a small house plus his fishing boat.

Summer would be both exciting and fearsome. Little did I know how true that premonition would be?

Last year Wil and I took a survival course. After that, we hiked dozens of trails in order to train for the Oregon Pacific Trail. That challenging trail spanned a distance of about 450 miles. The average elevation rose 5,200 feet. We experienced quite a trek. Beautiful scenery lurked around every grueling turn. Spending that time alone with Wil, turning off our gadgets and only sending a few photos, really clenched our relationship even closer. Though that was one of the toughest physical tasks I had ever undertaken, I became hooked on hiking. What a summer!

During the year, every chance we could find, we hit the hiking trails that were easily accessible from U of O. Slinging my 25-pound backpack over my shoulder now feels considerably easier than it felt on my first hiking experience. All year we trained for the next adventure - conquering Wyoming! To train, I even loaded my backpack with extra books just so walking to class I considered conditioning. Wil couldn't wait for me to experience the beauty of his home state of Wyoming packed with his favorite hiking trails. The way he described them, I couldn't wait either.

We'd be working regular jobs soon enough. Then our schedules might not allow us this much time for an adventure.

I had never traveled on an airplane before this coming venture. I prickled with excitement, but also trepidation, as I packed with everything I thought I would need.

The plan was for me to meet an old friend of the Warren family, Buck Johnson, at the Casper Natrona County Airport. Since he had to pick up some important papers in Casper, he could fly me in his private plane to Douglas. The short hop would take me from Casper to Douglas Converse County Airport where Wil would meet me. I had never ridden in a small aircraft before. That whole idea, though a bit scary, thrilled me. I fancied myself someday piloting such a plane. All I had to do was get over my fear of flying. Maybe I could pick up useful operations info during the flight.

Never very far away from Oregon except our trips to California to visit relatives and the trip to Yosemite, I anticipated this adventure with butterflies.

In the beginning, the plan went off without a hitch—unless you count the dither my Pop was in.

Papa worried about everything parents could be worried about.

I heard all about his concerns on the drive from Florence to the Portland airport.

"Oh Papa, I am inexperienced but not necessarily naïve."

"Yes, but there's a lot dangers out there in the wild."

"Yes, Papa. I know, Papa." Since I turned to the window watching Oregon pass by me, I didn't think he saw me roll my eyes every time he warned me about some danger or suggested his solutions for what he thought I might experience. I didn't want to admit I felt uneasy, too.

"Wil is not inexperienced when it comes to taking care of himself. He'll be taking care of me."

"Yes. Maybe that's what I'm worried about." Papa's last advice, "Watch yourself with that Wil."

"Why Papa, I thought you loved Wil."

"Yeah, I do but I remember when I was young."

I gave him a small punch in the shoulder.

Once at the airport, the flight departed on time. There was a stop over in Denver. I was spared dealing with turbulence, except the frizzy haired lady next to me must've been training for a marathon filibuster: "Then you'll never guess what she did next..."

Fortunately her waterfall of chatter allayed some fears I might have had about flying. My fingers eased up their desperate clutch on the armrest.

Maybe I should have been afraid.

Chapter 2
Thanks But No Thanks

It was a short stop over in Denver. Unfortunately for my ears, the same lovely but gabby woman remained in the seat next to me. A bit of turbulence had me white-knuckling again. She patted my hand. "It's okay, sweetie, I had a friend. . ."

Needing a break from my seat partner's chatter, when she ceased talking to blow her nose, I eased my way between the seat back and my neighbor's knees. "Excuse me for a minute."

With my arms stretched over my head, I stifled a yawn. I glanced around the compartment. A handsome young dark-haired man caught my eye. He smiled a broad smile proving his dentist had been taking great care of those perfectly chiseled teeth. His blue eyes twinkled. That friendly expression prompted a return smile.

My limbs tingled from tensing them during take off. So I cruised down the aisle, stretching as I roamed to the rear of the plane. My sleepy legs appreciated the little exercise.

A grungy man stared at me with his beady black eyes boring into mine. Abruptly, as I passed him, he smacked my backside. I gasped as his knotted hand grabbed mine. I halted with a jerk. Stunned, I peered down at the man's pocked face covered with a steely, gray, grisly beard. My attempt to extricate my hand from his clutch was met with a bone-crushing grasp.

"Pardon me, sir, may I have my hand back?" I glared at the canker of a man.

His whiskey breath soured the air as he pulled me toward him. He grimaced. "Not without a…"

I pulled free and stepped back but not fast enough. That time, his grip felt like a vice. "Not so fast, *chicky*." He sneered, exposing a set of crooked, gaping, yellow teeth, surrounded with pussy, red gums.

His shaggy friend next to the window raised his mini whiskey bottle and leered. His gold tooth glinted in the window's light.

"Sit down, *chicky*. How about a drink?" He gestured to the empty seat between them.

He tugged my arm.

"Let me go!" I twisted in his grip

Steam must've been escaping from my ears.

"Didn't you hear the young lady?"

Startled, I glanced up.

There in front of me stood the handsome young dark-haired man.

"Mind your own business." The grizzled man turned his attention toward me. "Now then *chicky*, take a seat." He tugged my arm down.

Just behind me, the stewardess addressed my aggressor. "Sir!"

"Hey, make this woman stop bothering me." He screwed up his face. "Huh, will ya?"

"Let her arm go." The dark haired man grabbed the troublemaker's wrist. "Sir, you'll have to behave yourself or be restrained for the rest of the flight."

With that threat, the young man drew his suede jacket aside. His marshal's badge shined from the side of his belt. It wasn't difficult to discern that the marshal was also armed. He squared his stance letting the two men see his impressive height tower over my five foot eight inch frame in protection and loom threateningly over them.

I wrenched my hand free and rubbed my wrist.

The sinister man mumbled something under his breath, aimed a squinted glare at me then turned away.

"Thank you," I gave a half smile up to my rescuer. "I'm okay." I rubbed my wrist.

"No problem, ma'am." His voiced raised. "There won't be any more problems, I'm sure." He eyed the two men. "Enjoy the rest of your flight."

I hadn't been called ma'am very often and I usually bristled thinking, *I am way too young at 22 to be called ma'am*. However, from his lips, I found it reassuring.

"We'll have no more trouble from you boys." He touched where his gun was located.

When I returned to my seat, I clutched my armrests. To blot out

---

the experience, I sat back imaging positive thoughts of seeing Wil again. I closed my eyes, and I imagined the two of us, hiking in the scenic
Wyoming wilderness. It'd be like we were the only two people in the world. That thought let me relax a little.

Struck silent only for a tiny moment, my stunned seatmate continued. "Sorry, hon. What an experience. . ."

She rattled on while I tried to get into my Wall Street Journal. So much distressing news sent me to my *Glamour* magazine and I flipped through it mindlessly.

"Bring your seats to an upright position . . ."

Concluding a smooth but tense landing, I unclenched my hands and smiled. *Not so bad.* I had nearly forgotten about the personal assault until I turned around. The two men retrieved their belongings from the overhead bin.

I checked the area, gathered my purse and belongings, but remained seated as my talkative friend, glanced awkwardly at me. "Nice talking to you."

"Likewise. Enjoy your visit." Totally relieved at the cessation of her chatter, I returned her smile as she slipped by me to the aisle.

Perhaps all the passengers felt as I did—let "those" men exit first. I didn't want to encounter them in the airport. I wanted them in front of me—not following me.

As I looked up, the two men had just reached the area where the stewardesses waited to greet the disembarking passengers. The men had donned their ragged Stetsons. The instigator tipped his hat, lasciviously leered then, raised his finger. With a jerk, he traced a slit across his throat. Emanating through his clenched yellow teeth, a grating, scratchy sound, like the ripping of cloth, accompanied his gesture. With a sidewise curl of his lip, he mouthed, "I won't forget you."

Noting the expressions of the passengers who were busy gathering up their carry-ons, it seemed no one else had even noticed the malevolent gesture.

A shiver enveloped my being.

Chapter 3
What Now?

While the intimidating idiots disappeared through the arch, the rest of the passengers continued opening the overhead bins, assembling their belongings and exiting the plane. A variety of scents passed by, mostly perfumes or aftershaves, but liquor had been consumed that mixed with their personal contributions. I waited until everyone else disembarked. Noticing the marshal by the exit reassured me, so I picked up my belongings and headed down the aisle.

His deep dimples tucked in as he smiled. "Are you okay, ma'am?"

"Gabi." I caught his very blue eyes smiling at me.

"Would you like me to walk you out, mm...Gabi?"

"Thank you, marshal." Silhouetted in the light from the open hatch door, his blue-black hair shone like a raven's breast.

"Greg."

"Yes," I smiled, "Greg. That would be...nice." I struggled with the word; 'nice', because I had worried that the men would be waiting for me. I didn't want to sound too fragile like I couldn't take care of myself.

I fumbled with my purse, magazines, and my bag. Greg took the bag. "Allow me."

As we walked out together, I checked the area cautiously for the two men. I exhaled deeply at not seeing them anywhere.

He handed my bag back to me. "Enjoy your visit, Gabi." Greg winked one of his impressive blue eyes and gave a singular wave of his hand.

The small airport in Casper surprised me a little. It was about the same size as the Eugene airport, except the huge murals on the walls rising like the Tetons made sure travelers were surrounded by the nature that evokes thoughts of Wyoming. The murals lining the walls exhibited open range and forests filled with bears, bob cats, wolves, cougars, buffalo, and big-horned sheep painted in their life-like forms.

Though not crowded, there were a fair number of cowboy hats bobbing around. I noted how different the folks looked from back home.

As I approached the baggage claim area, a man waited in the terminal holding a handmade sign, "Gabi".

Was I to assume that he was Buck?

Since he looked somewhat like my attacker on the plane, I was leery until he smiled. His eyes twinkled and his face lit in a hundred weathered lines, kindly wrinkles that testified to the fact that he smiled big and often.

My lips curled in a timid smile.

"You Gabi?"

I nodded.

He touched the brim at the tip of his ten-gallon. "I'm Buck."

Buck perfectly fit my vision of what someone who had lived 60 some years in rural Wyoming would look like - right down to the faded plaid western shirt, threadbare jeans, tattered ten gallon hat, and scuffed cowboy boots. He stroked his steel gray beard, before extending a gnarled, deeply tanned hand for a hardy shake. He eyed me up and down then whistled. "Boy, Wil shor picked a winner." He grinned.

I blushed and shuffled my boots on the slick floor then followed him to the baggage area.

I glimpsed Greg tipping his cowboy hat and waving farewell.

"Thank you, Greg." I waved then turned my attention to the circular luggage mover. *What a nice man.*

I focused on the baggage as it slid down the chute and circled the claim area.

"You got some bags?"

"There, with hot pink ribbons on them." I pointed as they tipped over the edge of the ramp.

As the bags drifted toward us, Buck picked up my luggage and my backpack like they were made of Styrofoam. He helped me transfer my luggage and hiking gear to one of those small airport mini trucks that he said belonged to his friend.

Chapter 4
Where To?

In a few short minutes we were at Buck's airplane hangar. Was his plane an older model or it had it landed a few too many times in a mud flat? I noticed the Cessna logo similar to the one Papa's friend flew out of Florence.

In the expansive hangar, his airplane lined up side by side with several other small aircraft. A shop area took up one side where I imagined the planes were checked and repaired. I hoped Buck had utilized the necessary tools to be sure his plane remained in good repair. I felt guilty entertaining that thought.

Settled in the plane, I fastened my seat belt and examined the dials and gadgets. Pointing here and there, I expressed interest in their use.

"Sometimes give lessons, case you was interested."

I nodded. "Well, I might just take you up on that kind offer. Learning to fly is something I've wanted to do since childhood."

The plane taxied out onto the runway as Buck waited for takeoff instructions. Butterflies flitted around in my stomach. The craft slowly moved into position. Before we received permission to take off, Buck showed me the location of the radio and how it worked.

Takeoff surprised me by being noisier than I had imagined, It also lifted of the ground so quickly it drew my breath away. The rumble of the engine served to intensify the excitement mixed with the fear I felt.

As I settled in with a thrust pushing me against the seat back, I noticed his dog, curled in a blanket, and harnessed beside some equipment in the back. "Hey, good looking. Who are you?" I unclenched my grip on the armrest and stretched over the seat to scratch behind his ear.

"That's Rambo. Been my dog for the last four years. Found him rustling around in my garbage. My ranch is several miles outta town. Don't know how long he was in the wild. Shor was a mess of matted fur, barbs and varmints. Good dog, come and meet my friend, Gabi." Buck patted the top of my gear.

The dog climbed atop my backpack.

"Shake hands."

I took his outstretched paw. "Well howdy, Rambo," I slipped into a slangy accent. "What kind of dog are you anyway?"

Buck cleared his throat. "Not shor. Maybe he's German shepherd, maybe an Alaskan Huskie, wolf or just maybe he's part all of them. Anyway, he's my huntin' pal."

In no time, with the roar of the small engine, we soared up into the sky. Rambo's company took away some of the fear of flying while I ruffled my hands through his fur. Watching Buck's every operation involved in the take off, I observed the world below shrinking until everything resembled toys. All that concentration didn't deter my stomach from doing a few flips.

Flying over the magnificent scenery took my breath away. Snow-blanketed mountains with steep rocky cliffs rose above the broad u-shaped valley. Switchback trails wound down to the valley floor. I wondered if they were some of the trails that Wil and I would hike.

"This country is so majestic and peaceful."

"Don't let its beauty fool you. That there's grizzly country—not to mention the coyotes and cougars. Always keep my rifle handy." His eyes shifted over his shoulder where I saw the gun strapped against the wall of the plane.

"Oh look!" I pointed. "There's a herd of elk grazing down there."

"Big horned sheep country too."

Feeling rather sleepy I began to nod. I had been up since four in the morning. I really wanted to pay close attention to all the flight procedures. Lulled by the mumble of the engine and cradled by the rumble and vibrations of the plane's pathway through the air currents, my eyelids kept drooping. I gave myself a little shake trying to rouse myself. Losing my battle with a snooze, I leaned against the window.

"Hey, don't worry. You can take a nap. I'll wake you when there's something to learn about landing. Be about half an hour."

If he said anything after that I didn't hear it.

A dream danced in my head. *With the sun setting, Wil and I chased each other on Heceta Beach. We leaped over logs washed up on the beach. Our feet splashed up water catching the rays like diamonds scattering to the sands. I'm tripping—falling, falling.*

Rambo's whining, as he pawed at my shoulder, woke me. When I opened my eyes. I shook the sleep away. I yawned with my arms stretched over my head. The view out the windshield spread like an oil painting in the brilliant sun.

"I suppose you're used to this gorgeous scenery, huh, Buck?"

That's when I looked left and noticed Buck.

"Buck?"

He was slumped over against the window.

"Don't tell me you fell asleep too," I smirked as I gave him a small shove. "Hey wake up, sleepy."

He didn't respond.

"Come on, Buck!"

"Buck! Are you okay?" I shook his shoulder and yelled over the roar of the plane, "Buck! What's wrong?"

He stared over at me and grunted.

It sounded like he said, "Off course."

"What, Buck. . . Answer me! Please Buck! Wake up!"

His glassy stare remained unbroken by a blink.

Chapter 5
Help Me

It's amazing how many thoughts process through your mind in an instant when the adrenaline takes over: *What's wrong with Buck? Is he dead? Can I revive him? What can I do? How long have we been in the air? How far off course? Am I going to have to bring this plane down? I saw my mother's face. Am I going to die?*

No, I am not going to die, at least not immediately. The plane flew level. *It must be on automatic pilot.* I sucked in a deep breath like it might be my last. My temples pulsated with each beat of my heart.

I put two fingers on the side of Buck's neck. No Pulse. I had to do something. Even though it was impossible to get in a good position for mouth to mouth, I decided to try. I undid my seatbelt and moved away from the steering wheel on my side. There was little space between his chest and his wheel but I pinched his nose then began breathing into his mouth. I alternated with as many pumps to his chest as my awkward position would allow. "C'mon Buck!" I sucked in another breath that I forced into Buck. "Breathe!" I kept pumping and breathing until I could barely breathe for myself.

When I couldn't blow another breath, I continued pumping on his chest until my hands and arms felt like Jell-O.

It was no use.

Buck was gone.

I looked at my phone for the time. Over an hour since Buck said we'd be there in half an hour. Surely someone would notice we're late. I tried to call but I couldn't get a signal. I stared at the dashboard. Had I listened carefully when Buck explained how to use the radio? I reached for the plane's radio.

Abruptly, my hand jerked away. The plane shuddered.

My stomach flipped as the craft suddenly dropped in altitude.

"Dear God. Help me!"

Was there something to stop myself from flying out of my seat? I grabbed the seatbelt and buckled up.

As instantaneously as the vibrating spasms came, the nose of the plane dipped. The plane aimed downward at a 45degree angle; we were on a collision course for the valley floor. *Did we hit a wind shear? What happened?* It felt like we hit a wall. The nose dipped again to a sharper angle.

Now what?

My heart raced.

My hands trembled.

What should I do?

Being equipped with dual steering wheels meant I might be able to fly the plane from my seat. After inhaling deeply and swallowing hard, I grabbed the w-shaped steering wheel right in front of me. Gripping tightly I pulled back. With my hands slipping in more sweat than I ever experienced, I fought to level the plane in a landing position.

The ground below raced toward me like one of those games on Wii.

A terrifying scream ripped through the plane.

Was that me?

The plane headed straight for a cliff. I steered left. "Gasp!" The wing barely skimmed by a rocky outcropping. With the ground fast approaching, my head seemed ready to burst and so did the plane.

I couldn't swallow the lump in my throat.

It wasn't until then that I noticed. Rambo rattled the windows with his ear-piercing howling, or was that the aircraft ready to explode.

Like one of those 3D movies, the ground seemed to travel at tremendous speed headed directly for my face. Just as we were about to smash nose first into the ground, I yanked back on the steering wheel. I managed to level the plane. The wheels touched down hard. We bounced like a giant ball, connected again with the valley floor then bounced several more times. The body of the craft screeched as though it was splitting at the seams. I literally wagged around like a ragdoll, before I clutched the wheel and held it steady for a few bumps as the wheels crashed against the ground. I ducked down and covered my head with my down jacket.

"I'm here Lord, Help me!"

Dizzying, spinning and disconnected from reality, the plunge and bouncing continued. Is it possible for your whole life to flash before you in a second?

I know that now - it is possible.

The wheels hit the rough ground again, bounced and came down with such force it seemed as though I soared through space, Rambo orbited along side of me. As the nose of the plane slammed into the ground, my head smacked against something.

Things went black though I could still hear the harsh noises of the plane banging, thudding, the frame screeching with me screaming.

The next thing I knew, I dangled upside down, suspended with the seatbelt cutting into my stomach and Rambo licking my face. Blood ran to my head. I felt dizzy. I had to get upright or my head would burst.

I struggled against the belt that left me still dangling.

By bracing myself against the side of the plane I eased my weight from against the belt while I grappled with the buckle. Suddenly it released. That sent me thudding to the ceiling, which was now beneath me.

I pulled the handle on the exit door. Again and again I yanked. Stuck. I shouldered into it with my best football block. It didn't budge. No wonder. The casings around the door were bent several inches out of whack. Tugging at Buck, I saw that his door sustained more damage than mine.

Hugging the whimpering dog, I sat with tears streaming down my face.

"What'll we do now?"

I sniffled and wiped my nose. Then I sniffed again to confirm. "What is that?" The reeking smell overwhelmed me. "Oh dear God. Gas!"

The thought ran through my mind that, at any moment, the plane could explode.

Could we get out? I scrutinized the cabin.

How? I ran my hand down Rambo's back.

I looked around for alternatives.

The scan of the interior showed no more exits.

The only way out was through the doors or the front windshield.

As I searched the cabin I also took a quick inventory of what I would need or could use if I got stuck here for...I sucked in a breath...for how long?

If I got out...that was the question.

Crammed between other parts of the crushed instrument panel, the radio was totally inaccessible.

I pulled my phone out of my pocket. No signal.

How long before someone missed the plane?

When would they start searching?

How long before someone found me?

Would they find me before this plane exploded?

I imagined a search party arriving. While examining the wreckage, they'd find two human corpses and one dog.

I shuddered. I bowed my head. "Help me dear Lord."

Now What?

The Lord helps those who help themselves.

Chapter 6
A Way Out?

After a few deep gulps of air, I stopped shaking. *Do not panic!*

My immediate problem - how do I get out of my confined space before the plane blew up?

I knew I couldn't move Buck with his dead weight piled against the door. His body hanging upside down against his seatbelt, further blocked the window on his side.

A quick assessment—his door was caved in worse than my side. I rummaged around in the back and saw a crowbar sticking out beneath a box. First I lodged the crowbar against the casing to pry my door open. I gouged the end of the crowbar into a gaping bend in the metal. I pulled as hard as I could. As it released I banged backward smacking my head. With my puny muscles, using the crowbar proved a waste of time.

I sunk back in a slump. "What now?" I rubbed my head.

All the minutes I squandered in my quandary, the gas smell swelled. Rambo's shrill barking continued at ear-splitting volume. I braced my hands against the window and willed my body to stop shaking.

"Easy Rambo." I ran my hand down his side, as much to comfort me as to stop his howling.

The front windshield came to mind first, but the nose was driven into the ground, upside down with the wingspan leaving no exit path. My side window looked like the only way out. A crack streaked across it. I kicked with both feet. It didn't give.

After I pushed Rambo out of the way, I scrunched my eyelids tight. Clutching the crowbar, I bashed the window. It crumbled into a thousand particles though it remained stuck together like a finished puzzle. A couple more direct hits with the crowbar sent glass shards flying everywhere.

With my hands covered in my shirttail, I pulled more splinters away from the frame. That produced a space large enough for Rambo and me to squeeze through.

After I cleared away the glass from around me, I threw the blanket over the ragged glass edges of the window rim. I lifted myself through the window and crawled out of the upside-down wreckage.

What are you thinking, Gabi? My brain raced as I looked around. I wouldn't survive without taking some provisions with me. There would just have to be time enough to grab some supplies that were strewn across and around the cabin.

So I eased back in through the shattered window. Rapidly I tossed everything I thought I would need from the plane out onto the ground.

I stuffed my down jacket through the hole, then the first-aid kit.

My hiking gear along with my backpack took something more than a shove. I braced against the seat as I kicked them through the opening.

The two-gallon water bottle went next with a little care not to burst it open.

I checked the grocery bag. Inside there I found a roll of duct tape, a sack filled with a Thermos, a bag of chips, peanuts and some doggie treats. I could check them later.

A box labeled tools rested upside down in the back. That box took a bit of a struggle getting through the space. When I thrust the box through with both feet, it clattered to the ground.

My suitcase just barely made it through the ragged opening. The butt of the rifle stuck out under some greasy machine parts behind the seat. I boosted it through the window.

The box of ammunition lay spilled and scattered among the wreckage. Scooping up the bullets with both hands, I crammed as many as I could in my pockets.

Rambo stopped his barking suddenly. He watched me for a moment then licked poor buck's head, which hung there before him, lifeless eyes still staring.

A shudder enveloped me.

I crawled out and moved all those items that blocked my passage.

Then I went back for the dog. The dog affixed himself to Buck.

I spoke softly. "How did you get out of your tether? Come on, Rambo." I pulled on his collar. He didn't budge. "Come, Rambo! We need to get out of here. Now!"

Stubbornly, he resisted my tugging.

The gas smell reminded me—time was dwindling.

After I grabbed a rope out of the back, I tied it around Rambo's neck. Remembering I had some candy in my shirt pocket, I unwrapped one. With the candy in hand, I teased Rambo up close to the opening before I climbed out dragging him after me.

That's when I saw the flames.

How much time did I have? Would the plane explode? What about all the provisions I unloaded? Much of it still sat close to the flaming aircraft?

With only minutes or even seconds to move the supplies still left beside the plane, I forced Rambo out from under the wing then yanked the blanket from the window frame. I spread the blanket on the ground. Rapidly I piled the supplies into the middle. That accomplished, I held the Thermos in hand, crawled away from the fuselage, while I dragged the blanket. I returned for a second blanket full of supplies as I moved the rest of the provisions away from the craft. I accomplished this, all the while trying to keep a raging dog from going back toward the plane for his Buck.

The first sprout of fire licked the front of the plane. Instantly the wreckage became engulfed in leaping, arm-like flames that encircled the body of the aircraft. I barely had time to bound away, put my arms around Rambo before the whole craft exploded.

A tremendous wall of heat rolled over us flattening me against the ground.

The explosion left my ears ringing. Poor Rambo whimpered and covered his snout with his paws. When I sat up, Rambo curled in my lap practically knocking me over. Panting, he breathed like a steamer. I hugged him tight, my heartbeat throbbing against him.

I coughed as the smoke filled my lungs and burned. I sucked in a horrific smell.

The sight, the smell, the fear of this incident created a moment that would remain with me for years to come.

Stunned, I sat for some time just watching the bonfire.

I looked heavenward. "Thank you, dear Lord. We're still here. Please, Lord, bless Buck and take him into your arms."

I glanced around hugging Rambo against me.

"What do I do next?"

Surely someone would notice our flight hadn't arrived. We would be missed. A rescue party would be coming soon. The fire should attract someone's attention.

I checked the wide blue sky. Nothing flew overhead but the puffy white clouds rapidly becoming obscured by volumes of black smoke.

Am I in shock? I'm not sure how long I sat, hugging the dog, watching the skies and craning my neck around for the rescue party that didn't come.

"Okay, Rambo. What are we going to do?"

He sniffed and whined.

"The best advice for someone stranded is to stay with your vehicle—plane in our case. For now we will be fine—but for how long?"

I remembered hearing something on the news a few years back. A dramatic rescue had taken place. A man had been traveling with his family. He took a small road that looked like a shortcut on his map. Their car became stranded when it plowed into snow bank. They were snowbound in the freak snowstorm. They weren't dressed for the severe weather. That same day the authorities closed the road for the winter.

With no food, water or emergency supplies, they had to make a decision. They had seen no other vehicles on the road. They weren't expected anywhere until the next week. So no one would be worried until then.

Knowing that they should, they decided to stay with their vehicle.

They had no way to know the road had been closed. Therefore no one would even know they were there.

After several days the man decided to hike for help. It took him a couple of days to return to civilization. They rescued him, however when they found his family they had frozen to death in their car.

I shivered at the thought.

Freezing was a distinct possibility in the area. I wrapped my arms around myself, using the blaze to warm up.

Graced with fairly mild weather right then, patches of snow still sat around like mounds of vanilla ice cream.

I knew this wouldn't last. Night would come soon. With the darkness, the thermometer would plummet. I would need to get down to a lower elevation to avoid the extreme temperature swing.

For now I had no shelter unless I could use the limited supplies I managed to save.

"Maybe I can construct something, huh Rambo?"

I surveyed the piles of things I had managed to stockpile. We had a limited supply of food and water. That I knew. There were also some supplies in my backpack.

After all Wil and I had planned to hike.

If only Wil were here, he'd know what to do.

"Okay Rambo. Wil is not here. It's just you and me."

Praying, with an upward glance, "Should I go or should I stay? Dear Lord. Help me."

Chapter 7
An Assessment
Day One

Assess. My mind rolled on super speed. *Stay here with no reasonable expectation that anyone knew where we were? Would help come for me or should I go? How long should I wait before I try to find help? What supplies did I manage to save? If I go what should I or could I take? If I let go of Rambo's rope, would he run off? After all, I wasn't his master. Would he be a hindrance with another mouth to feed or could he help me out?*

Leaning over the dog, I hugged him. "Let's face it. I don't want to be alone, Rambo." I patted his head then scratched his ears. "We've got each other."

Surveying the area, then a glance straight up presented an awesome view. Skyscraper cliffs rose to the miles of clear blue sky dotted with cotton ball clouds tinged by plumes of the black smoke. Beautiful or not, we had crashed at the base of the cliffs in a small narrow meadow that gave me no clue as to where we were.

Were we anywhere near the route we were supposed to take? Would anyone know where to search if we flew way off course? The plane crashed in a clearing. If someone flew over at that moment, they would probably see the smoldering wreckage. Tomorrow the plane would just be a smudge on the landscape.

I sat for a long moment hoping someone would notice the billowing smoke from what remained of the airplane, before I started to rifle through the stuff strewn across the grassy expanse. The black smoke dissipated as it rose into the puffy white clouds while they sailed silently across the sheet of azure sky.

As I sat there, the reality sunk in. *I might be injured.* I ached all over. My head pounded. *Whose blood was dripping into Rambo's fur?* I felt my neck. Drops of blood dripped from my fingers. *How badly am I injured?*

I had twisted my ankle as I jumped from the plane. Would I even be able to hike out of here if I wanted to?

The blood trailed down my neck bringing me back to the immediate problem.

When I touched the wound on my neck, I could feel a piece of glass embedded in the slit. Pulling my hand away, I stared at my fingers—covered in blood. I didn't want to force the glass further into the wound. I needed a mirror.

My purse! I hadn't thrown my purse from the plane. I put my face in my palms. That fact smacked me harder than I thought. My tears welled—what woman forgets her purse? A woman's purse almost has everything you could need.

Rambo pawed me.

My backpack has a mirror! I remembered Wil telling me to pack one for signaling, *or applying makeup which ever comes first* I remember him teasing me.

Pushing myself up from the ground, I discovered a few more aches. I touched my stomach where the seat belt bit into it while I hung upside down. Lifting my shirttail I checked out the raw strip of flesh across my midriff. I rubbed it. "This isn't too bad."

I took a few steps, limping at first. My ankle hurt. With the leg of my jeans pulled up I checked for swelling.

Not broken, not yet anyway.

I made my way over to my backpack, pausing to remember where I might have packed my makeup. I could almost hear Wil. "Don't bother with make up. You won't have time. Besides, you're beautiful without it." I packed it anyway.

The small zipper pocket on the side - I reached in and withdrew a handful of tissues. Inside I had wrapped a small pouch where I had SPF 30 lip balm, lotion, lipstick, makeup containing sun block, the small mirror on the bottom nested with my tweezers and mascara.

First things first—I unwrapped the mirror. As I clicked it open, I had forgotten. The mirror had a compass inside.

Was it luck that I threw in my tweezers? No, it was Wil. "You never know when you'll need tweezers."

"Like I want my eyebrows looking like walrus whiskers," I remember telling Wil.

He laughed. "You won't be having much time for tweezing."

I shook my head thinking how stupid could I be? I would not be thinking about how my eyebrows looked.

"No kidding, Wil."

Useful they proved. I dabbed the wound on my neck with a tissue. I focused my injury in the mirror before I plucked the menacing glass protruding from the gash. From the first aid kit, I found a large Band-Aid that said "antibiotic" on the wrapper, so I covered my wound, drawing the edges of the cut together. *That better keep away infection.*

"Whew! How close to my jugular was that, Rambo?" I patted my neck.

Rambo whined.

It felt less lonely to have someone to talk to as I rubbed my hand down his back. He rumbled a soft sound I likened to a purr. Wil, he seemed to be talking to me too.

The late afternoon sun, cool or not, with my fair freckled skin, I could already feel the heat on my cheeks. I smeared some make-up on my face and tops of my ears and lip balm across my lips.

"Hey Rambo," His ears peaked up. "Let's check what we've got."

He raised himself up slowly then limped behind me over to the pile of supplies. As he sat near me, I looked down at his paw. "Oh Rambo. What's wrong with your paw?"

Taking it in my hand, I checked for injury. With a short diagnosis, there wasn't anything stuck between his toes. It didn't appear to be broken. He whimpered and withdrew his paw. "Okay Ram. Sit." Surprising me, he sat right down. "We'll figure this out later."

Chapter 8
What's in it For Me?

I eyed my backpack and breathed deeply. "Thank goodness I have this, huh Rambo?"

Staples—I reviewed the contents of my backpack. There were eight power bars, a packet of dehydrated camp food left from our last hike. "Mm. Pasta Primivera!"

I had Buck's two-gallon jug of water. Around the area there were several piles of melting snow. *The sun might melt these piles quickly.* So I packed some snow into my canteen along with the other water bottles.

Plus we had Buck's snacks and whatever the Thermos contained. The old Thermos had a large metal cup for a lid. If nothing else I could fill it with water. Suspecting coffee when I unscrewed the lid, I caught a whiff of alcohol. "Eew!" I peered in—brownish liquid sloshed. Whiskey probably. I shook my head and tried to think how this might be valuable: to start fires, to disinfect a wound, to drink myself silly in the worst-case scenario?

I poured some whiskey on the tip of a tissue, which I daubed under the Band Aid on my cut. After removing Buck's snacks from the bag, I found a several apples. I set the bag aside.

Next I examined the tools in the box; a hammer, screwdriver, a box of nails, a pair of pliers, and a hunting knife. My eyes lit. I smiled. A small hatchet rested on the bottom next to a box of fishhooks and lures. I felt the smile grow into a grin. *A small grate might work for cooking.*

I held up the fishing lures. "These will probably be very useful, huh, Ram?" I surveyed the area. "All we need to do is find water." I glanced about at the lumps of snow. "No fish there."

All of these tools would be beneficial, even the crow bar. My mind's adding machine started calculating the pounds. If I had to hike out, every ounce would count. I'd have to decide on essentials.

Buck's hunting knife looked better than mine, so I switched it for the one I had in a sheath in my luggage.

Snorting a facetious laugh, I searched through the zipper pouches in my luggage. Knowing how useless, I pulled out the sundress with my sandals and threw them aside.

My water bottle was empty but I laid it with my belt over the blanket next to the knife and the hatchet.

I stuck the Duck's baseball cap on my head and pulled my ponytail through the back. I held up I my brown plaid Pendleton wool shirt. The color would be like camouflage if I needed it, but I would be hard to spot from a low flying aircraft. I kicked myself—I hadn't brought anything orange or bright red. Wil always brought his red jacket.

With a chill in the air I slipped on the shirt.

The two pairs of wool socks I stuffed into my backpack. That would make four pairs.

Not much else in the suitcase that would be of any use, unless I found a fancy restaurant where I could wear the dress. "Not likely, huh, Ram?" I patted his head, while I noticed a shadow eclipse the sun.

In a matter of moments, overhead, dark swift moving clouds quickly erased the sun. The temperature dropped. I sat up sharply when with clap of thunder exploded. It left no doubt - rain was imminent. I plucked some dry weeds I could use as kindling later. I pulled on my purple down filled parka, at least a bit colorful.

Fortunately the groundcloth was a large one as Wil and I intended to sleep pretty close. Unfortunately Wil was carrying the tent. Also unfortunately the ground cloth was camouflage - not a color that would make it easy for a pilot to see.

I looked at Rambo. "I'll remember that on the next hike." Stopping for a moment, I understood the optimism in that thought. "We are going to get out of here."

Surveying the area, I spotted a large rock. I dragged the ground cloth with Rambo sitting on it for a ride. "Get serious, Ram. You're not funny!" I caught myself laughing anyway.

I rolled him out on the ground. He quickly got to his feet with a shake.

I removed rocks and sticks out of the way for my bed.

"That'll be more comfortable."

The rise of the rocky outcropping began with the ground sloping. I attached my cloth around the rock, staked the corners into the ground thus creating a lean-to with enough cover to leave flaps at one end. I created, in effect, a half of a tent just tall enough to crawl into. "A pup tent, huh, Rambo, my pup?"

After I spread out a couple of trash-baggies with the blanket, I un-bungeed my sleeping bag from my backpack and rolled it out.

Quickly, I dragged all the things that I didn't want soaked and packed them undercover. When I laid the rifle in, I wondered. *What good would a gun be to someone who had never fired one before?* Something we'd have to worry about in the morning. I called the dog then I unrolled my sleeping bag.

We just made it inside before the downpour.

Rambo limped over. We curled together, hunched over, as the sky poured down, pelting our make shift tent.

With water all around I realized - I was dying of thirst. I poured some water in the Thermos cup and slurped some down before sharing it with Rambo.

"Well, boy, looks like we're becoming close buddies sharing the doggy bowl."

I lifted the flap. While he lapped up his share, I wondered if the rain would soak us. Thank goodness for a waterproof ground cover.

"Hey, Rambo. What if the rains melt all our snowdrifts?"

When he finished, I set the cup outside with a few items that could collect water. I knew the lack of that commodity could be a problem I might face.

Before I left Portland, I bought a ham and cheese sandwich. I only ate half on the plane. I almost forgot I still had it in my jacket pocket. "Mm, ham and cheese." I took it out—*smashed ham and cheese.*

"Well, Rambo. I don't think we can be choosy." He sniffed with his nose nearly glued to the plastic wrap as I extracted the squished roll.

He whined a very distinctive, '*I'm hungry*' whimper.

"Just you wait. I'm gonna share."

After I unwrapped the sandwich, I split it half and laid Rambo's share in front of him. I think I blinked twice before his half disappeared. I decided I would savor each bite, as I had no idea what we might be eating soon.

31

I sprinkled some chip crumbs down with a couple of doggie treats. That took him a little longer to sniff while I finished my sandwich then crunched some chips.

"Plenty salty."

Leery of eating too much of the salty snacks that Buck left us, I quit eating them, but for now we had enough water. I listened as the rain pelted down and pinged against our tiny home. Inside our hut it sounded as if someone had dumped a giant bathtub full of water on us.

When I lifted and peered out from the edge of the lean-to, a spray of lightening shot across the sky. It lit our space with an eerie light before another blast of thunder shook me to my bones.

Rambo scooted closer.

After an onslaught of drenching rain, thankfully, the sky let up to a soft even patter. I didn't know the words to very many songs but one came to mind. Wil was a big western music fan so we often sang on our camping trips.

I started singing, *I'll Fly Away* with Rambo trilling along in a very strange, raspy, whimper howl. "Yeah, Ram, wouldn't we love to fly away?"

We snuggled together. I patted his foot. "Dear Lord, heal this paw... and Lord, please show us the way. In Jesus' name, Amen."

Chapter 9
Reality Rains Down
Day Two

The ground raced toward me. Spinning. Stop! Buck wake up! I can't land this plane alone! Buck! Wake Up! I put my arms in front of my face. Rain came down in buckets. Lightning flamed the sky and thunder boomed. Help me Mama! Boom!

I woke in a sweat, heart racing, not sure where I was until Rambo yipped.

"It's okay. I must have had a nightmare." I shook my head. "Reliving our crash with sound effects!" Another clap of thunder reverberated as lightening lit the tent with a flash of eerie light.

I held him close. After a long while listening to the rain, I drifted off again.

The sunbeams rising over a distant mountain woke me as streaks of light slanted through the lean-to's opening casting a slit of light on my face. Or could it be Rambo's little noises, panting, with his moist tongue licking my cheek that woke me? I lifted the flap and checked the weather. The clouds were clearing as the white fluffy clouds raced in and chased away the thunderclouds.

I checked around the edge of the tent. Fortunately only a few of our supplies were dampened around the periphery of our humble abode.

I stretched, feeling a few sore spots from sleeping on the hard ground and the effects of my bouncy landing of the day before.

As I crawled out, Rambo pushed me aside and darted out with his rope trailing behind. He bounded away. "Hey Rambo! Where are you going?" I pushed the flap aside.

"Rambo!"

My heart thudded.

"Rambo! Come back!"

I scrambled out. "Rambo!" I stood studying the landscape.

He disappeared over a rise.

"Rambo! Come back!" Hurrying down to the slope I shaded my eyes and surveyed the empty panorama. "Rambo! Please!"

I tripped and rolled over.

When I rose to check the horizon for Rambo, he was nowhere in sight. Had he caught the scent of something? Was he coming back? No, apparently not. After 15 or 20 minutes of wandering toward where he had disappeared, I realized. Rambo had truly gone. That realization caught me unaware.

Like someone sat on my chest, I dragged myself back to camp and sank to the ground. I couldn't believe how quickly I had bonded with Rambo. My whole body slumped. My heart hurt. Tears rolled down my cheeks. I understood—alone is the worst feeling I had ever experienced. Completely and utterly alone with no help on the horizon, I wrapped my arms around myself in an effort to stop the shaking.

Wiping my eyes, I looked up, "God! Help me! I can't do this alone!"

Panic - the worst thing I could do. If I panicked I would accomplish little. *I can do this.* Sucking in several deep breaths, I did a few yoga, deep-breathing techniques hoping my body would quit shaking.

I had heard that soldiers often counted while waiting in stressful situations. So I started counting backwards from 100. At about 65, I breathed normally and I no longer felt like a vibrator.

Counting reminded me. Exercises! I usually did exercises in the morning so why break a routine that always made me feel better. After my stretches, I counted while I did 25 sit-ups. Finishing 50 bicycle kicks in the air, I picked myself off the ground then did 25 jumping jacks. Next I ran around camp for a few laps.

My cheeks felt rosy. I relished the warmth.

That made me aware of a more immediate problem. I had to go to the bathroom. How opportune it would be if I had been born male. Bundling up, created warmth, but all these layers of clothing were quite inconvenient for taking care of bodily functions.

Once that operation was completed, I began to snap out of my despair and just felt sad, lonely and afraid.

I tried my phone again. No signal. I felt like throwing the useless piece of technology a thousand miles away from me. Brought to my senses by the fact that maybe it would work if I just moved around. I dashed here and there trying the phone again. No such luck.

Not being a tech wizard, I didn't know. If I left it on - would it transmit signals for someone to locate me? If I did leave it on the batteries would be dead. Then I wouldn't be able to call if I did get within the range of a tower. I wished I were more into technology so I would know. *What is the best use of this phone? It must have some aps I don't know about.*

When I slid my finger across, several photos of Wil and me flashed in front of me. "Oh Wil. I need you."

Maybe I could listen to music for a while and leave it on. Maybe that was the best idea. Someone might hear the signal. I stuck the ear bud in, slipped the phone in my pocket. I cast about with the business of taking care of myself.

"Oh Wil, my great outdoorsman, why aren't you here with me? You'd know what to do."

I had to make some decisions. Should I stay here today? The rain had wiped out the last smolder of the plane wreckage,

Since I couldn't carry all the water I had right now, I should stay here one more day. "Yes, I'll stay." In this aloneness I took to talking to myself. I poured the collected water into my empty water bottle. I noticed that while shrunken, there were still snow mounds.

"If I stay, what's next?"

I looked up as if I could find the answer in the sky. Soft sunrays filtered down warming things up a bit. After my exercise, a comfortable warmth spread through me.

I stripped off my down jacket, to my wool shirt. *My makeup kit has SPF lotion.* With my mirror propped up on my backpack, I smoothed a film of makeup protection on my face, rubbed sunscreen on my arms and ears. I smeared lipstick across my lips for a lip-screen. I brushed my hair and put my U of O baseball cap on, poking my curly ponytail through the back.

Holding up the small mirror, I inspected myself with puckered my lips. "At least I'll look good if my rescuers show up."

After a breakfast of chips, peanuts, an apple and water, I brushed my teeth. *If I keep to the regular routine of living, I can hang on until I am rescued. If you are rescued*, trailed in my mind.

Surely by now, we are missed. How can I alert rescuers? Most likely they we would send planes or helicopters to search.

So for my next task, I set about to spell out HELP in big letters using everything I had thrown out of the plane and couldn't use for anything else. However, I drug myself about like a limp rag.

I had to conquer my depression over the loss of Rambo. It sapped my energy. I seemed to be dragging myself along as I tore up boxes and secured them with useless tools to spell out HELP in big letters.

Thoughts of Buddy, my papa's King Charles Cavalier Spaniel, reminded me that I had a dog.

I pictured Buddy racing across the wooden planked floor skidding to a halt to greet me whenever I came home from school. *When I get home it'll be me skidding across the floor to you, Buddy.* I smiled thinking of that cute brown and white fluff ball. *I could use you right now Buddy.*

I stood tall. I raised my fists in the air. "I don't need you, Rambo! So there!" I screamed at the top of my lungs.

I turned my attention to the box of books I had thrown out of the plane. I didn't know why I had kept them, only that books were special to me. They sat beneath the box of tools so the rain didn't soak them very much. I didn't have any idea of Buck's taste in reading matter and I knew I couldn't carry them with me if I hiked - still something in my love of books made me save them. I imagined myself lying on the blanket casually reading a book when my rescuers found me.

I sat by the box and sorted through Buck's *literature.* The top few books were wet from the rain. So I held them away from me while I carried them over to an open area.

From the book covers, I could see where he got the name Rambo for his dog. Buck was a real man's man with books about war, hunting and invasions of aliens. On closer examination, the raw subject matter of many of the books wasn't something that I thought would be very uplifting for me right now, but the books could be useful in my HELP spelling project.

I came to one book, *Cold Mountain* by Charles Frazier. It had a gold sticker on it that said, "National Book Award Winner". *That'll keep my mind off things I can't change right now. It'll keep me busy while I wait.* I threw it aside and continued working on the message to my rescuers.

The last piece of HELP in place, I took off my cap. Leaning back, I wiped my forehead congratulating myself, "Nice work, Gabi."

I piled the rest of the books with some trash that I might use as a burn pile near my help sign. I created a torch to light it for a signal fire. If a plane did fly over, I could light it. Hopefully it would flare up immediately. *That is—if it doesn't rain again. I could always steal a few books back if I need them for my cooking fire.*

Thirsty, I drank about a bottle of water. Afterward I made sure all the bottles and my canteen were full. Who knew when the snow would melt or when it would rain? I just appreciated that the rain didn't melt all the snow.

The day wore on with nothing to do, so I spread the blanket out and lay down. I stretched my sore muscles and rolled for a minute then positioned myself with my head resting on a couple of books. As I lay about reading, I remembered my thought that I'd be laying about reading when they came for me.

Before I got into the book, I checked the sky. A few high cirrus clouds streaked across.

Fortunately the book caught my attention quickly without a thought toward my predicament. It rescued me from my worries.

I munched down an apple and an energy bar, while I immersed myself in the complications of the Confederate soldier character in *Cold Mountain.* His troubles seemed similar to mine as he tried to survive and make it back to his home.

I thought of Papa worrying about me. "I'm okay Papa." Maybe thoughts could travel.

The sun sank lower in the sky with the shadow of the mountains shortening the daylight hours and bringing on the night as the rapidly diminishing sun rays hid behind the mountains. Shaking off a chill, I buttoned up my Pendleton over my turtleneck then zipped into my down jacket. The whole time, two days now, there had been no planes in the sky—not even high flying commercial airlines. I knew they wouldn't be able to see me, but it would show me a direction I could hike toward. I felt my face sag and my chest tighten as I contemplated that thought. A sighting would have given me hope just knowing that this location was on a travel lane.

Camping, so far, had been easy. It was as though I had planned a vacation—shelter, enough food and water, *except now I am totally alone.* With that thought, song came to mind from my choir days. I lifted my voice.

When you walk through a storm, hold your head up high,
And don't be afraid of the dark.
At the end of the storm there's a golden sky
and the sweet silver song of the lark.
Walk on through the wind
Walk on through the rain
Though your dreams be tossed and torn.
Walk on, walk on with hope in your heart,
and you'll never walk alone.

I wiped a tear from my cheek. I listened. I didn't really expect to hear Rambo's wailing accompaniment, and I didn't.

A feeling of calm came over me even though it wasn't hard to see that in a couple of days, adequate supplies would be gone. I would face an uncertain future. How long would I, could I survive?

Chapter 10
Dinner For One

When the sun began to set, I bundled up.

I decided to check my food supply. Sadly, I set the doggy treats aside. They'd be last on my list to eat if everything else was gone. I peered into the chip bag—half full. I found a full bag of peanuts, six apples, six energy bars, a handful of hard candy, two cans of Pepsi plus a freeze-dried packet of Pasta Primavera. I smiled. Did they also have a freeze-dried, handsome Italian waiter? Since I had plenty of water, pasta sounded good for dinner.

Inside my backpack, I found my cook wear kit; a flat pan and lid secured together, where I unpacked a set of airline size silverware, a plastic plate with a collapsible cup. My small waterproof case of wooden matches held only about 15. Those matches would go fast if I wasn't careful. Buck's stuff contained a Bic lighter. Luckily it fit in the case with the matches. I might need both.

I found Buck's Thermos of spirits. I unscrewed the cap and took another whiff. "Whew!" It practically burned my nose. If it were just regular Jack Daniels or such, it probably wouldn't light. However, maybe Buck's taste ran to the 100 proof Wild Turkey, which could be an accelerant. It should burn. I poured some from the Thermos. Tasted the brownish liquid. "Phew!" I spit it out. As if I could tell Jack Daniels from Wild Turkey.

I recalled the dry kindling in my pocket. "What a camper!" I congratulated myself for remembering to gather that before it rained again. I hunted some sticks, branches, and several unused books. Many of the supplies strewn around dried in the sunshine and breeze.

Using the hatchet, I chopped the branches into fire-sized logs. I poured a small amount of the Thermos contents onto the edge of the stacked brush and lit a match. The kindling caught and—Poof! One match had done the trick! I smiled as the dry books resisted then took flame. At least I knew what could quick-start a signal fire.

If Wil had been there it would have been a high-five moment.

Immediately catching on, the grasses snapped and sizzled as the yellow-orange tongues of flames leaped around the books.

The damp branches crackled, warm and friendly then finally flamed up. *Too bad I have no one with whom to share my fire.*

After I spaced out a couple of rocks around the fire, I laid the small grate over the flame. I hoped I had enough heat to boil the water or at least heat it. The pouch of Pasta Primavera contained four servings. With his appetite, that would have made enough for Wil and me. I smiled at how he wolfed down food when we were on our hikes. *Not much different than Rambo,* I lamented.

When the water was hot, I poured in half the pasta. I put the lid on the pan. *Would the smell of food attract any wild animals?* I scrutinized the area for the unseen eyes I felt sure were watching me. I didn't see anything, but that doesn't mean they weren't there.

I shook my head. *Don't be silly.* I busied myself watching the pot. I knew sometimes altitude made it take longer than what it would on the Oregon coast.

The fire started to peter out so, I added some more wood and books. Feeling quite hungry, I just cooked it until the pasta was al dente, Italiano style. I smiled. If I wasn't too ravenous, I could save half for a cold breakfast in the morning. The uncooked portion of the packet I put away for another dinner. I scooped the soft pasta into two lumps. I sampled a taste.

"Just eat it slowly. It might be your last regular meal." I spoke aloud as if I wasn't really alone. "Well, Pomadori's Ristorante this is not. But it is edible. Garcon!" I raised my hand in the air and snapped. "Bring some more wine." I held up my cup of water to the imaginary waiter.

The thought of Pomadori's restaurant reminded me of Wil and I dining there for our first year anniversary, just a few months ago. I closed my eyes remembering the way the candlelight lit his strong face creating shadows in his dimples and cleft. Strands of his rusty hair glinted auburn in the subdued light.

The pasta we ordered was delicious.

I hadn't ever seen Wil so smiley and antsy before.

He called the waitress who carried a bottle of champagne. She opened it with a pop then poured. "Happy Anniversary, you two."

He leaned over touching my cheek before he kissed me. It never ceased to amaze me that his kiss made my heart leap.

—

40

We toasted. "To many more anniversaries."

"I guess I'll have to give you a gift later." A quirky grin crossed his face.

"Oh, Wil, dinner is enough. We need to save that money for our hiking adventure. Besides, I only got you a card."

"Thanks. A card's all I need." That silly grin seemed stuck on his face while he opened my card. The greeting had a red candle in an elegant flower arrangement on the front. Inside it said, "When I hold a candle up to see the future, I'm glad it's you I see. I love you."

"Nice thought, Thanks." After we finished the first glass, he corked the bottle. "Let's go."

"What? Already?"

He held up my coat. I eyed him suspiciously while I donned my coat.

"I have something special I want to show you."

He took my hand and led me out the door. We hopped in his Volkswagen.

Once in the car, Wil headed to town.

"Where are we going?"

"You'll see. Midnight is the bewitching hour."

It wasn't long before he pulled into the parking lot next to the port docks. Boats tied up bobbed in place on the shimmering surface.

I checked my watch. Midnight. *The magic hour?* I thought. The chill moist air gave me a shiver.

The small downtown street had buttoned down tight, probably an hour before, though the lights still tinted the water with various dancing colors. What an exceptionally beautiful night. With a full moon nestled in the velvet sky, glazing the Siuslaw River with its silvery light, the twinkle of stars glistened over us.

Wil jumped out and opened my door. "Madam." He invited me out with a swish of his arm, holding the partial champagne bottle in the other. When I stood next to the car, he opened the glove compartment and took out two champagne glasses. I'm sure my face screwed into a perplexed look as he handed me the bottle and glasses.

Promptly he went to the trunk, opened it, and hauled out a large box as though it weighed a thousand pounds.

"Oh, my!"

"This is later. Over this way, Ma'am."

He led us over to a bench overlooking the docks.

"Let's sit over here while you open it." Once seated, he took the Champagne plus the glasses and traded me for the gift. It certainly wasn't as heavy as Wil pretended.

I positioned the box in front of me on the ground. I untied the quirky bow, obviously a Wil special. I lifted the lid. Inside I stared at one of those silly hand drawn smiley faces like young children draw. It smiled up from the lid of another smaller box. "And who might the artist be?" Lifting the next lid revealed yet another smiling box with an even sillier smiley face. I continued to open as Wil stood silently with a smile that grew into a broad grin.

Inside the third box I found an even smaller box. Finally on the fifth box, Wil whisked the mini box out of my hand. "Let me see that."

His eyes opened wide. "What's this? That's not what's supposed to be in there!"

I'm sure my mouth gaped.

He turned away. When he faced me, he dropped to his knee, holding out the velvet box. He flipped the open the lid and took my hand.

My hand trembled in his.

"Will you marry me?"

The heat of my face turning red brought on goose flesh from my toes clear up to my neck.

The solitary square-cut diamond sparkled in the moonlight. "Oh, Wil. It's beautiful! It's the one I saw in the jewelry store!" I had remarked how I loved that cut. The tears rolled down my face.

"Well..." His forehead wrinkled, "is it a yes?"

I slipped it on admiring it. "Yes. Oh yes!"

After his proposal, arm around my waist, he grabbed me off the bench. He spun me around and around until I felt dizzy.

It would be a long time before I forgot the smells wafting in the night air, the sparkle of the starlit night, the sheen of the harbor lights floating on the river accompanying the sheer joy I felt.

In my reverie, I closed my eyes as I remembered that kiss. A chill ran down my spine. *How long would it be before I'd feel that way again...?*

42

I kept my eyes closed to retain the image of that night.

"So what did we bring the champagne for if not to celebrate?"

He uncorked the bottle. "Here, hold this." He handed me my glass and poured. He clinked my glass. "To Us!"

After we chugged the rest of the champagne down, I felt giddy.

Alone here in the wilderness, I held my ring over the embers of my campfire while I watched the diamond gleam in the red glow. I closed my other hand around the diamond. *Solitary with a solitaire.*

I wished we had told Wil's parents about our engagement before, but he wanted to wait and tell them in person as we had my pop and my brother.

The evening cooled. Darkness settled in quickly, but a full moon floated in the sky, just like that night. Was that a sign telling me Wil was here with me? As the vast sky overhead filled with many more stars than Florence, I felt very small in the emptiness of my situation.

I threw some more books on the fire hoping that would keep me safe. After I brushed my teeth, I prepared for bed by reluctantly pulling off my boots. I rubbed my toes then added another layer of socks to my icy cold feet. I wiggled into my sleeping bag with Buck's rifle tight beside me. Chilled, I settled in with an overwhelming burden of loneliness.

Lying on my back, I wrapped my arms around myself in an attempt to warm the numbness from my bones. Closing my eyes just forced the tears out the corners as they found a pathway to my ears.

My face wet, I clenched my fists. "Why did you leave me here all alone!" My anger welled. *God abandoned me and took Rambo.*

If I couldn't talk to someone, being alone would be too much to handle.

"Are you there, Lord? Can you hear me? I made it through today. Please, show me the way. And send Rambo back, please. I need you. In Jesus' name, Amen."

Missing Rambo's comfort, I tossed and turned until I finally felt my hands and feet warming up. I fell asleep.

Wil! He was running toward me! Wil you're here! I am going home! Bushes in my way were slowing me down. Wil! Branches fell in my path. Brambles spread in front of me creating a barrier.

I tripped falling end over end down a huge precipice. I lay face down in the bushes.

No I wasn't saved. It was a dream. I lay face down in some grasses tracked into my tent. When I rolled over, I brushed off my face.

After I lay back down it took a while to become drowsy. Nearly asleep, my eyes popped open. I heard a noise outside. I lay perfectly still, listening. Slowly I pulled the gun out of the sleeping bag.

More sounds. I sat straight up.

"Rambo." *He's come back.* "Rambo, is that you?"

If he's there, he would have come running, wouldn't he?

Outside I saw a moving shadow. My pulse quickened. The hairs at the back of my neck prickled. If I crawled out now I'd be at a disadvantage before I could stand to take aim at whatever it was.

With my heart hammering, I slowly laid the tent flap back. The fire flickered, all but out. In the moonlit distance, I saw another movement at the edge of my vision.

I listened.

The silence was deafening. For a moment I lay paralyzed.

Soldiers in the movies crawled along belly down, pulling themselves ahead with their elbows, while they held their rifles in front of them. I removed the safety on the rifle. On my belly, I elbowed myself forward, out into the open.

My rifle raked the horizon as I searched for the origin of the sounds.

Something moved.

I bit my lip.

Chapter 11
A Surprise

Flat on the ground, I surveyed the area. With the rifle swaying slowly from side to side, I inched forward. The full moon glowed in the sky casting long eerie shadows. Grass ruffled in the breeze.

Maybe that's all it is—just a little wind.

That's when I saw the outline of the creature. It's head lowered. What was it? Not a dog, like Rambo, but bigger and scruffier. A wolf? It stood like a statue.

A suffocating stillness surrounded me.

Silently he crept toward me, each step steady and purposeful. His paws pressed almost noiselessly into the grass. Was that his breath I could hear, or the soft swish of the grass? The scene played out like a slow-motion movie sequence with me in the starring role.

Blood coursed through my heart one chamber at a time with me feeling each pump.

My hands twitched.

The star always wins? I thought with a question in my mind.

More questions careened through my brain.

Should I scream? Could that scare the beast off? Or would he charge toward the threat?

I saw his eyes glint in the moonlight. *Was I supposed to stare into his eyes to scare him off or would that antagonize him, making him more aggressive?* I couldn't remember what I'd been told about wild animals. But I couldn't take my eyes away. They were glued to his stare.

He raised his muzzle and howled.

Do wolves hunt alone?

He snarled with a growl that sent a chill ricocheting through my body.

I froze in the eerie silence that followed. A cold sweat broke out across my neck. I quivered with muscle spasms.

Would that howl bring a whole pack?

—

Crouched on the ground I knew I appeared as though I were a small animal. *Should I stand up and make myself big? It couldn't hurt, could it? Unless that should trigger an all out assault. Big. Big is better.*

Slowly, I stood, stretching my arms up and outward, growing myself as large as I could in this five foot eight body.

He froze though his eyes still fixated on me.

A scream. Could it scare him or stir him to attack? If nothing else maybe someone would hear me if I screamed. My throat burned as I screeched my loudest screech.

After a momentary pause, the wolf raced toward me in leaping strides.

Stunned, I aimed the rifle. I focused, trying to use the sight at the end of the barrel.

Tremors spread through my body. Frozen in time, I couldn't pull the trigger. *I'd have to make the first shot count. But how can I with the gun shaking.*

Should I aim at the head or a little lower for a chest shot? My hands dripped in sweat. *Should I wait until it's closer or shoot now?* How many seconds elapsed as these questions flashed thought my mind?

The rifle shook when I squeezed the trigger. "KaBlam!"

The butt of the rifle recoiled, smashed into my shoulder then flew out of my hands. I fell to the ground.

I missed.

Seconds ticked off.

He's coming for me.

Vulnerable, I lay sprawled on the ground. My ears rang, as I sat up and scanned the area.

Now about ten feet away from me, the startled wolf stood absolutely motionless. He wasn't scared off. He glanced around then zeroed in on me again. Deliberately, he padded toward me.

I remembered seeing dog trainers on TV. They always guarded themselves by putting their forearm up to block their face and throat. They wore a heavy cover on their arm. I stretched out and grabbed my blanket. I sucked my hand inside the jacket then I wrapped my forearm already thick with my down jacket.

Just then the wolf closed in speeding up.

He moved close enough for me to see his golden eyes glint in the moonlight.

With a pouncing leap, the beast soared toward me. His growls made my hairs tingle. His mid air silhouette towered over me. I flung my arm upward.

Chapter 12
Help me.

Just in time. My arm blocked my face.

His powerful jaws clamped down on my forearm with such force, I thought my arm had broken. His weighty body pounced on top of me, knocking away my breath.

My back slammed to the ground. My head whiplashed as it smacked the ground with a thud.

I think I blacked out for a moment. The fierce attack brought me back to reality. My arm secured in his jaws, the wolf shook his head from side to side. It felt like my arm would yank from my shoulder socket.

Tussling with his unbelievable strength, I tried to shake him off. My arm ached and throbbed.

I weakened under his weight. My arm collapsed. My chest compressed. I could barely breathe.

His bared teeth grimaced inches from my face as growls rolled in his throat. His hot, rank breath came in short pants as he gnawed on my arm. His jaws were so strong I thought he could rip off my whole arm.

His muzzle nearly butted against my face.

When I noticed the white cross of fur on his forehead, I said a quick prayer. "Give me strength, Lord."

As I shifted to the side, I felt the rifle butt with my free hand. I stretched to get my fingers around for a firm grip. The wolf shifted its weight. I pushed the wolf off my arm, however he quickly chomped down. I struggled again for the rifle, dragging it closer. With all the strength I could muster, I slammed the rifle butt into the side of the wolf's belly.

Before I could move away, he yelped, loosened his grip then bit down like a vise.

"Ahhhh!" I screamed, with no affect on my attacker.

This time I would aim higher.

I clenched my teeth, squeezed my eyes shut then screamed as I battered the butt into the side of the wolf's head.

He collapsed on top of me.

Dead weight. *Was he unconscious? Or was he playing with me?*

I pried my arm from his mouth as his jaws slackened.

After rolling this way and back again, I thrust him off to the side of me.

Gasping for air, unsteadily, I stood.

The wolf shook his head. Only stunned.

I held the rifle upside down in my hands. I kicked him as powerfully as I could. I jammed him hard in the gut with the rifle butt.

When he rose, I swung the gun like a baseball bat.

I missed his head but connected with his neck. He flew sideways.

The wolf whimpered, rose, turned and glared at me.

I glared right back at him. At the top of my lungs came a roaring screech, "Get outta here!"

He loped away in a fast trot.

The gun slid from my hand. I slumped to the ground, shaking all over. My lungs fought for air.

When I sat up, I examined the horizon. I couldn't see anything moving.

Was he really gone?

I could have shot him as he escaped. Why didn't I?

Would he return with his pack?

I pushed myself up barely able to use my right arm. When I stood, I ached all over. I bent and picked up the rifle. I realized a weapon becomes totally useless to someone who's not fired a gun before.

Cradling my aching forearm around the gun, I dragged my tattered blanket back into my lean-to. I bundled up inside with the rifle in my grasp. I faced outward and sat there trembling until the light of dawn.

We were only on day three. What more could happen before I was rescued?

Chapter 13
A Little Practice
Day 3

A short time later, I awoke. Crinked in a sitting position, I stretched out my legs then leaned against my backpack. Sitting upright with the rifle in my lap all night left me stiff and sore. I stretched and flexed. My neck ached as I rolled my head around trying to ease the stiffness. My right arm! I could barely move it. My shoulder stabbed me with pain. I recalled the recoiling rifle butt jamming me after I fired. My forearm sported a reddish purple bruise stretching from my fingers to my elbow, the residual damage from the wolf's powerful jaws. I flexed my fingers and rotated my arm. Nothing broken. Everything painful.

I checked the time, six. No signal on my cell.

Chilled, I set about gathering twigs and leaves to start up the fire. I remembered to tuck some dry ones in my pocket. With kindling, a few branches chopped, a couple of books, plus a splash of Buck's elixir, the flames soon leaped.

I had heard somewhere that exercising helps the muscles recover faster. Limited by my injuries, I forced myself awake with sit-ups and limited jumping jacks, though with less gusto and fewer repetitions. I grunted and groaned through the pain. Warming up, I took a couple of laps around the camp.

The leftover pasta still sat, a glutinous mass clumped in the skillet, so I heated it up. I opened a can of Pepsi and washed down the clumps of pasta.

If I decided to travel, I knew I couldn't carry all of my water. The two-gallon, plastic water bottle would be heavy and cumbersome. I had a canteen, two smaller water bottles and could fill one more extra bottle.

With the excess water, I splurged. After cleaning my food utensils, I heated water and washed up. Mom used to call a spit bath

Chris and Pits.

I imagined I saw wolf spittle clinging to my cheeks. *What a feeling to have a clean face!*

When I brushed my hair, I felt the soreness at the back of my head. Flexing I remembered how I had hit the ground. That thought kept me eying my surroundings lest the wolf return.

I laundered my underwear and hung them with my washcloth on sticks I staked in the ground. They'd dry in a sunny patch, out of my way. I smiled at my pink flowered bikinis fluttering in the breeze. Then I ignored them while I planned my day.

I discovered an interesting feeling. I had nothing scheduled to do. Days like that were few and far between with classes, studying and my job waiting tables. Unencumbered with obligations would be nice once in a while.

As I dressed, this time I drew on my silk long-john underwear beneath my clothes. Since no one was around, I didn't stifle my winces and groans. Every move was painful. Layering, I could thwart the cold until the sun crawled over the peaks to warm the air. Then I'd have to strip down again before the chill of night prompted a repeat layering.

Still there was no sign of aircraft or a rescue team. I checked my phone. I dashed here and there hoping a new position would locate a signal but no luck.

There seemed to be no reason to stay at my present location, out in the open. I felt vulnerable for predators, but with little prey for me to hunt or trap. I would have to make my way to a better place then just maybe I would find evidence of inhabitants other than wild animals.

"Today I pack and tomorrow, if I am not rescued, I will trek out of here."

I looked at the rifle poking out of the lean-to. I found the bullets and counted them. Twenty-three. There were still some in the rifle. I hated to waste any of them, but I needed to figure out how to fire the weapon without maiming myself and with more accuracy than in my last shooting experience. There must be more to holding the rifle. *Pressing it against my shoulder?*

At least this time I would be expecting the recoil and not drop the weapon. I made a pad of a rolled-up sock and sewed it into the shoulder of my shirt.

My first shot last night completely missed the wolf. *But by how far?*

How bad could my aim be? I excelled at batting in baseball. I shot a great game of pool because my brother knew how to teach skills to someone with no skill. Leo had also taught me to use a slingshot and his bow with pretty good accuracy. At one time I wished I were an only child. Leonardo got to do everything I was too young to do. What I wouldn't give to have Leo here right now. He was a crack shot with his rifle. Having a big brother around for protection can't be overstated. I could always depend on him. Even when he chided and teased me, I always knew he was on my side.

A neighbor boy, Teddy, loved chasing me. One day, Leo grabbed a hammer and chased after us. Poor Teddy shook in his tennis shoes when Leo threatened to create a new orifice if he didn't leave me alone.

I needed target practice—the only way I would feel confident, if I experienced another time like last night. Just thinking about what could have happened sent a shudder through my body.

I looked around for something to use for a target. A bunch of stuff still lay strewn around the campsite.

I smiled thinking about Mom. "What a mess! Clean your room, now!"

After I emptied the last of the books from a cardboard box, I set it up as my target. I stepped back about 60 feet. That seemed about how far I figured I might squeeze off two shots before a charging beast might come at me.

I stood practicing at what I thought was a suitable stance. My right arm quivered with the residual affect of the wolf's attack on my forearm. I willed myself steady.

"All right now, focus and pull the trigger and don't let the recoil blast you."

I concentrated and imagined I could stop that wolf in his tracks.

Without shaky hands, I squeezed the trigger deliberately.

The recoil knocked me back, but only a small step. I knew I hit the box because it moved if only just slightly. *I hit it!* Still holding the rifle, I raised my left arm, "Yeah!"

I trotted over and checked. Had that been an animal, I'd have missed because the bullet just scrapped the corner of the box! With one more shot blasting the center of the box, I realized this time I didn't react to the recoil.

After I set the Pepsi can on top of the box, I stepped back to about 70 feet. Feeling pretty confident, I squeezed off another shot. A miss! *Maybe it only missed by a grass blade.* I set it up again. Poised, I assumed my stance. I took aim and fired. The next shot sent the can flipping in the air.

While not perfect, my marksmanship would just have to do. I knew that if I needed to shoot, I might not have that much time to take aim, but I didn't want to waste any more ammo.

Next I sat down with my backpack. I sorted through everything, discarded useless things and folded all its necessary contents compactly noting where I packed everything.

One pocket contained a pack of cards. I set them aside for later.

I discarded my cotton socks and replaced them with wool ones. I remembered that cotton held more moisture against the skin—not a good thing if it rained.

Vacillating, I packed my small sketchbook and a lightweight container of art supplies that would only take up about the space of a paperback book.

I ripped up a blouse and made a rifle sling strap. My belt easily adapted to carry the hatchet, hunting knife, water bottle and my slingshot. I zipped some small stones in a jacket pocket.

My Swiss Army knife—I had almost forgotten about it. I opened it to flip out all the different blades to check what tools were in there. *The scissors might come in handy.* Having the knife zipped into another pocket of my down jacket would make me feel safer.

For tomorrow, I left out my waterproof pants to trade for my jeans. Once the denim got wet, I'd never get them dry. Too bad, I'd hate to leave my favorite jeans behind, but denim is heavy to carry.

As I repacked the backpack, I looked over my shoulder. Several birds circled around my flowery underwear and the wash pan I had left on the rise. I didn't know what kind of birds, but maybe raptors?

A sudden thought shot into my head. *Dinner!*

Was it possible to capture one of these birds? At home I'd caught a bird in the house once by thrusting a towel over it. That is probably not going to work without a wall to stop their flight.

I'd have to move very slowly so as not to scare them away.

My skills with a rifle aimed at a smallish target were marginal and besides, I thought maybe a bullet would make mincemeat of the bird leaving nothing but a few feathers to eat. I stood perfectly still.

In slow motion, I gripped my slingshot and placed a small stone in the sling. I took aim, pulled back and released. *Zap!*

Just as the bird dropped from the sky, I looked at the rise.

What was it?

What leaped up in the air?

Another wolf?

Did he come back?

I grabbed for the rifle. *How much time did I have?* This time he was he much closer.

What was it?

I braced with the rifle aimed at the creature loping toward me.

Chapter 14
Yeah!

Then the growling or whimpering started—whimpering? I thought I recognized that tone. The wolf padded closer, a bird flopping in its jaws. He's not going to attack with a bird in his mouth. *It's smaller than that wolf.* I lowered the rifle.

The sounds—whining—like Rambo? Not growling. A purring, a whine? I recalled Rambo's whining in the plane. "Rambo?" I squinted. "Rambo is that you?" He whined. I let go of the gun. "Rambo, it is you." He trotted toward me. I gathered him up in my arms, the tears blurring my eyes. "I could have shot you, you silly dog."

I sat up. "You came back." I jiggled the fur around his jowls.

Rambo dropped his bird next to me. He focused his eyes on mine, still whining, panting with his tongue hanging out as if to say, *Did I do good? Huh? Did I?*

Then he lunged at me putting both paws on my shoulders knocking me flat on my back as he licked tears off my face.

I pushed him back, "Ew! Don't lick me with dead bird breath!"

We tussled around and ended with a tummy rub. "I am so glad to see you!" The ragged rope was still tied around him. I untied it. "Okay. You stay or you go. You are free. But I never want you to leave me again. You hear!"

I tucked the dead bird's feet in my hand. Rambo followed me while I meandered over and picked up the bird I had nailed with my slingshot. I added that to the one that dangled from my hand. I raised them up. "Well we did it ol' boy. Albeit small, two birds for dinner!"

I scratched behind his ears. "Are you back for good?" He sniffed at our prey. "Maybe we should have lunch before we clean these guys up for dinner." I whisked the birds off the ground and tucked them into my suitcase so Rambo wouldn't devour them.

Roasted fowl is a better dinner entree than lunch.

I wondered if Rambo had found himself some wild creature for his meals in his absence. I was surprised that he would let me share his bird.

His doggy smell comforted me. I sniffed as I rubbed his back.

I got out the peanuts, chips, doggie treats, an energy bar, and the apple out of the lean-to. We dined in style sitting on the grass with the lunch spread on my sundress as a ground cloth. When I finished the apple I tossed the core aside. Rambo scrambled after it.

While I put the food away, Rambo hung around the tent. He kept sniffing at the blanket that I'd wrapped around my arm the night before. "Do you smell that wolf, ol' boy?"

I searched through my stuff to find the roll of tape. "Boy, duct tape is handy stuff."

That afternoon I spent time creating a saddlebag pack for Rambo. Since I had a couple of thermal space blankets, I hadn't planned to take the real blanket because of it's bulk, but it made a good saddle blanket for Rambo. We'd have it if needed. Who knew how cold it might get. I held it up and checked the lacey bite pattern left by the wolf's attack. Not needing to be reminded of that wolf-tussling experience, I ripped that tattered edge away leaving a smaller blanket just the perfect size. The cotton socks made sleeves for the extra water containers and the apples. I could use my regular belt to strap it on.

I did a practice packing to see if Rambo would shake it off while we hiked. He shook it once or twice. I gave him some dog treats when he walked along beside me, accepting the challenge of his backpack. "Good boy, Rambo. You're a smart dog, huh?"

I packed a few more things I thought we might need.

Finally Rambo wouldn't leave the suitcase with dinner birds stashed inside, so I began plucking the feathers out of them. Cleaned and ready to go, I rubbed the last of the potato chips on them for a little salty flavor. I built a fire, skewered the birds with a stick to suspend them over the fire between two Y-shaped sticks. Rambo thought the potato chips were a special treat, but I couldn't fathom eating raw bird-juiced-chips. Maybe later as our food dwindled, I would change my mind about what I would and wouldn't eat. *Not yet.*

For tonight, we didn't eat pheasant under glass but we ate our game birds with great relish. "Mm! Finger, *or paw licking*, good!" Rambo held his bird clamped in his paws gnawing off bits and pieces then licking those paws. I hoped the bones he devoured wouldn't hurt him. He gnawed on the bigger ones and crunched them in his jaws.

"You're wild, though, aren't you, boy?"

Settling down that night, I felt guilty for my anger at God.

I patted Rambo. "After all, He did send you back to me. I just have to trust." I thanked God for the return of Rambo and our good fortune as a hunting duo. I could see why Buck had called him his huntin' dog. "Maybe that's why you share, huh Ram? Did Buck teach you?"

The campfire glowed with red embers so I tossed on another log. Cinders like baby stars flitted into the sky. I sang a couple of songs with Rambo's wail rising to the skies as he sat next to me.

Not long after our songfest, we cuddled into our humble abode. I dozed off in a fitful sleep.

Darkness spread over me. The rain splashed down.

I could barely see anything but the lights glaring back from the slick street as they dimmed into the curves of the road.

Like slow motion, we skidded sideways. "No! No!" The semi truck barreled head on toward us. I threw my hands up in front of my face. "Ahh!" screamed, "Mama!" The car spun out of control round and round dizzying me in its spin "Mom! Stop! Help me!"

Shaking, I sat straight up with Rambo howling an ungodly yowl. *Had I been screaming?* I wrapped my arms around him. "It's okay, Ram. It's okay." I buried my face in his fur. "Just a bad dream."

As I lay back down still atremble, I thought, *"What will tomorrow bring?"*

Chapter 15
We're Off
Day Four

Sleep came again. I rested peacefully wrapped in the warmth and the companionship of Rambo. I woke to his moist tongue washing my face. "Okay, all right! I'll get up!" I pushed him away then sat up.

He whined.

"Ready to start day four, huh buddy?"

I peeked outside. The sun shone brightly and the patches of snow were melting fast. It would be a good day to take a hike.

We wrestled around for a few minutes before I crawled out of my sleeping bag with the dog squeezing past me.

For a moment I furrowed my brow wondering if he would dash off again. Instead, he shook himself off then pawed at me as if to say, *Get up lazy bones.* Stretching I turned to Rambo. "Hey, boy." I smiled, "My arm feels better after the attack from your brother beast!" I shrugged. As I lifted my sore arm in the air, I rotated my shoulder to try it out. "A little better, boy. I sure could have used your help with that wolf."

Exercises came next. Just into my third jumping jack, I glanced over at Rambo. I broke out laughing. "Are you mocking me?" He rose up on two legs jumping with me. I bent over I laughed so hard. When I lay down to do my sit ups, Rambo thought he'd give me more bath time with another good face licking before I wrestled with him and told him *no* in very uncertain tones.

Rambo thought it was great fun to race around the camp when I did my run. Afterward we collapsed in a great heap tussling around.

Before my morning wash-up ritual, a thought seeped into my mind. I wouldn't be able to carry all the water I had. *This could be my last Chris and Pits until I found a water source.* So I did it up good as I washed my hair.

"Maybe there'll be plenty of snow patches on our way, because

---

58

the shampoo sure felt good!"

I patted Rambo's head. "Oh, Rambo, I'm so glad to have you back. But I think it's time to get breakfast and then pack up."

I poured us each a cup of water, dumped a third of Rambo's treats in a cup, and peeled the energy bar for me. Rambo's food disappeared before I finished unwrapping mine. He sat licking his snout while I finished my apple.

"You know, the rest is yours." I tossed the core up toward the blue sky. "Fun to watch you catch it mid-air!" He leaped.

I folded our makeshift tent, filled my backpack and loaded Rambo's saddlebags.

Our lean-to tarp and the space blanket I used for a ground cloth were damp with dew from the grass. I shook them then laid them out to dry over a bush while I packed up the rest of our camp.

While I let him finish gnawing his apple core, I brushed my teeth and started planning out our day. First I needed to create an arrow at the end of my help sign. "Our rescuers need to know which way we went," I raked my fingers down Rambo's backside.

Following that task, I sat next to my backpack and checked our food supply. "Pasta Primavera tonight." I scratched the dog's ears. I counted out 5 energy bars. Rambo's treat bag—maybe he had two meals or three—if you count the apples. Rambo's nose sniffed on super speed. The chips were gone except for the crumbs that I shook into my hand. I licked them up with relish. We still had four apples. After we consumed that supply of delectable treats, I had no idea what we'd do.

I stared up at the sky, as though I'd find an answer there.

"Okay, Rambo. You're carrying the apples." I knelt. "Come here, boy." He whimpered as he padded over to me. I guess his whimpering, whining or whatever that noise he crooned must be his way of talking to me. Again the aroma from the blanket put Ram's nose sniffing on super speed. "It's okay Ram. I bested that beast! Though I could have used your help."

With the blanket folded just right, the saddlebags on, I packed the apples, two on each side tied in socks. I checked the sling I made for the rifle.

"Rambo, you're such a good boy." He sat quietly while I loaded him up. When I rose, he followed me over to where I finished packing my backpack with the water bottles.

Just before I slung my belt around me, I added notches to note the days I had been here and planned to do that each day until I was rescued. I fastened the belt around me, loaded with the hatchet, knife, slingshot, and my water bottle securely in place. The lean-to tarp and space blanket were dry. I folded them tightly so they'd easily slip in the side of my pack. I bungeed my sleeping bag to the top of my backpack.

For my last task, I made sure to bury any garbage that an animal wouldn't eat, wrappers, etcetera. There wasn't much when I saved the candy wrappers for fire starters. While I was down on my knees, I remembered a prayer that my gran used to pray, one that she said her grandmother prayed with her.

A visual picture of my Scottish grandma played like an old movie, her gnarled hands, palm to palm with her smile wrinkles sprayed across her face as she repeated the words. Mine blended with hers.

May God make safe to me each step
May God make open to me each pass
May God make clear to me each road
And may He take me in the clasp
of His own two hands

The weather warmed, so I took off my down jacket and did a few stretching exercises. With my jacket attached to the top of my rig, I hoisted the whole thing in place.

I loaded the rifle and put a few bullets in my shirt pocket. I fixed the rifle sling over my shoulder. It had been a couple of weeks since I had carried the pack. It seemed a lot heavier.

Did I add that much to it or could I just be a bit out of shape?

"See Ram, I have a burden too."

He answered with a mini whine.

"Are we ready?"

I checked another pocket and felt my mirror-compass compact is place.

We started off toward the west as I assumed that our flight path had overshot Douglas. Traveling that direction should bring us closer to civilization. My ultimate goal—get down from this mountain.

Maybe after all this time they weren't even spending their time for search and rescue rather just recovery.

I couldn't let myself dwell on that.

"Guess I'll fool them. Gabi is doing something other than sitting around waiting!"

Seeing the treat in my hand, Rambo pawed my foot. He begged me with his eyes. "Okay, Okay. Sit. Here ya go." I patted his head.

I pulled my clean, shiny ponytail through the back of my baseball cap, slipped on my sunglasses. I drew in a deep breath.

Wyoming boasted the record as the least populated state. I brushed that notion aside. Surely we weren't too far away from someone's ranch.

Feeling almost buoyant, I shifted the pack into a comfortable burden and took my first step into uncertainty.

I clicked my mental heels in the air. "Come on Rambo, we're off to see the wizard."

Chapter 16
The Hike

With the weather almost perfection, I paced ahead with Rambo beside me, jubilant that we were going somewhere, anywhere. Just because we had no idea where gave me no reason not to be optimistic.

Rambo occasionally darted after a butterfly, marked his territory, and sniffed wildly at everything as we passed. Moving slightly downhill permitted a jaunty pace, though one that required water to quench our growing thirst. Knowing that lack of water could be a problem didn't tarnish our stellar mood. There were still patches of snow that continually fed our emptying bottles. It hadn't escaped me that the snow patches were smaller, further apart, and the run off dwindling. Our water supply was shrinking. I hoped that there would be a spring or a creek somewhere in this green meadow but there hadn't been a sign of water in our first two hours.

Hiking along through the meadow, I bent to pick some purple wildflowers and tucked them behind my ear. As we neared the woods in the distance, bushes and thorny brambles sprouted up here and there. They not only sprouted, they attacked. I stopped to examine Rambo's fur for foxtails—my pants and socks! How could those spurs wheedle their way under my pants? My jaw tightened as I plucked the burrs out with a vengeance.

"There Rambo." I tucked my pants into my boots. "I wish I could tuck your fur away from those vicious bushes. What do wild varmints do, anyway?"

In the distance I could see that it wouldn't be long before we'd be in a forested area.

By midday, I felt hungry enough to eat a raw eagle. Fortunate for the endangered specie, there were no birds of any kind close by. A few high flyers escaped.

Shielding my eyes from the brilliant sun and swiveling around, I surveyed the area. I spotted a flat rock, about the size of an upside-down Stetson, just perfect for a stool.

Rambo followed me over. He sat at my feet, tongue hanging out with his head cocked in a questioning tilt. *What's next?*

Flipping off my baseball cap, I shook my ponytail and wiped off my forehead with my forearm. I off loaded my backpack. Rambo, relieved of his also shook himself off with great gusto.

"Is that better, Big Boy?" I dropped down cross-legged on the stone and drew the rifle close to me.

"Thirsty, Ram?" I poured out water for Rambo in his cup. He slurped with avid zeal as I sipped some of mine. That reminded me. My eyes scanned around looking for a snow pile, but for the first time on our hike, I didn't see one.

Meager as it was, I spread out our lunch. I unwrapped an energy bar. While I crunched into my bar, I polished an apple against my thigh. I sprinkled half of the remaining dog tidbits on the ground for Rambo. "Ready set go!" As usual it was no race, Rambo wolfed his up in seconds. His eyes remained glued to the apple that I finished at my leisure. "Okay, Rambo!" I tossed the core in the air. His eyes darted until the exact right moment before he leaped. He snagged it in mid air.

I fumbled in my pocket for my phone. Maybe. I moved around raising and lowering my cell. Just maybe. But no, there I still had no signal. Dead battery! I screamed, "No!" I almost hurled the cell, but stopped short. Maybe it still emits a charge someone could catch.

Rambo looked up at me then scanned the area, I assumed to see if we were threatened by anything. My shoulders slumped, but then I rationalized the loss of my phone. "It's okay, Rambo, just me loosing my cool." *Didn't matter anyway since there hadn't been any signal this whole time. This is the least populated state.* "They probably don't go about building cell towers where there's no one to use them."

As I finished my water, Rambo lay at my feet and soon began to snore. I forgot how much time my dog at home lay about and snoozed. Rambo was long overdue.

I took out my sketchpad and spent some time drawing the scenic meadow carpeted with the verdant lime-color of newly sprouted grass and dotted with wild flowers. I breathed in the fresh cleanness and faced heavenward, while appreciating God's gifts. A bevy of clouds puffs drifted across the bluest of skies. The meadow spread, like a blanket, to the rough-hewn mountains rising to snow capped peaks.

This topped the most beautiful places I had seen. I plucked a handful of grass running the blades through my teeth extracting the pulpy sweet ends. I breathed in the sparkling air's perfume and the fresh smell of grass.

"Ahhh." I had found a peaceful moment where I felt that an end to my life at this moment would be all right.

Rambo napped while I tried to capture this beauty in my sketch pad.

He caught my attention and broke my solace. He nosed into my pack sniffing for the rest of the food.

"Okay, Boy." I scattered a few doggy treats on the ground. "That's enough. Let's get ready to go." I knelt to secure his saddlebags in place. As I stood, I rubbed my back, flexed my shoulders as I swiveled my neck around loosening up for the next leg of our journey.

With the afternoon warmth, I stripped off my Pendleton shirt. I secured it with my jacket before slinging my pack back over my shoulders.

We set off again, revived, though not moving as jauntily as we had this morning.

It wasn't long before the woods seemed to grow around us. We traveled onward edging between and around the saplings. The towering firs engaged our senses with the mulch of leaves and pine needles strewn on our path. The scent of wilderness settled a smile on my face.

The light and shadow of sunlight streamed in through the spaces between the trunks and canopy of leaves overhead to lay down a brilliant spotted carpet on the forest floor. As a breeze rattled the leaves, the sunrays danced on the ground.

A few times I had to disentangle my boots from the overgrowth. I picked up my foot. This one unearthed the home of a lizard. With the shushing sound of the leaves and twigs around him, the lizard slithered through and disappeared in the overgrowth. He probably enjoyed his lunch as the ground below was teeming with tiny insects, the other world we seldom see. I guess I should have thought about catching the lizard for food. The scant meal I planned for tonight's

—

dinner represented the last of our food except for power bars and apples. I rationalized. Pasta Primavera definitely sounded a little bit better than roasted lizard.

The forest was alive with sounds of life. I wasn't sure. Were we hearing chirping of birds or chipmunks? Whatever it was, Rambo's nose twitched as his line of sight took in all the wonder of the forest. Enraptured by the beauty and not terribly hungry, I forgot that I would need to locate food very soon.

No birds had ventured close enough for my slingshot, though a flock of geese flew high overhead in a V formation maybe heading north for the summer. I shaded my eyes and watched them fly over, as they created their symphony of honking.

In the beauty of Wyoming, our routine became easy to get used to. We set up camp. We sang around a campfire. Spending time with Ram was fun. If the food hadn't been fast dwindling, I would have thought we were on a pleasure trip.

We stepped into a clearing. The sun felt soft on my skin. I paused and leaned back, letting it splash warmth on my face. I listened again expecting to hear the gentle sounds of twittering birds.

It was eerily silent.

Then I heard it. Not the voices of birds, not the shushing lizard, an unmistakable sound, soft but menacing.

Rigid, I glanced around.

Where are you Rambo?

Chapter 17
In His territory

Rambo had vanished. I took a step. Standing still I scrutinized the brush around me. No dog anywhere. I had ceased the worry that Rambo would leave me, but still I became unnerved. The quirky noise kept growing slightly louder. I thought I saw a movement in the grasses behind a tree.

"Rambo?"

Louder now, I cringed at the threatening sound. It came from the ground close to my left boot. I glanced down. Instantly, sweat broke out on my upper lip. A cool breeze swept across the dampness on my neck. Shudders bounded down my back. I clenched my teeth. I searched my brain for the proper response. *Think!*

It slithered closer.

Paralyzed with fear, my sensibilities recognized the scaly beauty of its patterned back. I had only seen them in zoos because there are none in Oregon.

However, there was no mistake. Coiled, head cocked with rattle extended behind him—it was definitely a rattlesnake.

The rattle's voice intensified with the quick swishes of the rattler's tail.

Goose flesh rose up my arms.

Thoughts rolled through my mind as though I stood frozen in the spear of light, like I had all the time in the world, yet probably only seconds passed as I assessed my situation.

What were my options? Run! No. Snakes can slither faster than a person can run. Snakes have poor eyesight. What if I backed slowly away? They have good hearing. Would he hear me move? Wouldn't any movement elicit a strike? I wanted to call Rambo, but with the snake's acute sense of hearing, in seconds it would be too late. *I could be dead*—I choked a yell in my throat.

My heart pounded in my chest.

I stood for the longest moment. How long could I stay like a rock?

I screamed inside my head. At that moment I thought of Wil. I had never known him to back off anything. He'd just face it—face it with spunk, just like he did in his graduation stunt. How I wished he were here. I saw him fight off a drunk who harassed me in a bar.

Do something, Gabi.

The snake's head swirled up from his coiled body making sure a plunge toward my leg would land calf high—definitely above my boot.

What if the snake did bite me? Rattlesnakes are definitely poisonous. How long could I expect to live after such snakebite?

In survival class, I learned how to lance the snakebite then suck out the venom. *What if he bit me someplace I couldn't reach or lean my mouth toward.*

My mind conjured a picture of me all alone, laying on the ground, the night closing around me, slowly succumbing to the poison of a snake bite—or worse—being attacked by wolves or mountain lions before the venom drained away my life. The idea of being eaten alive, my flesh being torn from my bones, tensed every muscle in my body.

You can't stand here forever, I warned myself. I looked up. "Help me, Lord," I whispered under my breath.

When I felt dizzy, I realized I held my breath. I let out a huge air stream before gasping for another breath. An experience like this made me understand. *This is what heart palpitations are.*

It seemed like an hour that I stood sculpted like a statue, staring down at the snake's coiled body. With heart hammering, I listened to the incessant rattle, and watched the sun glint off his beady eyes.

Back up, I felt wobbly. *I can't stand here forever.*

I willed myself. *"You can do it."* I lifted my right leg like a slow motion replay.

Swift as the dart of a hummingbird, I saw the snake thrust forward. I clamped my eyes closed and waited for snake's fangs to penetrate my leg. When I felt his head slam against my shin I almost felt the venom course through my system,

Snarling and growling resounded with crackling, swishing, whipping sounds that emanated from the ground next to me.

My eyes snapped open in expectation of being further assaulted by some other vicious creature.

By the time I reacted, Rambo's teeth were clamped just behind the snake's head. Rambo shook the viper until it resembled a limp rope swaying, suspended in his jaws. He dropped the creature in front of me.

I slipped the rifle from my shoulder sling and butted the snake around with the barrel. I kicked it. Lifeless. "Yes!" I thrust the rifle in the air. Like I'd seen Indians on TV, I danced over to Rambo, whooping and holding the rifle overhead in one hand.

Ram nosed the serpent, stood back with his tongue hanging out, panting and looking at me like, *"Did I do good, Ma?"*

I knelt. "Rambo. You're my hero!" I wrapped my arms around him.

I didn't think the snake fangs penetrated my pants, but I couldn't tell. Even though I didn't feel pain, maybe snake venom numbs the strike zone.

I looked down.

"What's that?" I inspected the area where I felt the snake strike against my leg.

I noticed two ivory spikes below my knee on my pant leg. Two ivory fangs had been yanked from the snake's jaws when Rambo pulled him off me. The fangs had penetrated the thickness of my pants when Rambo jerked my predator away from me. They protruded from the fabric, but hadn't managed to reach my shin. "These'll make a great necklace when I get home." I plucked them out and dropped them into my pocket realizing that somehow I intended to get home.

"Wow! We had a close one, there." Rambo had snatched the snake within millimeters from my shin.

I took one last poke to make sure the snake didn't just play dead. "Looks like you just went shopping for dinner, Rambo, old buddy." We had an hour left of daylight. "Let's bleed him. We can eat him later, though I'm not sure that's what you'd like." Motorized, Rambo's sniffer went wild.

With my hunting knife, I scooped the snake up. I sliced off his head to let him bleed out. I didn't want to watch Rambo devour the head. So I turned away while the snake's blood drained. I tried to ignore Rambo's grunts while he gnawed on his snake snack.

I coiled the snake so it fit into a Ziploc baggie. I hadn't many of the bags. They might be very valuable for preserving, storing and carrying things, so I would have to be judicious in their use.

Beheading the snake I had been careful not to bloody myself. I knew that would just attract other more dangerous animals. Besides I couldn't afford to use our precious water to wash. I cleaned up with some of Buck's whiskey.

All day there had been no sighting of any planes. I took a moment to check for a cell signal. "Well here goes nothing." I shook my head. Nothing is what I got. I had forgotten my batteries were dead.

Before I became bereft of this loss, I suddenly remembered we had some hard candy. I unzipped a pocket in my jacket, unwrapped a couple of pieces and shared my find. "There, Rambo, see how much I love you. Nothing like a bit of sweet to make life sweeter, and a mint to camouflage your snake-breath."

Maybe the candy would give us an energy boost. I felt exhausted after our encounter with the serpent, which slowed us up considerably. I shook the tension from my muscles and laughed when Ram imitated me.

I didn't want to waste daylight yet I felt more like a nap. That kind of rest would need the safety of our nighttime campsite. *What else could happen?* I wondered, though I rationalized the worst must be over.

After a mumbled prayer of thanks, I took a couple deep breaths "Let's be on our way!"

Chapter 18
Evening Vespers

We hiked about an hour. The approaching darkness showed its beauty as the shadows lengthened and light faded into filtered spears poking through the trees.

When Rambo sat in the middle of a small clearing refusing to move, I knew. We both were more than ready to make camp.

"All right, you win." After I swung the backpack over my shoulder, I dropped to the ground in a heap.

I guess I had been too busy hiking to notice. I screamed, "Aah, Ow!" as a spasm ripped through my calf. I jumped up. Leaping around for a moment, the muscle contraction eased. Then I realized the rest of my muscles quivered in throbbing masses. I rubbed my legs, my neck, and my arms before I collapsed to the ground in an exhausted heap of cramping muscles.

"I must've run full speed into a locomotive!" I grabbed Rambo's head and ruffled behind his ears. "A bit outta shape, am I?" He licked my face. "Okay! Enough!" I removed his pack, rolled him over, as I snuggled down for a playful wrestle. I finished off with a tummy rub. Thinking his muscles might also be a bit sore too, I continued with a complete rub down. He lay on his back, legs splayed midair, eyes squinted and I swear his snout wore a smile. "Well, Ram, wish you could do the same for me."

A dreamy glaze blurred my eyes as my mind flipped back to Wil and our camping trips. We'd lie back alternately rubbing and kneading each other's sore muscles. I took off my boots to rub my burning feet remembering this action was pure luxury when Wil alternately messaged then tickled my feet. "Ouch! Blisters."

"Well if I don't have Wil, Ram, I have you to protect me."

Time to get to work. First I checked the wind direction. In placing the tent I selected a flat spot.

I was safe in front of two large trees that grew together.

Next I laid out two trash baggies as the ground cover. I had begun to leave the shiny silver thermal camp blanket spread outside the tent in case a plane should fly over it might see the glare through the trees. Then I attached a bungee cord between two smaller trees, flopped the ground cloth over it. I laid out the sleeping bag then staked the corners of the ground cloth with my pegs.

Resting his snout on his paws, Rambo had been watching me set up camp.

When I pegged the tent in place, he meandered over. I chuckled when he curled up inside. "You lazy bones!"

After I gathered some kindling and chopped a couple of larger branches, I scraped a hole in the ground where I built a fire. Purposely I had carefully set up the tent with my backside protected by the trees. The fire protected my front side.

Rambo wouldn't mind eating our snake delicacy raw, "But I still am not that desperate—yet!"

Besides, while the sun dipped lower, the cold settled in. I swung my shirt and jacket on before preparing the *Viper a la DiCarlo.* That's when I wished for some of my mother's herbs.

I had never eaten snake before. I bet there were recipes that would make it tastier than enjoying this repast without benefit of even salt and pepper, let alone marinara, pesto or wine sauce.

Those thoughts had me almost drooling thinking of mom's cooking. She could throw any pasta together with olive oil or butter, mince in a little garlic then add some shrimp, or chicken or calamari—it was to die for. Remembering had me drooling.

The fire caught as it engulfed the logs in tickles of flame, I grabbed my preparation tools. I unzipped the pouch taking out the baggie full of the snake. To avoid messing up camp, I took the coil just outside of camp to a fallen log as my counter space.

When I brought out the snake to clean, I hoped Rambo would stay and snooze just long enough to get most of my task completed. He would not be a big help trying to grab and devour spare snake parts, but he would be a good scavenger to clean up the mess.

I can't draw any bigger creatures to share our dinner.

My Swiss army knife had a pair of scissors, which I used to snip off the rattle. I slipped the rattle in my shirt pocket. Maybe using it could scare off some predators. However, I discovered, the scissors weren't sharp enough to cut the length of the skin with any degree of comfort. After I located the snake's anal vent, I eased my hunting knife under the skin and slit it to the end where the head once resided.

The skin was way tougher than I thought it would be. Equally tough was the job of prying away the muscles from the skin.

Once I finished that job, I began to scrape away the entrails, I heard Rambo whining as he made his way to my makeshift kitchen. "Just in time, Ram." I dropped the innards down to his level He made quick work of them while I used my scissors to snip the meat into smaller lengths and drop them back into the baggie.

Carving the skewer sticks with four Y-shaped sticks, I created a perfect roasting apparatus for two skewers of meat. After I poked the meat onto the sticks, I placed them over the fire and sat idly turning them as they roasted. I used a bit of Buck's whiskey to flavor the meat and to clean up.

Rambo joined me, cuddling next to my leg. My mind wandered as darkness engulfed us. Dimming light still let us see things close to our blaze, edging things in the gold fire light, but leaving the forest shrouded in shades of gray. That thought made me smile thinking of the book of that name which had nothing to do with these shadowy shades of gray.

As the fire popped and crackled, sprays of embers flitted above the flames like fireflies. I turned the skewers sniffing the aroma. It had been a while since I had thought about my Mom's cooking. This just made me miss her more and more as our food supply dwindled.

Mom's expertise was so much a part of our family's restaurant's success. Papa had run it by himself after her death with me trying to fill in as cook when I wasn't in school. It worked for a while before he sold it. Then he started using his fishing boat to generate income. As a partial retirement, he sold most of his catch.

The smell of the roasting snake reminded me of Mom's Veal Scaloppini. Mm. I inhaled deeply appreciating the aroma. *Oh for a bit of garlic.* Her manicotti and lasagna were legendary. The thought of her Fettuccini Alfredo had me drooling again. *I might never taste those delectable delights ever again.*

Rambo's nose twitched as the bouquet of the cooking meat grew with each turn of the spit.

He sat up twitching his nose at the *Viper a la DiCarlo.* I ran my hand down Ram's back. "Thanks, Ram, Thanks for dinner. Smells pretty darn good, huh?"

I couldn't believe the depth of love I felt for him in such a short time. Having him save my life bonded us even closer.

With a fork, I slipped the meat onto the plate. I decided to give him hunks of meat from my plate one at a time. If I thought I could teach him to savor food by portioning it out, I was wrong. There's a pretty good reason why they describe some methods of eating as *wolfing it down.*

I licked my lips and my fingers as I finished my share of our roasted delicacy. I'd have to give *snake* three and a half checks. I didn't know how much a robust dog like Rambo should eat, but after all, he had scarfed down the entrails, and devoured the snake's head since our last repast. So I reserved part of the second skewer to smoke during the night. That meant we'd have breakfast and lunch for tomorrow. Smoking should preserve them for at least 24 hours.

If we didn't find water soon, we'd be having our last portion of primavera with crispy uncooked noodles. I didn't want to think about that or face the fact that we might run out of water.

While the sky darkened, I found myself less tired and sore as I ran my hands over my arms and neck. I thought about what to do before I tucked in for the night, besides crash. Not quite ready to go to sleep, I sat by the firelight.

Amazing what you'll do for entertainment and what little can amuse you. I started to sing just like I did when I was young and posed in front of my mirror. I posed, pretending I stood on some vast stage with a band accompanying me. My voice rose, master soloist in the forest, with no other competition but Rambo, I sang, *I went down to the River to Pray.*

Rambo titled his head back, howled with a shrill, whiney quality that made him the soprano. I missed Wil's booming tenor to complete a trio.

By the time we finished a couple of songs, I was rolling with laughter and playfully wrestling with my beast. Panting, we sat for a moment heads tilted skyward, taking in the deep velvet sky, dotted with a twinkling array of stars peeking through the branches. I thought of the childish song and wished upon a bright star in the sky. "I wish I may, I wish I might…"

I kissed the top of his head. "No Ram, I can't tell you what I wished. It wouldn't come true if I did."

Ram gave it one more howl before we settled into our tent.

I took off my socks. "Ouch. Eew! I think I'm getting blisters!" I'll have to bandage these up before we take off tomorrow!"

The two of us cuddled together, chasing the chill of the night air out of our tight quarters. Sore muscles accompanying a day filled with adventure left a sense of contentment surrounding me as warm as my gran's quilt.

Sinking into a deep sleep, I snoozed in a matter of seconds.

"This is the heaviest rain storm that I have seen in a long time," Mom said. *I leaned forward, tensely gripping the dashboard. Deluged with a downpour worse than buckets of water being dumped on us—faster than the wipers could swish across in a smear, the car slushed ahead. "I can hardly see the road in front of us." Mom hunched over the steering wheel, neck craning. Suddenly she pumped the brakes. The deafening screech sent spasms through me. Spinning, spinning! Stop the spinning! I tightened every muscle.*

"Watch out, Mom!"

The scream woke me. The realization that it was me who was screaming set me trembling. Rambo barked wildly. I sat up in a cold sweat. I leaned over and hugged him. "It's okay, Ram. Just a dream." I laid back down not wanting to let go of my Ram. "A nightmare."

Chapter 19
In Search
Day 5

Amazing, after a couple of days hiking how I slept like a rock even following my nightmare. The morning light woke us, Rambo taking his morning constitutional and I mine. We must have had a bit of rain through the night. The soft patter had been gentle enough not to wake me from my sound sleep. So, unfortunately, I hadn't put out containers to collect it.

Before I dressed I notched my belt for day 5.

I noticed Rambo licking the leaves. "You clever beast." I copied Ram by following with my bottle. I collected water a couple of drops or leaf-fuls at a time. I checked the rest of the water supply. With not enough to waste on my Cris and Pits, I yearned for a nice a long hot shower. *We'll be okay if we find water during the day.* I caught Ram's tail and ran it through my fingers.

I split a piece of snake with my buddy, leaving a total of three hunks for lunch. Rambo sniffed as I unwrapped a power bar for him and one for me. I cut an apple in half. Rambo totaled his in a matter of seconds. Never mind that the apples had been banging in their saddlebag. I savored mine noticing the juiciness of the apple and ignoring the still edible, yet mushy, bruised spots, that I might have cut out if I were at home in my own kitchen. I spoke with a mouth full. "I hope this will suffice as our water intake." We would be thirsty soon enough. That thought made me thirstier.

I brushed my teeth followed with a leaf full of water. Actually the minty tang with the meager wash of leaf water satisfied my momentary thirst.

After I put Band-Aids on my budding blisters, I pulled on two pairs of socks before shoving them into my boots.

There were streaky clouds floating overhead but the rain clouds were long gone.

"Oh well. C'mon, Ram. We'll stop later for a drink when we're really thirsty. Let's get packed!"

Stowing the tent and ground cloth in the least amount of space, became a skill I had mastered.

"Here Rambo." He paused for a moment realizing he was about to don his pack. "It's okay. I'm loading up too."

As I put the burden on Ram, I couldn't ignore the socks full of apples. "Good news, Rambo. Your burden is lighter. Bad news. You're carrying only two apples." Those, the last power bar with half pack of primavera, constituted our grand store of food. I patted the breast pocket of my shirt noting we still had two pieces of hard candy.

After I slung my pack on, we started off in a zigzag walk through the trees.

The taste of the forest grit with the leaf water, became something I began to savor. At least it was wet. Though not enough to collect much, both of us stopped periodically to grab a slurp of leaf water here and there for the first part of the day, until any remnants of rainwater were just a fading remembrance.

I kept watch for any prey, as I wasn't looking forward to eating the rest of the Pasta Primavera without water. I heard that forests often had springs - though why hadn't we been lucky enough to find one?

The trail I followed must have been matted down by an animal and wasn't leading anywhere. It might have been worthwhile to follow had I been sure I'd find the animal to invite for our dinner guest, or that it might lead to a waterhole. Tracking wasn't my best suit. What if this path followed a mountain lion or another wolf?

A squirrel sped up a tree. I fumbled to get my rifle. "Drat! I'm too slow." I watched its furry tail flair as it bounded across a wide expanse to another tree, bouncing as he landed and then he disappeared in the foliage.

Ram's tongue hung out as he panted in tune with our steps. With a raspy throat, I poured out a half a cup of water for each of us, to accompany our 'delicious' cold snake luncheon entree. The water sloshed around in my nearly empty stomach.

I checked the compass and readjusted our path. We trudged along at a much slower pace.

By afternoon we hadn't found any water and I tried to not to even think about my thirst. Funny, when you try not to think of something, it's the only thing that runs through your mind. It brought to mind someone thirsty watching a placid lake lap against the shore from behind a high barbed wire, electrified fence.

The next thought I couldn't ignore—we had nothing but dry noodles for dinner.

If I hadn't removed my baseball cap to wipe my sweaty forehead, I might not have noticed.

A quick movement in the tree caught my attention—a bird's nest resting in the crook of a branch on a fir tree, nearly eclipsed with the leafage.

I whispered, "Sit." Rambo sat sniffing the air with his nose pointed right at my target, a fairly large gray bird, maybe a hawk.

Slowly I reached for my slingshot. Not a very large target to aim for—a bird whose head barely rose above the edge of the woven nest of twigs. I retrieved a pebble from my pocket, loaded and fired.

A squawk, a mad flap of wings with a flutter of twigs accompanied the bird as it jetted away. Not only had the bird escaped, the nest still sat firmly attached to the tree. "Sorry, Ram. I really thought we had a lunch guest." Still staring at the nest an idea sparked. "Hey, how about egg salad?"

I off loaded my backpack. A single thought of fear shivered through me as laid my rifle next to it. I had promised myself never to put more than a few feet of distance between my gun and me. However, eggs would surely be cradled in those twigs. Eggs sounded pretty tasty to me. Birds twittered here and there. Though I couldn't see them, their song let me know there were no predators around.

I took a sock out and tucked it in my belt.

"Stay, Ram. I'll be right back with dinner."

Ram sat with his head tilting this way and that, like *What are you going to do?"*

I stood below the tree plotting my path through the branches and up to the nest.

"I can do this."

Just barely able to touch the branch closest to the ground, I hunched down, sprang up and grabbed the outstretched branch. Hanging felt good to my tired muscles.

—

Swinging and steadying my hands, I heaved myself up and balanced my stomach on it before I hurled my leg over. I climbed up and straddled the bough determining how to approach the branch just above me.

After another easy up, I looked down—a big mistake. Not that I am queasy about heights, but my next move! Standing I couldn't even touch the limb above me. I hugged the trunk. On my tiptoes, I strained to make contact with the bough. I'm not good at shinnying up. I would have to jump.

Rambo whined.

I had a decision to make. How hungry was I?

My options to climb down appeared to be equally unsteady. The nest seemed pretty close.

"Lord, please." I looked heavenward.

I teetered on the branch knocking bits of bark that sprayed down. I took a deep breath. "Okay, Gabi. Nothing to it!" I sprang up. First with fingertips then I worked my hands around. Focusing down again, I watched my toes swing back and forth. No choice at this point to change my mind even if my stomach felt a bit jittery.

I hung, dangled, kicking, as I willed myself up.

"Almost there!" With another swing and a thrust, I landed near the crook of the limb, leaning on my midriff, next to where the nest sat. I swung my leg up and over. I took a couple of gulps of air. "Boy I'm literally out on a limb here, Ram." I called down to him. He circled, antsy, rearranging himself and alternately sitting here and there while he watched me.

I thought back to the last time I had climbed tree. Wil and I were at my pop's house after a BBQ. I told him that I always climbed up a spruce out in the yard. "Yeah but you're too weak and girly to do it now. Anyway you're chicken!" he taunted. He had the nerve to call me chicken!

"Oh yeah! I bet you ten bucks I still can."

So I did it quite effortlessly while he jeered me from below. As I plunked down, I held out my hand. "My ten."

"Okay…" he slowly extracted two fives from his wallet.

Then I dared him. Being so much bigger plus heavier, he was the one to chicken out because he couldn't go as high as I did.

"Chicken, huh?" I greeted him when he came down.

Just when my heart calmed down from reaching my goal of the nest and I felt secure, I heard the unmistakable flapping of wings. Choppy wafts of air whooshed around my ears.

I turned to face one angry mother bird, malevolent eyes staring into mine. My face, more specifically, my eyes were her trajectory's target. She screeched as she gouged my cheek.

"Ouch!" I screeched back. I turned my face away.

I visualized a scene I had watched on TV where a murder victim lay stretched on the ground with crows pecking out the eyes. When I looked down where I'd land if I fell I shuddered.

She dove in again aiming for my eyes.

Holding tightly to the limb with my left hand, I smacked her away. Not wanting this whole operation to be for nothing, I retrieved the sock from my belt, gently scooped the speckled eggs into it. I tucked the top of the sock safely into my belt.

Seconds later she came back with a vengeance. While I tucked my chin in, I thrust my arm in front of my face.

Instead she landed on my head stabbing her beak into my scalp and forehead. While her talons clung to my scalp, she pulled at my hair with each lunge of her beak.

Being mad enough to knock her all the way to Florence, I swatted my enemy. I whacked her quite a distance away from me but not before she took a bite out of the base of my thumb. I sucked on it for a minute to stop the sting.

With one hand on the limb, I felt around to find a handhold in the bark of the tree. I hopped down. Swinging down from branch to branch, I barely escaped the onslaught of renewed fowl attacks.

Rambo leaped and growled at her. Dropping like a sack of potatoes, I thudded to the ground with my legs collapsing beneath me.

While the bird dive-bombed us, Ram almost caught her for dinner, but she zoomed up and away.

Apparently Mrs. Bird wasn't ready to take on both of us because she flew off shrieking in the breeze.

I found a Kleenex in a zipped pouch in my backpack and dabbed my face. I couldn't blame her, but I felt very lucky. The bite near my eye didn't hit the target, I hadn't fallen and we had dinner.

With a little of Buck's elixir patted on my wounds, I felt disinfected though my heart still fluttered.

Afterward I used the tissue to wrap the eggs so they wouldn't break. I eased them back into the sock.

This experience of a bird attack reminded me of the time when I found one of those old VCR tapes of Mom's. I watched Hitchcock's "The Birds"—a movie to teach you how to hate birds. It would be long time before I liked birds again.

I checked the time, forgetting that my cell had died. Tilting my head up I guessed from the angle of the sun it was mid afternoon.

We only took a limited gulp of water as we hiked. That probably added to our exhaustion.

And we were hungry.

It crossed my mind to wait around and take down the mom bird for dinner. *Though with the eggs gone, would she come back? Did I want to stay there at the scene of the egg robbery not sure if she would return. With my limited aim at a moving target, would I be able to stop an angry mom returning to finish me off? I even missed her with my slingshot while she sat in her nest. I consoled myself that I only had her head to aim for.* So I swung my backpack on.

As we hiked further into the forest, I paid careful consideration to the raw eggs, all six of them. I carried them like they were English bone china.

Soon we found a perfect spot to camp, I dumped everything down. With the thought of scrambled eggs tickling my hunger, I started a fire first.

While the fire took hold, I finished setting up camp. As I evened out the ground for the sleeping bag to lay flat, I raked through the sticks and matted leaves.

A deep breath took in the fecund odor under the carpet of fallen leaves on the forest floor. The underworld of tiny creatures undulated before me. Would these, one day soon be on the menu for our evening's meal? Or would we find larger animals to hunt? We had been lucky so far.

I addressed the clouds. "Or have You been there keeping an eye out for us?"

I patted Ram's head. "He's watching over us, Ram."

I set out the eggs from their sock sheath. Rambo came next to me sniffing. I kissed his forehead.

"Rambo, I'm sure you wouldn't think even one second about eating your share raw, huh? Wouldya? Yuck! Though, for mine I'm thinking scrambled."

The thought occurred to me, that the eggs might not be just yolk and white, but could be embryonic.

"Ew!" A shudder of revulsion went through me with a shake.

After a moment of attitude adjustment, I announced. "Mm. Cooked embryos. Yum! Yum!"

It was almost beginning to feel like home.

Chapter 20
The End of a Camping Trip

We had conveniently eaten a small lunch consisting of a couple of bites of smoked snake. By the time I prepared to fix our eggs—the sun descended behind the mountains. The sun setting behind the trees stretched long shadows across the forest floor. My stomach growled or was that a roar? Never in my life had I experience real hunger. I didn't know how much worse it could feel than the knots I currently felt. I shuddered to think I was getting close to finding that out.

I carefully unwrapped my precious eggs.

"Dinner it is."

So I began meal preparation. Rambo frittered around, whining, sniffing. "You hungry too, Ram?"

First, I consolidated our remaining water and calculated that we had roughly a half-gallon of water. Thank goodness for the infusion of leaf rain drips to stave off the lack of water. Ram still had a bit of water in his bottles.

Making a quick decision, I took a half a cup of water to soak the Pasta Primavera in the bottom of the skillet. Meanwhile I approached the eggs with trepidation. Had I waited because I feared what the insides might contain? Were there little featherless birdlets curled in embryonic balls? Or would the contents of the shell pour out yolk and egg white as though I'd just picked them up at the market?

"Well here goes, Ram." I held the first egg over the cup then with a quick tap, I split the shell. The egg plopped into the metal cup from the Thermos bottle. "Yeah!"

I peered into the cup and examined the contents. What's this? Well…" Something had happened. "Maybe a fertilized egg, but not developed enough to put me off."

82

Actually it was twins with a double yolk. I wondered how often that occurred in nature.

I finished cracking the eggs then whipped them up with my fork until no gooey egg white existed.

"What's that noise?" A crunching noise rose from the ground. Checking it out, I noticed the shells had disappeared.

"You'll eat anything, huh, Ram?"

I poured in the little water left from soaking the noodles and heated it before I dumped the scrambled eggs into the skillet. The pasta came next. I stirred my *Eggs Primavera* around while Rambo shifted from side to side licking his lips or hanging his tongue out panting. His nose pointed directly at the skillet.

I had to admit, even though my body hadn't been fortified with its usual intake of fluids, my mouth filled as I salivated over my gourmet mixture. It smelled like real food—with seasoning.

It had been days since Wil entered my mind, except on my tree-climbing episode. A new love had taken over—food. I never thought of myself as a foodie before, however food dominated my thoughts and even floated through my dreams—Mexican food, Chinese, hamburgers, lobster—there was no end to the delectables that tickled my thoughts, my dreams, and my taste buds.

"Just a minute, boy." I scooped half the *Eggs Primavera* into the large metal cup for Rambo. The skillet became my plate. I licked my lips then picked up my fork. Before I had swallowed my first bite, Rambo had nosed into his cup. He proceeded to push the nearly empty container around the campsite while he snorted like a hungry pig.

Holding my stomach, I couldn't stop laughing.

When his food was gone, Rambo sat by my feet, snout about an inch from my food platter.

"It's mine, you little piggy. All mine!"

I stowed a small portion for breakfast.

Rambo set his tail to wagging. So I didn't scrape the very last remnants stuck to the bottom of the skillet, I set it down. Rambo licked and licked, scouring the skillet. I hadn't enough water to wash the implements. So I sat back on my haunches, took hold of the cup with a sock for hot pad and held it over the heat from the fire. Then I did the same with the fork, skillet and my hunting knife. I watched the flames finish licking them clean.

"There Mr. Rambo. Sanitized with a clean bill of health. No ptomaine for us."

He jumped with his forepaws on my knees, squatting in front of me, licking my fingers.

I put one hand on his paw and drew my hand down the length of it. Then quick as a fly escapes, he plucked his paw out from under mine and put it on top of my hand. I tried the action and once again his paw withdrew and landed on mine. We played this little hand-paw game until my stomach hurt from giggling.

That interrupted our plight with levity. However my next activity proved more serious.

I pretty much knew that we were almost out of food. Maybe I thought if I took a closer look, some candies or power bars would magically appear.

"It's time to take stock of the food still left so I can decide how we could plan to increase our store—Insects, Eeeew!"

Ram tilted his head to the side as if to ask, *"What did you say?"*

"Well I know you catch some of those moths that flitter around the light but I am not excited about fricasseed worms or moths." I ran my hand up his throat. He smiled as he laid his snout in my hand and closed his eyes while I massaged.

I turned to my backpack and checked all the compartments.

A small portion of the cooked *Eggs Primivera*—just about enough to feed a finicky mouse, still remained—that is if the mouse didn't mind gummy noodles. We'd have that for breakfast. I checked Ram's pack for the apple sock. It held but one, bruised as it was. The remaining power bar was crunched in two pieces with crumbs rattling around in its wrapper.

There was water left. I listened as it sloshed in the canteen. "Not much, my boy." I shook my head. "But a little more in yours."

"Okay, Rambo." I combed his fur with my hands, extracting a few foxtails from his belly. "We're not camping any more."

I took a deep breath and let it out.

"We're surviving."

84

Chapter 21
Sweet Dreams?
Day Six

Before we lay down for the night, I brushed my teeth hoping to cleanse away the thick feeling of the eggs and pasta that clung like glue to the inside of my mouth. Afterward I swished my tongue—a cotton ball rolling around—I hoped the minty flavor of the toothpaste would disguise the thirst that had enveloped my being.

"Okay Rambo. Just one slurp of water." I poured a small amount into his cup and drew in a dry breath as I watched. I wondered. If I once put my lips to the bottle I held in my hand, could I stop with one gulp, "Here goes." I took a couple of gulps right from the bottle then capped it up.

I patted myself on the back. "Only two gulps." Did Rambo roll his eyes at that one? He picked up his back foot and gave himself a good scratch.

I took in the view straight up, feeling very small. Millions of stars twinkled between the branches that sliced a huge moon in pie-shaped pieces.

As Rambo and I lay cuddled together in our meager abode, I kissed his head lying curled against my chin. I wrapped my arm around him. Exertion is a marvelous sleep aid. So is Rambo. "Thank you Lord. Tomorrow we're really going to need your help." I heard a soft snore from Ram. I spent a few minutes worrying about our lack of food, before I drifted off into fitful sleep.

The rain beat down and I smiled. I was so thirsty. Finally more water than I could have wished for, all around me. My clothes were soaked. I tilted my head up and felt the drips pelting my forehead, my cheeks, and my chin, though no water to drink. I thrashed about trying to catch the drops in my mouth. I spread my hands to collect— just a small drink. Why couldn't I? My mouth felt like sandpaper. Come on! Just one little drink! I shivered with the drenched clothes

---

clinging to me.
What's wrong? I can't move my legs. Pain blinded me.
"Mama! Mama! Help me!

I woke up screaming with my arms hugged around my whimpering Rambo.

"I'm okay, Rambo. I'm okay."

I buried my head in his fur as I sniffled. "Just another bad dream. I'm sorry, boy."

Curled again around Rambo, I fought with my eyelids to stay shut. Even my eyes were dry as I remembered my dream. Water, water everywhere and not a drop to drink. My nose had clogged from crying. As I breathed through my mouth I felt even more parched.

The thought that I had completely erased Wil from my dreams, that he had been replaced by food and water surprised me.

Each breath I drew, dried away what was left of the saliva in my mouth. As soon as I grabbed a moment of sleep, a raspy cough erupted from my dry throat.

Visions of those giant juicy hamburgers served at the Restobar sat just out of my reach as I dozed on and off until the light of dawn.

Slow motion, how I would describe our morning as I packed up camp and planned our limited breakfast.

Not knowing how long we might be here, I realized we hadn't eaten any vegetables. They could keep us from starving plus they probably had some water content—not that I knew which of the growth of flora abounding around the forest was edible. I had seen mushrooms that looked delicious. I imagined sautéing them in butter and garlic. Then I would picture myself dying of a gut-wrenching poisonous mushroom churning around in my stomach. Wil and I were going to take a class to learn more about harvesting wild mushrooms though we hadn't—yet. I liked thinking 'yet'.

I grabbed up a handful of grass. I felt safe with munching on the ends of the grasses—after all I had seen Rambo eat grass sometimes.

Before this hunger had set in, I had seen some dandelions. I must've been getting hungry enough because I kept thinking of salads full of dandelion leaves. *How about some rich blue cheese dressing? Maybe I will find some greens as we walk along.*

I did know that pine needles possessed a good amount of vitamin C. *Too many bitter pine needles could bring on an adverse*

---

affect on my system, I thought as I picked a few more needles to chew on.

I patted my flat stomach.

"Well at least it'll be fun to eat what I want when I get back and not worry about the calories."

I cinched up my belt another link.

First I ate the couple of bites of pasta.

Salivating I located the last apple and cut it in half. There was some moisture in the squishy apple, which might help us wait until later to use our limited water supply.

Rambo took his share of eggs in one gulp while he munched the apple in about three bites. As he demolished his breakfast, I savored my juicy breakfast smiling at his voraciousness.

"What's that Rambo?"

He whined.

I swiveled around listening to determine the origin of the sound.

A noise?

Ram whined again.

I grabbed his muzzle and held it shut. "Shh! Ram, listen!" I swiveled my head around trying to determine the direction from which the sound came.

I turned my ear toward the noise.

Again I heard it—a low rumble.

An animal?

No, it's not an animal.

What was it?

The noise grew. Coming closer?

Chapter 22
Rescued?

Could it be the noise of an engine? Was it really? I could be imagining it. I peered upward through the jumble of tree branches that cut through the early morning sky. Nothing.

The noise grew louder. I wanted to be sure that it was an engine. I could only catch glimpses of it. What ever it was, it wasn't close yet.

A helicopter? A chopper would be able to land near here. I would be saved! A plane could go for help. I should be patient and wait!

Then I saw it.

Between the branches, the airplane flew through and across the spaces between in the foliage—my scant view of the sky.

It wasn't a tiny low flying aircraft. Neither was it a jumbo airliner that flew miles high in the clouds.

Is it a search and rescue plane? Are they still searching for us? Are we invisible to the pilot? Could he even see there is someone down here?

Covered over with leaves and branches of the thick pines and the camouflage tent, our camp blended into our surroundings. Overhead the branches embraced each other nearly as thick as a roof. Probably a pilot would only see the green canopy of trees covering the ground like a thick green carpet.

I thought about starting a fire. I grabbed a couple of branches. *Don't be ridiculous—that would take too long.* The plane would be gone by the time I could make enough to smoke signal.

Don't waste time!

I had no bright clothes or objects. I hadn't left out the shiny thermal blanket.

I grabbed my backpack scrounging through underwear, socks, and I found it. *My white turtleneck!* From a zipper pocket I yanked it out by its sleeve. A small opening in the forest lay just ahead. I sped for treeless space swinging the shirt over my head. I grabbed up the silver thermal camp blanket dragging it and swishing it.

"Yes! Yes! It's a plane!" I jumped up and down. Rambo barked and leaped at my feet. "I'm here!" I yelled. "Down here!" I waved my white shirt wildly until my arms ached while I jumped up and down on the silver blanket.

"My mirror!" I fumbled around until I found it. "Here! I'm here! Down here!" As I caught a sunbeam, I flashed my mirror at the distant plane. I continued flashing as the plane neared.

The pilot flew directly overhead. I flashed my mirror repeatedly. Had the pilot dipped his wing?

I screeched until my throat stung. I flicked the mirror as I ran to another opening in the forest, waving and flashing, but the plane jetted out of my sight.

My shoulders slumped.

I listened.

"Come back! Please! Come Back."

Maybe it would turn around and come back. It would just need a bit of space to turn around. *Yes, it would come back. I'll just wait.*

I sank to the ground in a heap, draped myself with the silver blanket to flash at the empty sky.

For a long moment, I strained my ears as the very last of the engine roar whispered in the wind.

How long had I waited? I swallowed hard. Maybe I stopped when I realized that my screaming had made me even thirstier.

I dragged my blanket and myself back to our camp to finish packing up.

Because I really didn't need the white shirt, I staked it out in the clearing. I took a piece of charcoal to write, "help" on it. I completed my artwork with an arrow.

"I know. With one rainstorm, the message will be lost." Rambo watched with his eyes questioning my behavior. "But if they come back they'll know something, someone needs help. It might look like a body from the air."

I'm not sure I convinced Rambo.

As the last gesture, I chose to treat Ram and myself to a swig of water.

"Let's go, Ram. It's just you and me." I scratched behind his ears.

I packed up my disarray of items pulled from my backpack, replaced my Band-Aids and stood up. *I guess I'm ready.*

"Let's survive!"

Chapter 23
We're Buffaloed
Day Six

Rambo and I pressed ahead adjusting our pathway in the direction from which the plane had been traveling with nothing in our bellies but half an apple, a mouthful of eggs, and half a cup of water. I cinched up my belt another notch, leaving the end of the belt dangling out in front of me. I wrapped it around the belt loop next to it. "This is not my idea of the perfect 5-day diet."

It didn't take long before my hunger pangs returned. I fixated on the last bit of food we had, one crumbled Power Bar—a dry crumbled Power Bar.

"Not an extensive menu, Ram."

The trek through the woods sapped my strength. I split the Power Bar. "Here ya go, Ram." I took tiny bites of mine, then dumped the crumbs in my hand to let Rambo lick them up.

When we came to the edge of a large meadow, I paused, ready for a rest. I ambled out to the middle in the tall grassy area hoping to find a spring or a creek running through.

Rambo's nose sniffed wildly as he stared off.

Wondering what made him so nervous, I followed the direction of his snout. He always pointed his nose at whatever he wanted me to notice.

We were down wind from a herd of buffalo or perhaps bison, I didn't know the difference. The woolly creatures calmly grazed with their backs to the midday sun. The scene reminded me of a glossy picture out of a travel magazine. I wished for my camera to be working.

I glanced to the side when I saw something moving. It was creeping through the grasses. *A cougar!*

We were also down wind of the cougar so I hoped he wouldn't notice us.

The cat eyed the beasts, picking out his lunch from the edge of the herd, where a calf had strayed to the side becoming semi-isolated from the group.

To a cougar, Ram and I could represent a much easier take down than a buffalo. I just hoped he wouldn't notice us.

Hunching down, I assumed we were safe for the time being undetected in the gentle breeze that ruffled the grasses in our direction.

I bobbed up to watch the cougar's stealth, creeping toward the calf that had lingered beside the herd nibbling grass. I had to admire the grace with which the cougar stalked his prey, his sleek muscles orchestrating his ballet as each paw touched down. Apparently neither the calf nor its mother had noticed the threat.

With a snort, the mother picked up her head from feeding. She turned, braying for her calf to come back. The baby's bleating tugged at my heart, knowing no way could I stop this attack. This was the way of the wild. I knew I would do the same if we were to eat tonight.

Before I knew what happened, the cougar lunged at the calf in his sights.

The cougar's attack of the baby caused a ruckus among the herd.

The mother tried to intervene, however, she was too far away from her calf. She could do nothing but watch.

In seconds, the babe lay on the ground with the cougar looming over it. The assailant's teeth embedded in the neck of his victim, the cat shook his head back and forth. The cougar then lunged at the calf, tearing meat from its body.

I turned away. "Ew!"

Though repulsed, I felt relieved to know that he hadn't targeted us when suddenly a new problem arose.

When my eyes shifted back to the herd, I observed their reaction. Startled, they paused a moment then drew their heads up from their feeding stance to assess the situation. First the snorting, then loud bellowing followed. One or two buffalo started to amble ahead. A single braying came from the front of the herd. Slowly the beasts began to move. Starting at a mild trot then their speed ramped up.

I stared disbelieving my eyes and ears. A sudden stomping of hooves shook the earth. In the blink of my eye the rampaging buffalo stampeded straight forward—straight for us.

The thudding of hooves against the ground caused the earth to shake, an earthquake beneath my feet. As the bison advanced, the pounding, the roaring, the thundering of an unbelievably deafening tumult tore through the air.

Where could I hide? I surveyed my surroundings—nothing behind me.

Off to my left I saw a stand of trees. Several boulders were located to my right. Both were quite a distance away.

My heart thumped clear into my brain.

Another split second decision. *I had to do something. Run? Which way?* I pulled out my rifle. *Could I manage to shoot one? Would that leave me in their midst to be trampled? Or could it turn the herd.*

The broad wall of a hundred tons sped toward me close enough to smell the distinct odor of wild animal - not unlike the smell of a barn.

I couldn't run fast enough to get clear. I knew it. What now?

A scream roared in my throat as I raised the rifle, aimed and pulled the trigger. The sound of the exploding shot could scarcely be heard over the booming roar of the herd.

Just yards ahead of me, down went a buffalo. A harrowing dying squeal barely rose above the deep rumbling of hooves. The fallen buffalo lay trampled by several charging bulls.

I squeezed my eyes shut while I waited to be stomped to death.

A whoosh of air blew past me like the passing of a train. The smell of trampled grass and dirt wafted up with the strong animal odor.

When I opened my eyes, I stood in the middle of the herd as they parted and charged around me. I froze, a rock in their midst that they avoided.

I better not move!

Erect, I remained perfectly still not daring to move to either side as the buffalo sped past me only inches on both sides of me. My jaws ached from clenching.

The moments I stood there trembling seemed like hours before the noise of the rioting herd diminished and the dust settled.

I crumbled to the ground. Pausing before I gathered myself up, I sat cross-legged staring straight forward.

I unclenched my teeth.

"Oh, Dear God. What just happened?"

Every muscle in my body had tensed. When they relaxed, I ached everywhere.

As the dust settled, I perused the flattened area around me feeling the breeze chill my sweaty skin. The odor of the bent and broken grass combined with the waning smell of animals permeated the air.

The cougar had totally ignored the trauma that had just played out at his dinner table while he ripped pieces of flesh from the calf's carcass. Assessing the situation, the cougar ate heartily, and he'd not probably want us as dessert for this meal. He wouldn't be hungry for a while.

If we didn't try to share his meal, he likely wouldn't bother us.

I finally felt safe savoring the utter quiet and calm that spread across the meadow.

I patted next to me where Rambo had been.

"Rambo?" Behind me, to the side of me, or straight forward, I saw no sign of Rambo. "No! No!" My heart pounded as panic gripped me. I couldn't see him anywhere.

"Rambo where are you?" I screamed. "Rambo!"

After I buried my face in my palms, I let the tears flow.

"Oh!" I sucked in a sob. "Please, oh please, God—not Rambo! Trampled? NO…"

Chapter 23
My Cup Runneth Over

I dragged myself off the ground as though there were a hook attached to the nape of my neck. Muscles aching and nerves fractured, my heart finally slowed to a normal pace.

Standing gave me a better view. Turning from side to side, ahead of me I saw a hump between the grasses. Not in hurry to find out if Rambo lay there, I paused.

Surely he could go fast enough. He could have outrun the herd and made his way clear, couldn't he?

My throat swelled shut as the image of Rambo pummeled and heaped on the ground filled my mind. *No, please no!*

As I neared the hump I plodded at the rate of a two-legged turtle.

It became obvious, it was the buffalo that had fallen.

Relief spread through me like a warm breeze. "It's not Rambo." The lump rose too tall and more brownish in color than Rambo. That obstacle probably saved my life as the herd parted to avoid tripping on their herd-mate. Standing next to it, its shear size gave me goose bumps. Even laying down, the beast rose from the ground almost hip-high.

I pulled my cap off and wiped my forehead with my forearm. Sweaty grit sanded across my brow. With my hand shielding the sun, I scoured the area. There was no evidence of another body protruding from the flattened grass.

"Thank you, God." *That must mean Rambo is still alive. He's alive. I know he is.*

My eyes strained at the brightness as I checked the area once more. I knelt next to the beast. The buffalo hadn't just fallen. I found a bullet hole in his neck where I had shot him. Without the trauma of the stampede, I might have been overcome with guilt, the way his open eye stared back at me.

I had never killed a furred creature. Somehow mammals seemed more humanoid, therefore harder to kill with no purpose. *I did have a purpose. Didn't I? I believe I saved my own life by dropping him in front of the herd. Hadn't I?*

Then I envisioned a ranger, riding up and ticketing me for hunting without a license.

I smiled. If only. Then I would be rescued.

My next thought surprised me—nearly sickened me. Maybe instinct just takes over when you are in dire straights. Blood flowed from the gunshot wound like a trickle of red water.

Thirst.

With my forearm I wiped the dust from my lips and ground my teeth against the grit.

Only a few swallows of water remained in my water bottle. Rambo had the rest of the water bottles. Even if he came back those bottles were nearly empty.

Blood from the mangled beast oozed out from its injuries.

After off loading my backpack, I located a cup. My hand shook a little as I used my hunting knife to slit the throat of the buffalo. This allowed a stream of blood to flow into my cup. I watched it fill.

I paused a minute before I raised the cup to my lips.

Could I? Could I do this?

Being parched combined with my hiking had sapped my strength. *Without replacing the fluids, I would weaken. Then would I become prey for the wild animals that I knew were all around me?* I remembered info from the survival class. *This blood would also fuel my energy.*

"Yes Gabi, you can!"

A sip at first, the slightly salty liquid filled my mouth. *Not so bad,* came the fleeting thought before I could force myself to swallow. I gulped the rest down so fast I couldn't think myself out of it. After downing another cup, I took a tiny swig of water to wash off my lips and my mouth.

Without water, I knew I couldn't bring any blood with me. I'd compromise the container. That could make me sick if I found water and wanted to fill my bottles. At first I tossed the plastic cup, then my guilty conscience made me bury it. This pristine part of nature should stay that way.

I needed to assess my situation.

96

The cougar was satiated with his prey, though other animals might smell this kill. They might be here shortly to feed.

No other creatures were visible then, but I wouldn't have much time before they would come. I rolled up my sleeves to keep from bloodying myself and thus be a magnet for hungry beasts.

Quickly I pulled out a large Ziploc baggie.

How much meat could I take?

Using my hatchet with my hunting knife, I sliced into the hindquarter of the bison. I filled the baggie with slices of meat from the rump of the creature.

As I carved away I heard sounds, sounds like an animal running through the grass would make, a pounding and swishing.

I shifted my eyes from side to side. Clear.

I turned just in time to see a dark shadow leap toward me. Blinded by the beam of light, I flung my arms up across my face. My eyes scrinched shut waiting for the attack.

Instead of pouncing on me, the animal had landed next to me with a thud. It gnawed, grunting loudly as it fed on the carcass.

"Rambo!" I threw my arms around him. He totally ignored me as my hungry dog attacked his lunch.

"Sorry Ram." I patted his backside. "I'm still not hungry enough to gnaw on it raw." Careful not to bloody my clothes, I leaned back in with my knife.

I kept on slicing off hunks of meat—so glad to know that I gathered enough food for two. "This hunk's for you Ram."

When the bag filled, I allowed it to fill with blood. I remembered that I actually liked cooked blood when my mom had seared a hunk of beef, I always asked for the fried blood.

"I guess we're all just wild animals, huh, Ram?"

I wiped my hands, best as I could on the grass, rinsed with Buck's whiskey. Then I sloshed some on my knife and hatchet.

Grateful for the last apple, I enjoyed each bite that rescued me from the taste of blood. I felt somewhat nourished and not so parched.

By the time Rambo had eaten his fill, he wasn't interested in the apple core. "Stripped to the core" I held up the core. I realized what that saying meant when I noticed nothing left of the apple but some seeds and thready parts of the core.

As I picked up my belongings, I couldn't find it.

"Where?" I patted the matted grasses.

I stood and searched the area around me. "Where is it, Ram?" Rambo continued ripping hunks of meat from the carcass.

"It's gone! Rambo! Where is it?"

He ignored me.

"My rifle is missing!"

I felt around me.

"Maybe it's buried in the smashed down grass."

I felt something. Was it the barrel?

"Oh! There it is!" I lunged toward it.

Trampled on the ground, I saw the rifle. My heart quickened. "Yes!"

I bent over and picked up the stock. The barrel fell away, completely separated from the stock.

"Oh! Rambo, No!"

I hadn't realized how safe I had felt because I had the gun for protection.

Fear crawled over me as I swept the area for the predators that I could keep at bay with a rifle. *But I don't have one now.* The vast sky with open grassland spread around me. I felt very small.

The bravado the gun gave me had disappeared. I studied my surroundings, feeling the eyes of the wilderness focused on me.

Now what? What would I do without a weapon?

"Okay, Rambo." I bit my lip. That held in my tears. "It is just you, and me, and my slingshot."

He sat for a moment licking his lips, his paws and his chest cleaning away the remnants of his lunch. While I stood, round-shouldered feeling incredulous at my loss.

I searched my pocket where the last of the hard candies bulged. At least we could sweeten this moment. I unwrapped the candies and stuck the wrappers in my pocket. Fire starters. I smiled at my resourcefulness.

"I am beginning to feel like a real outdoorswoman, Ram." The round sweetness of the mint filled my mouth with moisture, almost like a drink. Almost.

I offered Rambo a candy. It didn't take much to make Rambo sit down and take notice. He wasn't too full to enjoy a hard candy for desert.

The way he looked up at me, I felt better.

—

98

"We have food and…at least we're not alone." I patted Rambo on the head. "We take care of each other."

"*Shoulders back. Head up.*" I could hear my mom. "Okay Mama." I straightened myself.

"C'mon, Ram."

The blue heavens overhead seemed to say, *Never alone.*

Chapter 24
Unprotected

I could tell Rambo had eaten so much he just wanted to nap. The experience with the herd accompanied by the loss of my rifle had left me exhausted too.

However we had to leave the bison carcass or face some other wild animal like another hungry cougar. Without my rifle, that thought brought images of a leaping beast headed straight for my neck with a full set of flesh-tearing teeth.

On my second night, when Rambo left me stranded alone, when Rambo had run off. . .I winced at the thought of the wolf. *I couldn't be that lucky again.*

I shuddered.

"Let's go, Rambo."

If water flowed in this meadow, Rambo's sixth sense hadn't picked it up. We moseyed along at a slow pace.

Some of the grasses reminded me of wheat. The tall slender stocks mixed with the grasses weren't foxtails as the kernels were plumper. I picked the head of one. I rubbed it between my palms and removed the hulls leaving several kernels in my palm. I chewed one. Yes it was wheat, or at least it tasted pretty good, kind of nutty. "How did you get here, Mrs. Wheat?" I ate another grain. Without water, I knew I shouldn't eat too much of the grain. It would swell in my stomach as it absorbed water. Not completely satiated with my day's intake of food and blood, I picked some spears of wheat and held them while I found a baggie.

"Wheat. Not bad Rambo. Want to try?" I offered him several grains in my hand.

He sniffed with an expression like, *"You've got to be kidding!"* He turned his snout toward a more interesting smell.

Thirst. I couldn't forget the thought of cool fresh water. Dandelions. I stopped and plucked some leaves. I munched a couple.

"They're moist at least." Even their bitter flavor tasted kind of good. Maybe because I had not eaten any seasoned food for a while. When I offered Ram a long leaf, he offered me not even a sniff.

"Turned me away again? I know Rambo. You wonder why I am eating such tasteless grains and green things, but you eat grass sometimes. Besides you had a lot more lunch than I did." I munched a few more leaves.

There were a bunch of the pretty yellow flowers in clumps among the grasses. Dandelions didn't have the aroma or the mouth-watering appeal that roasted bison did, but maybe they'd be useful if I made soup or salad. While I munched a few, I gathered a baggie full of them and nibbled a few leaves as I collected. They'd only be good today before they turned limp, though who knew when I'd find them again.

Soon we were in a forested area once more.

I sat down, dropped my backpack and braced against a tree.

"Let's take a nap." I undid Ram's pack, though there was nothing in it except the nearly empty water bottles. I drained some into my canteen. Just watching the liquid trickling between the containers made me aware of just how thirsty I was. "I should save this." However I gave Ram a lick and took swig for myself.

"We have to keep these containers. If, I mean when we find water." I stuffed them into my pack. "Empty they don't weigh much."

I messaged his back, cleaning away barbs stuck in his fur.

Rambo worked up a snore in minutes. He lay sprawled out with his over-filled tummy stretched taut like a football.

Suddenly I didn't feel sleepy.

I didn't have the rifle. The rifle became a friend that I had been relying on to keep me safe. Now I feared closing my eyes. My brain rationalized. I had not used it successfully to save myself except when I clobbered the wolf and when the bison closed in on me. The bison was the only food gained from the use of the rifle.

I checked my belt. I still had my hunting knife, my slingshot, and...the hatchet. I hadn't thought of it as a weapon until this moment. I unsnapped its leather strap and lifted it out. I felt the heft of it in my hand. Being in close enough quarters to use it on a wild animal gave me a shiver.

Though I could. Couldn't I?

When I stood I took aim at a tree about 15 feet away. I lifted the hatchet above my shoulder, drew it back and flung the hatchet at the tree in front of me. I missed. The next fling scraped the side of the tree. "Okay, right in the center of the trunk!" Thwap! It hacked into a tree, just about where I aimed it, imbedded in the bark.

"Yahoo!" I congratulated myself. "Well if it's a big animal." It took some doing to yank it back out.

Grinning, I raised my arm like a body builder showing off my muscles as though I had an audience other than a snoozing pooch to admire my prowess. "I'm queen of the wilderness." While I yelled that little affirmation, I realized I still feared what might lie ahead.

Would I ever feel safe again?

I glanced at Ram who barely reacted to my pronouncement by rolling over.

The action of using my axe with some accuracy eased my mind a little.

With my head on a thick leafy plant, clutching the shaft of my new friend - my hatchet, I closed my eyes. "Lord, please watch over me."

Reality faded as I fell asleep.

Chapter 25
Where There's Smoke, There's fire.

Floating on an air mattress, the river lolled along at a leisurely pace, lulling me in the luxury of enough water to drown a desert. The sky spread overhead, azure blue with fluffy white clouds drifting by. I dipped my hand in the water and raised it over my head. In slow motion I watched the crystal droplets trickle down my wrist to my fingertips. The droplets dripped into the placid water with a tiny splash. Ahh ,bliss. I raised up my hand another time to drizzle some cool water into my mouth, but I missed. Again I stretched out my hand for a handful of water. But no, my hand came up dry and full of sand. I rolled my head around to discover dry land surrounded me. My air mattress teetered out of the water. "No!" My eyes squinted tight to block the scorching rays of the sun.

When my eyes opened, I saw him there. His broad smile tilted a bit to the side showing those perfect teeth glinting in the sun. He ran the back of his hand down my cheek. My face tickled where he touched it. He stood over me extending his hand toward me. "Thank you, marshal."

As I grabbed out to accept his help, I clutched a hand full of fur. Rambo's faced me nose to nose. Rambo licked my cheek.

"Oh, it's you tickling my cheek. You beast. I was having a wonderful dream. Gallons of water flowed everywhere. We were rescued by that handsome marshal." I scratched my head. "Maybe my dream is a sign." I got up and dusted myself off. "Maybe that plane really did see me waving and flashing. And it's coming back."

I picked up my pack, "And just maybe that handsome marshal will come and save my life! Yours too, Ram."

With the angle of the sun, I estimated the time at about one PM.

"C'mon, boy. I don't suppose you'll eat much after your feast. Let's make a fire. A little buffalo snack will make me less hungry."

Rambo might not be starving, but I am.

I gathered some dry grasses and leaves, then hacked some bushes. After I tossed in the candy wrappers, I had a fire going in minutes.

Rambo acted a little disinterested as I prepared the spits and created brochettes of buffalo. Earlier Rambo had eaten his buffalo with more relish than he had with the snake meat.

I sat dreamily turning the spits. Not wasting a drop of blood, I ate my fill. Ready to eat food would make our next meal easier, without wasting a match. I had already used half of the strips so I finished roasting the rest of the buffalo meat and smoking it. I did still have the lighter, I noted as I used one of the few matches left.

"This gives new meaning to the phrase, *Fast Food.*" I whispered as I gave the meat a fast spin, acting like a real frontierswoman.

I had never eaten buffalo meat. *Not too bad—a little gamey and chewy—but not bad.*

While I munched on dandelion greens and some wheat kernels, I realized how one could miss the change in tastes, textures or temperature, aspects of a regular meal that most of us consume.

Rambo slept through my lunch, his tummy distended from his own buffalo feast. He breathed steadily with his underbelly looking like a balloon ready to burst.

Afterward I felt full. Somehow I didn't feel as thirsty either. Knowing what my next meal or two would be gave me some comfort.

From the angle of sun, I figured it to be early afternoon.

"Hey sleepy, wake up." I pushed on Ram's back. "We can maybe go a little longer today."

With a herd of buffalo feeding so peacefully until the cougar arrived, there had to be water close by. All we had to do was find it.

As we sauntered along, the forest filled with the sound of birds. "Wouldn't you know it? Just when we have plenty of food, it's everywhere. Those birds are close enough for me to use my slingshot, too."

The twittering of birds meant we were probably safe from other larger more menacing animals. Their silence was the first warning of danger. I stopped for a moment to check my surroundings. They twittered, as they hopped along the tree branches. "Are you trying to taunt me?" Anyway, our bag of BBQ buffalo steaks would feed us for a while.

I inhaled the fresh air laden with the rich scent of pine. This place brought to mind walks I'd taken with Mama and Papa behind our house though the woods. Boy Mom could sure make Papa smile—the way she'd pick a wild flower and tuck it behind her ear, then one for me. I wondered if he'd ever smile like that again.

I plucked up a little white flower. "For you, Papa." I tucked it behind my ear. There was a song in my heart. Knowing singing would just tantalize my thirst I listened in my mind.

After I pulled up some grass, I chewed on the ends and ran my teeth along the shaft where the sweet tender moist insides slid into my mouth. *There must be some water content in here,* I thought as I plucked another one. I walked along, shaded by the pines, still nibbling on grass.

Before I thought about it, dusk settled around us transforming the surroundings into subdued grays under the pale twilight sky.

I shook off a chill. "We should stop for the night, huh buddy?" I looked around. "This is as good a spot as any we've had." I sighed as I took off our backpacks and dropped to the ground, resting for a moment while I slipped on my jacket.

Ram's nose twitched on super sniff. "Ram? What are you smelling?"

I drew in a big whiff. I sniffed a strong smell? We were well away from the fire I made at lunch. I knew that I had put that fire out very thoroughly, but I couldn't mistake the smell of fire.

Was it the smoked meat?

Was it a forest fire?

After perusing my surroundings, I could see a plume of smoke rising to the sky. It wasn't a raging fire. "Can't be too far away."

It was definitely fire.

"It must be a campfire! A Camper! Yeah! Rambo we're saved!"

I leaped up.

"C'mon boy. Let's go get saved!"

Chapter 26
We Meet Again

My heart leapt in my chest matching the pounding of my feet as I took off jogging toward the tendrils of smoke.

"We're going home, Ram. We're going home!"

Rambo's nose twitched as he padded along side of me. "Good boy. Stay with me."

As I raced along, I barely noticed the grass, brush, and branches that I kicked or hacked out of the way. Though I didn't fall, I caught my foot on a raised root. That sent me wind-milling. I didn't actually fall, if you don't count putting out my hands to stop myself against a mossy tree. I stayed there a moment catching my breath and brushing off my stinging hands.

I gulped in some air then I just kept on going, elbows bent, swinging alternately at my sides unless I had to chop away brush. Bushes snapped back and scratched my face as I hurtled through.

What would I find when we got there? Was there a campsite with a homey fire going? Would they have plenty of food to share? Would there be water, lots of water? That thought made me remember my thirst. My mouth felt as dry as a Kleenex as I sucked in the cool evening air.

I slowed a minute, placing my hands on my knees and breathing deeply.

Single minded I moved ahead. *Just get there and everything will be okay.* I pictured myself walking into some small town with a search party cheering. *Wil will be waiting there. We'll be racing for each other, his arms open wide, waiting to enfold me like the happy ending to Hallmark movie, sun highlighting his auburn hair dancing like bits of fire caught in a breeze.* My face stretched into a grin.

With one hand on the trunk of a tree and the other clutching my waist, I bent over to ease the pain in my side. I inhaled several gulps.

I imagined the slow motion scene of my reunion with Wil. *He'll grab me up dancing me round and round caught in the exciting moment of time.*

Papa would be there. Reporters would want to know every exciting part of my adventure.

Rambo paused then sat beside the tree, panting. "Just a minute, Ram. I'm panting too. Let me catch my breath. It's nighttime. They're not going anywhere."

I stood up with my hands on my hips until I finally regained my stamina.

The excitement grew though I slowed my full-force run into a manageable jog.

There's no rush.

Rambo stayed right at my side. Knowing he could have raced ahead, I appreciated that he stayed with me.

"Pack animals, Rambo. They could have mules or horses. We won't even have to be loaded down with our excess baggage." I imagined a leisurely trip back to civilization, back to my Wil.

"Maybe it's a cabin and there's a nice warm fire…" I paused for several deep breaths. "And maybe even a bed… A nice soft bed."

As we drew nearer, I wondered if I should call out. *No, I don't want them to be alarmed. I'll just walk up softly to say hello.*

I stopped again. I bent forward with both hands on my knees, gasping as I struggled for a breath.

When I glanced up I could see a campfire with perhaps two men lounging around it. Their backs were toward me with the warm glow of their fire highlighting the surrounding brush, a halo around their darkened forms.

They were laughing and joking. I couldn't exactly hear the words. In between their banter, I thought I heard the gentle rumbling of a horse.

I listened again. Did they sound drunk? Were they were slurring their words so I couldn't understand what they were saying? Maybe I should get closer.

I inched ahead not feeling exactly comfortable.

Rambo whined.

A smell of danger hung in the air.

One of the men grabbed his rifle.

"Hey! Who's there?" He faced my way.

I looked down the barrel of his gun as he panned the forest.

I stopped. My arms flew up in an automatic reaction. "Hello. It's just me. I need help." I gave a small wave.

Rambo whimpered again.

"Just me and my dog." He leveled the rifle, still pointed in my direction.

The other man flashed a strong flashlight in my eyes. "Well, lookie who's there."

I raised my hand to block the bright glare.

"Hey, Chicky. Join the party."

His greeting crawled like a snake up my back.

Even with my vision impaired, I recognized the voice, the intonation of threat. *The same men who bothered me on the plane? Could it be?*

My heart thumped in my chest.

"C'mon over and have a little drink to warm you up." The seated man lifted a large bottle of Jack Daniels. He tipped it toward me.

There was a venomous quality to the invitation.

And the gun—still leveled at me.

What I needed was help. I wasn't just camping like they were. *Could I trust that these men meant me no harm? Would they help me? Or did they have something sinister in mind?*

A sudden vision of the last time I saw them came to mind, the gesture, the mouthed warning as they exited the plane.

A shiver trekked across my back and crawled up my neck.

"Uh, no thanks." I backed away slowly setting one foot down then the other.

The man on the ground jumped up. "Hey, stop!"

The man with the rifle started toward me, his toad-like face glowering in the eerie flashlight glow. The rifle still pointed my direction.

"A sign, Lord. Just a small one."

Rambo growled. Like a wolf, he howled an eerie shriek. Then came his sharp barking.

The man yelled, "Shut the mutt!"

When the rifle rose again, I stared down the barrel.

Would he shoot me? Would he shoot Rambo?

Would he?

I thought through my options—my defensive weapons. *My knife? No, I didn't throw a knife well. My hatchet? That was a deadly weapon.*

I couldn't be sure that they really were going to harm me. My mind flashed to the scene of a courtroom, me on trial for murder. The vision stopped me from reaching for my hatchet. Besides he could shoot me before I unsnapped it from my belt.

Slowly I withdrew some pebbles from my breast pocket. Taking aim I hurled them at my aggressor. The gun fell away as he blocked the stones from hitting him in the face.

I didn't wait to see what they would do next.

"C'mon, Rambo."

I took off like a gust of wind.

Chapter 27
The chase

The darkness descended like doom with only a partial moon to light the way. Were they following me? I wasted a moment to check over my shoulder. The men were just behind me. Straight ahead, we dashed through the dim tunnel of light emanating from their flashlight. The branches and brush crunched and snapped to my rear as the men trampled through the brush trying to close the gap.

Step it up, Gabi.

I lungs ached and my side cramped.

How long had I been running? How long could I keep it up? Could I voluntarily induce my adrenalin to kick in? These men are older and definitely out of shape, maybe even drunk. I can do this!

My arms scraped and scratched against the brush. When a branch slapped across my face, I paused at the stinging scratches, rubbed my side then snapped up into my fastest pace.

Their bobbing flashlight poorly lit the pathway where Rambo raced beside me.

Rambo sped up. He moved in front of me. Recovering from the branch attack, I followed.

"Hey, there. Stop!" His voice scratched the air.

"We're not gonna hurt you."

Maybe they're harmless. I took a quick glance backward. All I could see were the rifle, wild eyes, and a fierce grimace in the glare from the flashlight.

In my haste, could I remember where I dropped our packs? We needed to get back to our own campsite to pick up our stuff or I really couldn't imagine what we'd do to survive.

Fortunately we had left a trail of mashed down grass, and bushes with broken twigs. Rambo took the easiest pathway cleared from our dash toward their campsite.

I followed.

Our path continued zigzagging through the trees. Unfortunately there would be an easy trail for the men to follow.

I bent over to give my side a mini-rest then continued on.

My mind kept wandering back, trying to assess this situation. *Were we running for our safety or were we passing up the chance of a rescue?*

I just knew that those men frightened me more than the threat of trying to survive by ourselves.

There were two of them. They had a rifle. I did not. They were not young. I had gained a little on them, or was that my imagination. *Surely I can out run them.*

Every time I looked back I slowed my progress, but it looked as though they were falling back.

So I kept eyes forward until I could see the lumps of our packs just ahead of us splayed on the ground where I'd dumped them.

Still on the move, I leaned down grabbing one in each hand and kept going. This process gave my foe a couple of seconds gain.

If I stopped would Rambo, in his fiercest growling, be enough to scare them off, or would they shoot him? I couldn't take that chance.

After we passed our campsite I had no idea where we were headed but it seemed like I could trust Rambo to lead me.

Old men should be tired by now. Surely they wouldn't continue to chase us.

However, they did.

I could hear them however their flashlight became dimmer on the brush ahead.

I've gained on them!

Rambo sped up. The adrenaline coursed through my system as I strained to catch up.

I wanted to call out, "Help! Somebody please help me!" *Who would be able to hear my plea?* This wasn't a campground. Somehow these men hiked in or maybe rode on horseback, but the only other sign of civilization had been the plane that flew over days ago.

I couldn't see the men behind me. *Maybe we could lose them, but not if I screamed and let them know my whereabouts.*

Scanning the path ahead of us, the trees became further apart. Twilight sky backed the trees, suggesting there was a clearing ahead.

What would that mean? A meadow? Would we be targets crossing a moonlit glade?

Hurry! You don't have time to waste.

It took a second to slip my backpack on my back. I fumbled with the straps to buckle it around me. I bent and belted Rambo.

Wasting this moment brought the men closer. I could hear them thrashing through the saplings and brush, though I couldn't see them, just the bobbing flashlight.

I chanced a glance. There they were. One of the men waved at me. "Wait!"

I paused to contemplate whether I should just see if they would or could help us.

Rambo bared his teeth, glinting in the moonlight. When the vicious growl roared in his throat, I set out running again.

It seemed like only seconds until I stood at the edge of the forest. Sprinting forward another 30 or 40 feet I slowed. A space, dark and ominous stretched ahead of me. I paused and stared across the moonlit gully of some sort just below us.

Even with the pounding of my heartbeat in my ears, I could hear something else. Was it Water? It sounded like a rushing river. I couldn't see it, but I was sure. *That's water near by.* Even the air felt moist. Heading this direction, maybe Rambo knew it was there and brought us to it.

The men burst from the forest.

Shivering I wrapped my arms around myself. I turned and started to take a step further. Rambo's fierce bark stopped my forward motion.

I gasped.

The shear drop off had me teetering on my toes.

How far down would the next step have taken me? I couldn't really tell. I just knew I stood on a precipice, with the darkness clothing its depth in deep shadows like a bottomless pit.

I felt for my flashlight and unhooked it as I listened. The water was not the only sound I heard.

I clicked on the switch. I pointed the light downward. It hadn't flashed long enough for me to determine how far the drop would be before I turned to face what was behind me.

The men were about 30 feet away.

Rambo growled as he leaned toward them baring his teeth.

112

"No Rambo." I grabbed hold of his collar. "Stay!"

What would happen if Rambo charged them? They would shoot him. I just couldn't lose him.

"Stay." Quivering, I knelt with my arms around him.

I could smell my own fear.

The sound of tumbling of gravel and rocks toppling over the edge of the cliff reached my ears just as I felt the ground give away beneath me.

My scream died away like an echo in the wind.

Chapter 28
Shelter For the Night?

What just happened? Falling. My arms flailed out touching nothing but air. While I flew, the flashlight flipped out of my grasp. Just before I could wonder how far I would fall or whether I might die, I landed with a thud on a very hard surface. My head whipped backward with a thump. Rambo collided with me, ending up sprawled out on my chest. I clutched my arms around him. Flat on my back, I could hear my flashlight as it tumbled end over end down the side of the mountain followed by the crumbled debris that it knocked loose. When its light finally went out, my teeth clenched, muscles taut, heart drumming, I began to relax one muscle at a time.

I sat up.

A raw wind swept by me in a fury. My body shivered. Yet the sweat dripped down my forehead collecting in my ears. An icy chill ran the length of my spine.

My eyes became accustomed to the darkness with the moonlight allowing me to make out shapes.

Where was I? I tried to figure that out. I didn't have enough light to make out more than shapes.

We must've landed on a ledge, because we were not at the bottom of whatever this was. It almost appeared as though we were in a cave carved into the side of the wall of rock. Without light, I resorted to Braille. I felt around the icy, rough-hewn rocks. It wasn't a cave but rather an overhang of a boulder, sort of like a saucer with a teacup sitting on it. We were under the slope of the cup.

Above us, the men's voices grumbled. I grabbed Rambo by the snout gently pulling him beneath the overhang. If the men looked over, we would be hidden from their view.

A shot of their flashlight slowly trawled the rocky terrain. I wanted to look down to see how far away the bottom might be. *Then they'd know where we were.*

Sucking in tightly against the rock, I sat still as a doll on a shelf.

"Gawd. . .It looks like she went over."

"That's a mighty long way down. Think she could still be alive?"

"I wonder. Did you hear that rumble down the side? It sounded like she fell a hundred feet?"

He flashed a wedge of light back and forth across the rock face and down into the depths.

"See anything?"

"Naw. You?"

"Hey, Chicky! You down there?"

I held my breath.

"You okay?" He hollered.

The air tasted of danger.

"You hear something?"

A long silence blanketed the air.

"Naw."

They continued pacing down and back at the edge flashing the cliff and the wall of rock with triangles of light. "Are you there?"

My gran would hold my hand when I thrashed around in some teenage agony. She'd say, "Be still and know that I am God. Psalms 14 verse 10."

I am still, still as an elk caught in a headlight.

"Anyone down there?"

I held my breath.

"Nothing we can do right now. It's too dark."

"Come back tomorrow?"

"Yeah. Let's go."

I heard their footsteps pacing away. A huge breath seeped through my tight lips. Maybe Rambo held his breath too because I suddenly heard his panting.

Did I hear concern in their voices? Should I have let them know we were here? With his growling, I had trusted Rambo's assessment of the men. Dogs know whom they can trust. I hoped we weren't wrong.

Hugging Rambo tight, I listened to the drumbeat of my heart, while I felt each throb radiate through my body.

Running my hand through Rambo's fur soothed me.

"Too late now, Rambo. If they come back tomorrow, and we're still here…maybe?"

Meanwhile I knew I could do nothing. To climb either up or down, without light, would be way more than foolish.

Rambo whined, probably wondering exactly what I wondered. *"What should we do now?"*

The darkness kept me from finding out exactly where we were, therefore what we could or should do.

"I have no idea what to do, boy. We are probably going to have to stay right here until tomorrow. Then we'll figure it out." The remembrance of all we'd been through calmed me. "Haven't we always figured it out?"

I think I said that as a comfort to buoy me up.

"Yeah, we've always figured things out before, but this is really different."

Chapter 29
Up In the Air

Settling down for the night would be hard if I didn't make an assessment. *How much room did we have in this space?* Investigating, I ran my fingers over the rock. It felt like a stack of ice blocks, only rougher. Height wise I could just sit up under the overhang. *Is there enough space to take off my backpack?* That was like asking myself if it mattered to me if I got separated from all our supplies. A wrong move this way or that, and the pack would be gone down the abyss or worse, half way down.

Could I lie down? What if I fell asleep? What if I should roll over while I slept? I could be part of a landslide down the mountain. Or maybe I'd just knock poor Rambo over the edge. I shuddered at either idea.

I brushed a strand of hair that blew across my face. A raw wind gusted by. I had no idea what that might mean.

I pictured myself uprooted by a gust of wind, plunging off the mountainside, bouncing off the rocks and landing with a thwack, splattered on the ground covered by an avalanche of rubble. I winced at the thought of being pelted with an army of rocks.

Rock hard? I found out what they meant by that expression. I took out Ram's blanket from his pack to scoot it under my bum. Getting out the sleeping bag didn't seem possible. Too much moving around and we'd be over the edge.

The rigid surface chilled my tortured bony rear. I had to decide if I wanted to sit on the blanket or wrap it around us.

My stomach growled so loud, I thought the men above might hear it.

Like studying, when your mind has been busy, hunger sets in. Fear kept my mind busy until it wasn't. My tremors had stopped.

In all this process of escaping, plus the time I took to assess our situation, I hadn't thought about anything but staying alive.

With my mind clear, another thought occupied my mind. Food. At that moment, food was the only thought I had. Visions of a hamburger floated in my brain. I was starving.

One bright moment in a field of chaos—I had a Ziploc Baggie filled with smoked bison meat and it had been a long time since lunch. "How does BBQ bison sound Rambo?"

After loosening my backpack, I decided against taking it clear off. I struggled but finally unzipped the pocket where I stashed our dinner. I pulled out the baggie. "Ta Dah!" Dangling it in my hand, I jiggled it. "Dinner my boy!" As I listened to his sniffing, I pictured his black nose twitching as he pointed to the bag.

My eyes adjusted to the darkness allowing me to discern his furry outline. Every so often I caught a glimpse of the glint in his dark eyes from a moonbeam.

"Good boy." I fed him the first hunk.

If those men had stayed around they would've had heard the chomping, the slurping as we finished off our buffalo meat. I tucked a little back in the baggie, saving just a small bit for tomorrow morning. I nibbled dandelion greens between bison bites, though I couldn't persuade Ram to try any greens.

Still a slurp of water remained in the canteen that I shared with Rambo. I reserved a slosh for the morning. That just reminded me to listen as the rushing water below sang out.

"We need the blanket." I scooted it out from under me. I propped myself up against my backpack which leaned against the rock. I stretched out my legs. Shivering, I drew Rambo close where I found just enough space for him to curl up next to me with his head on my lap. I wrapped the blanket over us.

The wind whistled as it swept into our sheltered crevice.

I smoothed my hands across his head and back. Then I felt around for the gloves that I had hooked to the outside of my backpack.

"Let's warm each other up," I said as I slipped my fingers inside the gloves. "That's a bit better." I rubbed his paws. "I wish we had mutt mitts, Ram."

I wrapped myself around Rambo, and tucked in the blanket. "Dear Lord, thanks for another day. Please be with us tomorrow." He brought us here for a reason. Just what was it?

"Thank you, Rambo, for your warmth."

I listened.

The wind eased up. Smiling, I suddenly realized that this predicament wasn't all bad. *At least we weren't hungry. I needn't fear those men. Our whereabouts rules out an attack, sort of like a castle with a moat around it. Our moat is air. The wind had ceased. And water! It flowed very near. But could we get to it?*

No sounds were left but a hoot from an owl, Rambo's snore, a moaning wind with the rushing water that flowed somewhere below. I created another sound—as I shivered, my pack knocked against the rock.

Exhaustion set in and my shivering finally stopped.

That tantalizing slushing of streaming water somewhere close touched my taste buds. Closing my eyes I hoped would induce sleep while I listened. A vivid vision of a crystal clear mountain stream gurgling past dominated my mind.

Would I be able to sleep? Was it even safe to sleep? Maybe I'd roll over. Could I knock Rambo over the edge or fall myself? Was I tired enough to forget how thirsty I was?

That formed my last thought.

Chapter 30
A New Day
Day 7

Darkness engulfed me. I could see nothing. Then how did I know I was falling end over end like being thrown into outer space. I reached out to grab a passing limb but the branch slipped through my hands. Help me! Dizziness had me churned around and over and under. The darkness of the sky surrounded me like a velvet blanket. Stars twinkled. I tumbled off the ledge. Help! My arms wind-milled. I found nothing to grab onto. Help me! I'm falling! A strong hand extended toward me. Papa?

The next thing I knew Rambo pawed my leg while the sun rose over the adjacent mountain. Slanted rays of morning light angled into our resting place.

I rubbed my eyes almost forgetting what had happened.

Ram's thick tail beat a rhythm against the rock when he saw I was wakening.

"Thank you, I just dreamt of falling into a dark abyss. You saved me—again!"

After a quick peek over the edge, I gasped. "Thank you God. How lucky you stopped my fall that last night or I couldn't see how far down we could have fallen." I scooted to the edge with my legs bent over the ledge. I sucked in a breath. A river, at least a pretty healthy stream flowed below us. It rumbled splashing over the rocks. I licked my lips as I envisioned scooping up a handful of that cool, clear, pristine water and gulping it down. From where we were, that would be no easy feat. It was a long way down.

With daylight I could assess our situation. There was no way to climb up because the overhang was a rounded boulder with no foot niches or hand holds. The only way out of our current campsite was down.

As scary as that proposition was, that's where the water waited for us.

Should we stay here for a while? What if the men came back? Would they bring a rope? 'If' is a big part of that equation.

Below us, a small ledge woven into the mountainside appeared to be about 10 or maybe 15 feet away, almost like someone had carved a path from this ledge right to it. *Would that just put us further in the middle of this shear drop? If I went down this way, would Rambo follow?*

I couldn't go without him. I held his face in my hands and stared into his eyes. "It's both of us, boy. That means we'll figure this out together."

Perhaps I could put a leash on him. From this vantage point there didn't appear to be another trail leading from that next ledge to the ground.

What should I do? Since down is the only option, we have to face the next hurdle when we get past the first one.

That decided I listened to my stomach grumbling, reminding me it might be a good idea to eat breakfast first.

"Okay Rambo. While we contemplate our escape, let's finish off our BBQ bison. Maybe if we gulp down the last of our water, we'll have to find a way down." I took out the baggie then the canteen. "Breakfast?" I handed him a piece of buffalo meat. Being a bit tough to chew a large hunk, I nibbled on mine. Anyway, if I gobbled mine too fast, I would just have to make some big decisions.

"No use rushing into anything, huh Ram?"

The water sloshing around in the bottom of the canteen told me that this was it. "It's okay, Rambo." I poured some in the cup for me then gave the rest to Rambo.

"Don't worry, boy. There's plenty of water down there," I said while I viewed our escape route over the edge. "The problem is—how do we get to it?"

A thought of my Gran came to mind. She always had something to say when I came to her with a problem. As a teenager, every problem seemed like the end of the world. I inspected my position. "Now this does seem like the end of the world, huh, Gran? What should I do?"

I patted Rambo. When I finished my meager breakfast, a Bible verse immediately came to mind—a verse Gran used to say.

I cocked my head to the side just the way Gran would. She'd smooth the tendrils of her white curls up into the twist of hair at the top of her head. I smiled remembering how she always included the chapter and verse. "Psalms 46 verse one; God is our refuge and strength, a present help in trouble."

"Well, we're in trouble and we need help, Lord."

Sitting straight up, I closed my eyes. I took in a deep breath of cool fresh Wyoming air, put my hands together, "Okay God, it's up to you and me."

I found the duct tape. Were my blisters better? Maybe. I tapped some duct tape over the Band-Aid and laced up my boots.

First, I didn't want to lose my backpack on the way down. *If I throw it, how could I be sure it would make it to the bottom? I have to secure it before we started down. Besides, if it isn't secure it might flop around and keep me off balance.* I shivered in the breeze thinking of me losing my balance and rearranging the rocks on way down the side of the mountain.

First I secured all the straps for my backpack around me. After I unrolled a length of duct tape, I kept wrapping it around me like I was a mummy.

"There. I won't loose you while we're climbing down." I patted my pack like it was alive, like it could really understand me.

"See how silly you get when no one's around—talking to inanimate objects and you. Okay, Rambo. It's time for your harness."

I strapped the belt of Rambo's saddlebag around his middle. Then I hooked a bungee cord onto Rambo's collar and threaded it under the belt attaching it to the back of his collar. This created a harness that I could lower or raise. With the end wrapped around my wrist or my waist, I could help him down with me.

My ponytail whipped against my face.

When I leaned out and peered over, the wind whistled past us catching the outgrowths of vegetation that protruded from the rock and whipping them back in its force.

"Hmm. I hadn't counted on that wind." I took Ram's snout in my hand so I looked straight into his eyes. "It doesn't matter. We're out of water and food. We have no choice."

I kissed the top of his head.

"Here we go."

Chapter 31
Down

This wind reminded me of being a child, facing into a strong gust. You'd hold your coat outstretched, while you ran across a field. You just knew you could fly at any moment. This was one moment I didn't want to fly. *Could this wind be strong enough to blow me off the slim trail? What could I hang onto?* My eyes scanned the rocks for handholds.

I grabbed my baseball cap as the wind caught under the bill and it nearly blew off. I stashed the cap in between my backpack and my upper back. I brushed my tangled, matted hair then tightened it into the elastic band. The wind caught my ponytail and lashed it around my eyes. So I rolled the ponytail and tucked it into another coil of elastic making a knot on the top of my head.

Rock face climbers do this and on much higher and steeper grades than this. My only experience with rock climbing was a onetime visit to a gym that had a small cement rock wall to climb. It was a thrilling experience, but they had you harnessed up with belts while they suspended you with cords.

"Okay, we wait."

Maybe the men would return. Maybe the wind would die away. Yeah, sure—maybe a helicopter would fly by just to pluck us off this ledge!

After waiting for what seemed like a long time, I had to assess this new situation. No Food. No water. *Maybe those men would come back to help, maybe not. It had been at least an hour since sun up. If they were really concerned about me, they would have come back right away. Wouldn't they?*

The wind seemed to die down but hadn't ceased. Just when I thought it stopped, it often resurrected its might in gusting blasts. I wiped a strand of hair out of my eyes.

I scanned the wall of the mountain checking for handholds.

The footpath was wide enough with sketchy gaps that made me wonder if I could stretch between the spaces.

"Could I wait? Tomorrow might be better or not. Nothing would be different tomorrow except I'd be weaker, hungrier and thirstier.

I kept in mind those rock climbers on TV. They scaled steeper, smoother heights than this like a slow crawl of a cat climbing a tree. Most weren't hooked in a harness.

I attached the end of Rambo's Bungee cord around my waist. "Okay, we're going, Rambo."

I planned to let him down slowly then set him on the ledge.

"C'mon, boy. You can do it." Rambo braced against the wall of our temporary campsite. He wouldn't budge.

This time I didn't have a candy or even a bison bite to lure him. I couldn't blame him. The crumbling of the small debris tumbling away, bouncing downward wasn't helping my confidence.

"I got you, Ram." I gave a gentle tug. "Please, Ram. I can't leave you there."

He wasn't going anywhere.

My second assessment, the cord might not be long enough. *Would he bob around on the bungee cord and what if he couldn't get his feet on the ledge and balance?*

"What are we gonna do, boy?"

Chapter 32
I've Got You

Evaluating my options by surveying the space between the next ledge and us, I realized there were few.

I could drag him down. No, his paws probably would not be able to find the spaces that I had used.

I could throw him over and hope he landed all balanced on the ledge. Impossible! I'd have to be there to catch him.

I could rope him against my chest. Could I hang on tight enough to cling to the rocks? No, I had enough trouble hanging on for myself.

Those rock climbers must train for their climbs to build up strength in their fingers, hands as well as their arms, legs and toes. Plus I don't think they carry 25-pound packs on their backs. My fingers are not strong enough and besides, they are ice cold. Is it possible to have fingers snap like an icicle?

My gloves wouldn't work in this situation.

I could lower him down. In our tiny cramped camp, there was nothing for me to hold onto. What if he's too heavy? What if he started swinging? Bungee cords bounce. He could drag me over.

What about this wind?

After locating handholds, I eased myself down one step, then two, but I firmly had hold of the ledge. Rambo stared at me as if to say, *"Just what are you doing?"* He backed away from me, coiling at the back of the indentation of rock. I climbed up and hoisted myself back on the ledge. I leaned over in observation.

Then I saw it. *Yes, I've got it. I think I can make this work.*

After my initial descent, my confidence to climb down had built. I lowered myself, inch by inch, one handhold to the next, my feet finding the narrow bands of stone. As soon as I found holes for my hands, my toe probed for the next toehold. Finding it, I jammed my boot into the crevice.

Between each maneuver, the loosened rocks plummeted down, reminding me how far I would fall if I let go—a great motivator for maneuvering carefully and hanging on tight.

This journey was a realization of how tenuous life is.

Swallowing hard, I took the next step. Hand and foot coordinated, I moved on.

I rested for a moment. The way my heart knocked around inside, I thought I might be able to see it hammering on my ribcage.

I let go of the breath I was holding. I counted backwards from 100 until I quit shaking.

Breathe normally.

I gave a tug on the cord. Ram still resisting, pulled his head back like, *"What do ya think? I'm crazy?"*

"C'mon. Come to the edge, boy. I need you to help."

Rambo approached the edge slowly. He peered over.

He yipped a sharp yip as if to say, *"No Way."*

A substantial root looped out of the rocks then looped back in— a possible anchor for me to hold onto.

I gasped in a few dusty breaths.

Then I glanced down.

Big mistake.

I imagined my body bouncing, tumbling to the bottom followed by a rockslide, pelting and pummeling my bloody body all the way down, then being buried until my lungs sucked their last breath.

A strong gust of wind blasted my body.

Involuntarily my right hand plus my right foot abruptly slid from the safety of their holds.

I wailed. "AHHH!"

The blast blew my right side away from the wall. A scream of horror ripped thought my being as my limbs dangled free. I clutched desperately with my left side. Then just as suddenly as the gust attacked, it ceased. When the wind died, my body swung back to the wall with a smack. I shrieked.

Rambo howled.

Do not panic!

I scrambled for a handhold, raking the rocks until finally I felt it. I gripped a protruding rock with my right hand and jabbed my foot against the wall searching by braille until I kicked into a crevice.

Trembling in every corner of my being, my toe found a resting place.

I froze for a moment contemplating my close brush with death. Pausing, I settled into a dubious moment of safety. Determined, I continued shaking as I carefully planted one foot, one hand and one mind on my downward trek.

Breathe.

I made it to the ledge! When at last my feet plunked onto the solid surface, I let out a huge breath and gasped. I leaned against the wall. Until I became calm, I inhaled slowly then exhaled.

It felt like it took an hour to reach this plateau.

"There Ram. I made it. See. I'm okay."

Assessing my new position, I found my observation to be correct. I yanked hard against the thick root to test its strength. A bit of debris cascaded down the face of the wall, but the root didn't budge. It was strong, strong enough I prayed.

One glimpse over the brim caused a shudder that engulfed me. "Okay Rambo. You have to trust me."

The trouble though—could I trust myself? You can do this. Be with me Lord.

Inhaling another deep breath, as though I could fortify myself with air, I hooked the bungee leash and my elbow around the root leaving my other hand free. I braced my foot against the wall and clung to the root.

Looking up became impossible because, Rambo resisted against the edge. His stance knocked a small cascade of dirt over the edge that dusted my face.

"It's your turn Ram!"

Whimpering he peered over the edge like, *"Help me, please."*

I grabbed the cord of Rambo's leash with my free hand.

Am I strong enough? I have to be.

"Rambo, are you ready?" I said that as much for me as for him. If I was wrong he might fall all the way down. If I was wrong, we might both be part of an avalanche.

I do not have a choice. I will not leave Rambo!

Time suspended, passing like a set of frame-by-frame display of images.

The debris spillage ceased for a moment.

With Rambo's eyes fixed on mine, I could see whites around the edges of his big brown eyes—white that I didn't know was there.

"It's okay Rambo. I'm here. Trust me."

A broad base is stronger so I spread my legs like you prepare to do jumping jacks.

Eyes cast upward, I whispered. "Okay God. It's you and me and Rambo."

I jerked hard.

Dragging behind him a barrage of dust and debris, Rambo flew over the brink.

Chapter 33
Now What?

I willed myself to squint but to keep my eyes open through the minor avalanche. I needed to see him to be able to pluck him out of his fall. As Rambo came flying near, I stretched my arm out to hook him in.

While I had an alternate plan, the dynamic catch seemed the one I hoped would work.

It didn't.

I broke his fall but he slid through my grasp almost in slow motion.

"No! Rambo!"

He whined and whimpered, as he slipped through my arms. I grabbed for the bungee cord. It slid through my burning hand. I clamped hard, finally gripping the cord. Dangling at first then bouncing on the end of the bungee, he stuck out a rear paw just in time to hang onto the shelf.

When I looked down I had caught his cord just a foot or so away from his back. He didn't exactly dangle loose as he had an actual hold with his hind paw pressed onto to ledge. His body stiffened. The odd angle of his haunch appeared as though one false move and he'd break his leg.

He must have been more scared than I felt. He didn't even bark, just whined a pitiful pleading for help. *"Please Gabi. I saved your life. Please save mine."*

"I know I—I owe you." I grunted as I strained to keep hold of him. My fingers smarted as the cord chafed against my grip.

Three of his legs hung over the edge. I strained to hang on. So did he. "Don't let go Rambo. Don't let go!"

A gust of wind tested my tenuous grasp. "Help me, Lord."

With my one elbow still hooked onto the root, it felt as if my other arm would pop out of its socket.

Loose weight, Ram proved heavier than I expected. I had only one arm to work with.

Can I do it? I have to.

"Ugh! Hold on, ugh!" I grunted.

The root shifted then held, halting abruptly, creating a jerk to my arm that set Rambo swinging back and forth.

My arm ached all the way up through my shoulder and into my neck. My hand and fingers quivered. I feared they'd release involuntarily.

I concentrated, willing my adrenaline to boost my strength. I clenched my teeth. "Urg!" Then I yanked with all the force that I could muster.

Rambo scuffed onto the narrow ledge lying on his side, but I still straddled him. A gush of air burst from my lungs. Before I released my grip on the root, Rambo righted himself. Whether he had room or not, he shook himself.

My awkward straddle-stance made my position seem even more precarious.

Clinging tightly to the root, I slowly worked to get both my legs on one side of Rambo without knocking him off the sill.

We didn't have enough space to turn or to shuffle one way or another. Ram scooted a few inches as I pushed him with my calf. My two feet found each other. I released the bite on my lip. I had bitten so hard I could taste the blood.

One glance over the edge proved there we still a great deal of space between us and the ground below—we were not even half way down. The hairs crinkled at the back of my neck.

"Hey Rambo. People pay a lot of money to go bungee jumping like that!"

Could we try that same plan again with the ledge further down? Rambo might not cooperate this time seeing how precarious and scary our last maneuver was and considering that I almost dropped him. The bungee cord probably wasn't long enough.

Finally I registered where we were headed. I surveyed the terrain below us. A lush narrow meadow lined the river edged with aspen trees. The new green leaves fluttered with the flexing branches whipping the wind. A rolling stream cut through the space, rushing past us. The sight of which compounded my thirst.

130

Rugged mountains across the meadow, jutted like white-roofed castles into blue, blue skies. Cotton ball clouds sped along pushed by the strong wind. Taken by its beauty, I felt as though I floated along with the clouds, catching the wind until I soared like a bird.

The serenity offered a moment to breathe, to gather strength and thank God for getting us this far.

With all our struggles I had forgotten my thirst. Now the river reminded me. Who knew just the sound of water could evoke insatiable thirst.

The wet scent of the vegetation, the effervescence, the sound of the river splashing by, plus the dampness against my skin made me keenly aware of how close we were. Although, looking down reminded me of how far away we were.

The wind howled past us like wash drying on a line, flapping my hair out from my ponytail knot. It also sucked the moisture from my mouth as I breathed. Rambo's fur ruffled when he nosed into the wind. As dry as a weathered board and just about as stiff, I couldn't imagine where the sweat running down my neck came from.

The wind pushed against me buffeting my backpack. I clung with every muscle.

As I raised my line of sight I glimpsed a movement just above us.

A shadow floated on the rock formation.

A fresh cascade of debris rolled past us on its downward path, debris that we were not causing. I ducked with my eyes clamped shut against the showering dust.

A silhouette blocked the sun.

What could be there?

Chapter 34
We Are Not Alone

All of my senses seemed heightened. I clung with every nerve on alert.

Did I hear breathing, a minimal snort? I sensed another being, not that I saw anything but a shadowy movement. An odor wafted in the wind. Fear?

I didn't think it could be the two men from the camp. It wasn't booze breath or unwashed male body odor. Did I wish it were the men? Maybe. Maybe then we'd be rescued.

It wasn't Rambo.

Maybe it was myself without a bath for several days now.

I sniffed in a breath using all my olfactory perceptions. The gamey smell, not unlike the barnyard odor, reminded me of my gran's farm. She raised sheep plus the goats that leaped around in the field. *Oh, that delicious cheese and milk!*

Traversing of the rock face had masked my need, my thirst. I sighed. The thought of fresh goat milk puckered up my taste buds as it evoked a longing for a moment at Granny's breakfast table, sun streaming through the lacey curtains with me drinking an iced cold glass of goat's milk.

Before I could regain my sense of reality, Rambo blasted the air with a volley of threatening barks followed by snarls.

Then a large shadow flew overhead. I held up my arm blocking a sharp ray of sun combined with the exploding grit.

Then it registered. I watched the graceful leap of a big horned sheep, legs spread as it aimed for a landing on the small outcropping of rock. I marveled at all four hooves neatly perched together on a mini ledge making the animal poised like an upside down triangle.

Rambo ceased his barking. Could he be as fascinated as I was?

The ram turned his head eyeing us with a beady-stare. Did we constitute a threat?

He glanced at the ewe feeding at the bottom of the cliff.

So nimble and beautiful, I wanted to reach out and touch the circular twist of his massive horns.

"Now where to Mr. Bighorn?" I couldn't see how he would ever find his way off that ledge.

Abruptly, as quickly as he came, the ram leaped, strode and picked his path down the face of our shear wall. In a diagonal trail, he zigzagged down, a direction I never would have figured out.

I shook my head.

"Bet you've done that before, Mr. Bighorn."

Deftly, he elegantly traversed the mountainside—the very dilemma that faced the two of us novices. We watched with wonder. Nearly to the bottom, he vaulted a seemingly impossible distance. He landed on the ground next to the female with the grace of a dismounting gymnast.

Taking a backward glance at us with a tip of his horn-crowned head, he followed his mate. Another peek at us as he wandered off, seemed to say, "Sorry, we can't help you." They continued on to the placid edge where the water swirled into a pond-like extension of the river. Alternately they bent for a long drink and lifted up to check their surroundings. For all of us, a sense of distrust existed. In the wild one must always be wary.

The ram took one more look at us before they moved on.

"Are you trying to rub it in?"

"I got my drink. Let's see if you can get yours."

The thought of a lengthy, cool, refreshing, gulping drink tugged at my thirst strings. I inhaled the coolness, the moist plants, the damp earth, with the certainty that water does have a smell. That's how animals in the wild found water. The same thought must have occurred to Rambo. He whined a small yip. As though he had been hit by a spark, Rambo bounded down the same pathway as the ram.

Since we were attached by the bungee cord, I had no choice but to follow. "Hold it! Rambo." I jerked on the bungee. "Wait for me." Fortunately Rambo slowed enough for me to catch up, pace him so we could pick our way down. The descent proved relatively easy compared to what we experienced higher up, but we were no bighorn sheep. A long nosedive awaited us if we lost footing and crashed.

When at last we were about 15 feet or so from the bottom, as we perched on a small outcropping, I could see no more path carved for us on the smooth lump of rock.

We landed where the ram had taken his last giant leap. The ledge sat high enough for Rambo to pause whimpering on the edge, teetering like he wanted to jump but not believing he could do it safely. The distance looked great enough for me to realize the danger. Nor did I think I could make the jump.

"No, Rambo. It's too far for us to imitate that ram."

Rambo wagged his tail and looked up at me as if I again could figure this out.

He was right. I would figure this out. Not because I'm so smart, but because I had to. Being completely consumed by my thirst, I would leap, break my leg then drag myself to the water, if I had to.

I took a moment drawing in a lung full of moist air.

What to do?

My options involved jumping or hanging down and dropping the remaining distance. Both choices included the threat of injury. If either one of us were injured badly enough so we couldn't travel, we might not be able to find our way out of here.

It could mean death.

My thoughts went back to my gymnastics class and also the time I had taken a parachute jump with my papa. We had practiced how to fall.

So. . .I can do this. However, what about Rambo? If he jumped he could break a leg then what? I could put him on the blanket to drag him. However, he couldn't do the same for me.

"Okay Rambo. Here's what I am going to do." I wiped the sweat from my forehead. "I'm going to hang from this ledge and then drop. I am not going to hurt myself." I patted Ram's head and looked into his eyes. "Then you're going to jump. And this time I'm going to catch you. That okay, Ram?"

He lifted his paw with a whine. We shook. "Okay partner."

Was I convincing him or me?

I bent down, grabbed the edge. Carefully I eased myself over. Swinging I hung by aching fingers.

Rambo's whine turned much louder, ending with sharp barks. "*Jump Gabi!*" I imagined him barking.

"All right, Ram."

I swung in the breeze as I convinced myself to let go. "You can. You can do this. Don't look down. Just do it! One, two, three—go!"

"Ahh..." I plunked down with a thud, flexed knees continuing into a roll in the grass.

I stood up slowly as I stretched myself. A bit sore from our ordeal of the descent, plus my ankle did feel a little stiff, however, I was intact. I shook my leg.

Nothing felt broken. Nothing sprained.

I checked the bungee between Rambo and me. Not surprisingly it felt taut with Rambo resisting at the rim of the sill of rock.

"Here we go again, Ram!"

Not stopping to think, I gave the bungee a quick yank then opened my arms. Down he came. He landed with his front paws on my shoulders. The next thing I knew, I lay sprawled on the ground, Rambo on top of me. He made sure my face got a good washing.

"Oh Rambo. I love you!" I buried my face in his fur as I gathered him in my arms.

The next instant we were up racing for the water. Rambo reached the edge first and lapped like crazy.

After I unhooked my backpack, I struggled with the duct tape I had secured it with. Then I sprinted forward. At the edge of the river, I dropped on my knees and I dunked my face in. I sucked in mouthfuls of the cold crystal water. "Ahhh!"

My tool belt came off next. I plopped it on the ground, removed my boots then stripped off my grungy socks. With my clothes slipped off, I wore nothing but gooseflesh as I raced ahead.

I didn't care if it was cold or not, we swam around. I plunged under and came up with a mouthful of water. When Rambo's head popped up, I squirted water at him. He crawled up on shore, shook himself, and ended up with a long cool drink.

"Delicious! Water is the most delicious taste in the world!"

I threw myself backward, arms flailing and plunked under again. When I came up, I thought of how dirty I was. I dashed ashore, retrieved my soap and sudsed myself until the water floated with islands of bubbles.

"Clean at last!" I swam around dispersing the bubbles.

Rambo had found the perfect spot. He waded in, stood like a statue. He stared into the water without moving a muscle. His eyes darted this way and that.

"What are you doing, boy? Are you fishing?"

Standing still to let the water settle, I peered below the water line. Not only could I see them I could feel the fish swimming around.

Could he really catch a fish in his mouth? His nose just skimmed the water and a slight movement seemed to follow a moving target.

If I hadn't been so hungry, I would have luxuriated a while longer, scrubbing plus swimming around. But the thought of a fish dinner had me drooling. I finished a quick shampoo then splashed out of the water, gooseflesh rising. I shook off my hair with the wet tail slapping my shoulders.

Staring up to the top of the mountain, my adversary. Feeling a burst of hubris, I raised my arm and yelled at the top of my lungs, "I conquered you! I am the sovereign ruler of my world!"

Rambo joined me in a howl. Afterward he resumed his quiet watchful stance.

I continued to study my nemesis with my hands plunked on my naked hips.

How long it had taken us to descend from the cliff? Checking the sun's position in the sky I figured the time to be about three in the afternoon.

Not bad for conquering the impossible.

Chapter 35
Fish Fry

Rambo remained motionless midstream while I got on my underwear and a shirt. Poking around in my backpack pockets, I located the fishing hooks and line that Buck had so generously left me.

After swimming around with the fish, I had no doubt there were plenty of them. *However, could we catch any?*

I thought through my ability to fish. Papa and I had gone fishing, fly-fishing, but not that many times. I'd gone out on his boat, but net fishing wouldn't help me with the task at hand. I didn't think I could hang on to a fishing line in my bare hands even if I was lucky enough to snag a fish. Nor did I think I could catch one in my hands or—as Ram attempted—catch one in my bare teeth.

I opened the tin with the fishing line coiled next to the hooks. Two fancy little flies were there too. Since I had no food for bait, I hoped the flies just might do.

First I got the fire going then I searched around until I found a sapling. I chopped it down. Using my knife or my hatchet, I cleaned away the twigs and branches.

Rambo remained haunch-high positioned for a fish to swim by. He struck the water once or twice while I fashioned my fishing pole. *Even though my hungry stomach growled, what if I hook a giant fish? My makeshift rod might not be capable of handling much more than a small fish. With no reel I'd have to be strong enough to just pull it in. There wasn't that much fishing line so I'd have to hang on tight no matter what. I couldn't afford to lose it or my hook to a runaway fish.*

I admired the beautiful fly. *Did Buck tie his own?*

Rambo struck again, He reared his head up empty-mouthed as he watched me cast my line.

I tramped knee-high into the icy water.

"Ew! Chilly huh?" It's a race, Ram. Who's gonna catch one first? Then the bigger question—who is the one gonna haul in the biggest?"

Not more than about 15 minutes went by before Rambo dunked his snout into the river. Like it was as easy as stirring soup and scooping up a vegetable, he yanked up a silvery flapping fish. He held the fish out of the water with it struggling against the steely grip of his jaws.

"Okay. You win the first. Just wait'll you see the one I'm gonna catch! It's gonna be a monster."

I jerked in my line in. I drew back and cast again.

Would he be kind enough to share his catch with me or would he gobble it down right then? After all, he is a wild beast. He's probably starving. We hadn't eaten very much for hours. Surely he's as hungry as I am, hungry enough to be shaking while I just thought of swallowing a bite of tasty fish.

The fish head hung out one side of his mouth. The tail flapped out the other side. Ram shook his head until the fish settled down. He trotted back to shore and dropped it near the pack. The fish, about seven or eight inches long, flopped around on the ground. Ram subdued it with his paw until it accepted its fate. He gave me a look, *"Did I do good, huh?"*

"You're my good boy!" To my surprise, he waded back into the water where he took up his watch again. "Did Buck teach you to share?" I couldn't believe he didn't scarf it down in a bite or two. We wouldn't starve if we didn't catch any more fish. Though I was really hungry.

This part of the river pooled up. Maybe fish came by to rest from the current, because I got a bite not long after. "Strong little bugger, aren't you." I wrestled with it, until it stopped struggling for a moment. I raced for the shore, yanking as I went. Once I dragged the fish on shore, I tried to grasp it but it flipped out of my hands. I copied Ram's trick. Extending my bare foot, I held the fish down. "Eew! You tickle!"

When I finally settled the fish down and was able to get the hook out of his mouth, I measured Rambo's fish. "Mine's bigger, ol' boy."

A while later Rambo trotted back on shore with another fish a good two inches longer than mine.

"Okay, Ram, you win. First and biggest."

This time he didn't drop the fish.

He sat down, sprawled out as he held the fish in his paws like a lollipop then proceeded to rip the small beast apart.

"Yuck! You are something, Ram."

The fact that he gave me his first fish seemed incredible.

After that it was only minutes before I pulled in another plump fish. I drew out my knife, cleaned and boned the fish. Once I had boned and separated them from their head and tails, I scraped the entrails in a pile with the head and tail. Ram took no time at all to clean up the mess.

I had to look away noting in my mind, how lucky so far on this adventure, I hadn't been hungry enough to eat raw meat or to grovel for insects. Those options might come up soon but for now, "Thank you God." I smiled at my thought, 'adventure'.

"So far, Rambo, we are on an 'adventure'."

After I plopped our silvery beauties into the skillet, I set the skillet on the grate over the fire. By cooking more than we could eat at night, breakfast and lunch would be cooked. I didn't need to waste a match to start another fire.

While the fish sautéed, I noticed some dandelions. "Oh, boy! Salad with dinner." The little purple flowers scattered around with the dandelions looked lovely, but I had no idea if they were poisonous.

I gathered enough greens for my salad and saved some to make tea for later.

"Mm." With savage hunger, I picked my fish apart, licking my fingers as I went along. "Listen to me! I sound even worse than you do engulfing your food."

Rambo sidled up to me. While I ate, he knew I was a sucker for his big brown eyes that he rolled up at me. He poised his snout on my knee as I sat cross-legged.

"You already ate yours." I scrunched my nose, thinking he ate his raw. Sushi, I had never tasted it. *Maybe next time I'll venture a bite raw.*

I alternated my fish bites with my dandelion greens.

"Here you go, best friend." I dropped the skins down for him to finish off. Anymore, we didn't generate much garbage to bury after our meals. "Thanks for cleaning up my mess."

While smoking the other fish, I watched the sun slip toward the vee of the mountains in a beautiful twilight blue sky. The last sunrays clothed the surroundings in an amber light. The beams gilded the rims of the new spring leaves with an amber glow. The rays danced like golden glitter on the ever-changing river as it journeyed past us. *How wonderful to find a peaceful moment to recoup from our harrowing experience.*

Then I remembered my laundry. I took some time to wash my filthy clothes.

Rambo sat scratching while I headed for a flat rock hanging just about the right height to dip and scrub. "I am glad I fished first before doing my wash. Those fish critters would have beat their tails away from here pretty fast in the opposite direction when I dipped my foul duds in the river." I sat on the rock, dunking my bikinis, pants, and tee shirt in the water, scrubbing then rinsing. I included the blessed bungee cord in the suds, *blessed* because without it I don't think Rambo would be here. After I made a clothes line stretched between the branches of a couple of aspen, I draped my laundry across. Not so cold as it had been, with the evening so beautiful that night, I decided to sleep *al fresco,* so I could use my bungee cord for the clothesline. The clothes would be dry in the morning.

After cleaning the pan, I filled it with water dropping in a handful of dandelion greens. I had never tasted tea made that way before but had read that it was very good for you. Sipping it warmed me as I sat with Ram by the fire. I hummed, as my gaze turned toward the open expanse of indigo skies. The sky filled with glistening stars that settled around a soft moon. They sometimes became veiled with passing wisps of clouds.

"I wished I'd listened better in science classes so I would understand how this beautiful orb had any influence on the tides."

As I hummed, Ram had found a new voice, a gentle whine so different than his begging or frightened whines also softer than his howls when I sang out loud.

Experiencing the quietude, a respite, a pleasurable feeling of confidence and contentment filled my being as I rested my arm around Rambo. "We've been lost for a week, Ram. But I am sure it's not much longer until..." My voice trailed off as I watched a shooting star sail across the sky. I smiled and pointed. "Look Ram!"

A good omen, I thought.

Wil and Papa might be looking at the same expanse of sky, while they wonder where I am. That thought took me out of the moment while a feeling of melancholy shrouded my thoughts. *My papa must be so worried. So must Wil. They probably think I am dead. I wished I could let them know I was okay.*

Tears welled in my eyes when I recalled how devastated Papa became when Mama was taken from us. That day in the cemetery he delayed coming to the car after the graveside service.

Impatient, I went back to see what was taking him so long. I paused behind a tree while I observed him kneeling by the grave and pounding his fists on the lawn. I waited while his body shook, sobbing with his face buried in his hands. That was almost more than I could stand. I had never seen him cry before. I fell to the ground my wails accompanying his and I didn't stop even when he picked me up and carried me to the car.

My eyes blurred as I sipped on my dandelion tea. Warming my hands around the cup, I thanked God that I was okay. I would be seeing Papa and Wil—soon I hoped. "Hey my favorite men. I'm coming home." *If only my message could tiptoe through the stars so it could find it's way to them.*

Tomorrow's journey would take us down stream where surely civilization could not be far away.

Food and water aplenty, in the safety of this serene place, I could not imagine any more traumatic events could befall us.

Chapter 36
A River Travels with Us
Day 8

After I drank my warm tea, I luxuriated in the exhaustion that crept into my being. With Rambo nestled close in my arms, I sprawled out in the comfort of an easy sleep under the stars.

When the dream began I felt joy exploding in my spirit. *Just a short distance away, down the river and through the meadow I saw Wil's silhouette shimmering illusively in the setting sun. Nevertheless I knew for sure it was Wil. "Wil, Oh Wil!" I raced though the grasses. I passed a thicket of bushes that I slashed out of my way. "Wil, it's me! I'm here!" As fast as I hacked them away, branches swung slapping me again and again, hindering me as Wil dashed toward me. Although I hurled myself at maximum speed, as fast as I ran, and as fast as he ran, we were getting further and further away from each other. "Wil, I'm safe! Wil. I'm coming!" Darkness closed in and he faded in the distance. "Wil? Come back!"*

When I woke, the tears slid from my cheeks down the sides of my face. *Tears of happiness* I thought as I sat up. This dream wasn't happening just yet—but it was coming.

As I sat up transfixed, I didn't want to scare them.

Several mule deer dipped their graceful heads into the river with their black-tipped tail ends facing me while they drank. I wished my phone were functional. I had missed so many beautiful photos. *What an album I could have made with photos of all the adventures we've had.* I still had the ink/water color sketches I made.

Trying to move in stealth, I eased out my pen and pad. I sketched quickly. I knew that Rambo would scare them away.

And I was right. As soon as he lifted his head, took a sniff, he rose to his feet barking viciously. He rushed forward filling the air with his voice.

In unison the deer popped their heads up.

With Ram at their heels, the deer dashed off. His chase didn't last long. He stopped to take care of business. His nose worked overtime sniffing where the deer had stood. Hunger must have caught his attention as he sniffed the baggie full of fish from the night before that I had tucked into my backpack.

"Okay, okay. I have business to take care of too. Then we'll have breakfast."

I pulled myself out of the sleeping bag with a big stretch. "I guess you wanted deer for breakfast but we have fish. Did you really think a mule deer would be an easy take down even for a wolf-dog like you?" I patted his head. "Then it's fish again for dinner. There's a whole school of them that beg to be caught right here in our own private river. We don't have a gun, remember? Besides I'd have to be very hungry to take down a deer. Should I have tried to lasso one with my bungee cord?"

I felt sore everywhere as I did a few morning exercises. Ram kept me going with my jumping jacks because his version, with his front paws wagging while he danced about on his hind legs, had me chuckling.

Rambo kept reminding me about breakfast, so we finished off a portion of the fish. After I munched a few dandelion greens, I plucked some pine needles for vitamin C. I took one more bite bit of fish then brushed my teeth.

To begin our hike, I prayed for a day filled with positives. Starting with washing my face, I didn't rush my morning. I folded my clean clothes breathing the fresh scent. One appreciates the small things in life—being clean was the top of my list at that moment. How unpleasant to smell my sweaty self. Perhaps being clean also meant that wild animals might not smell me either. After a nice hike today, along the river, at least I knew I had the possibility of another bath in the evening.

I waded in ankle deep to fill a couple of water bottles for convenience even though with the river, I could stop whenever I wanted. Besides one gets used to gulping from a bottle or cup.

Rambo splashed about, then shook himself sending a fine spray all over me.

"Okay, Ram. You win."

I shed my clothes and dove in. We splashed around playing chase.

"Time to go, boy." I imitated Rambo as we shook ourselves off. My ponytail slapped around. I twisted it to wring it out dripping it on Rambo who looked at me like, *"What?"*

Lying face up on a rock to dry off, the morning sun began to warm the air.

The chirping birds filled the air. Across the river, more mule deer fed on the rich new spring grass. Knowing that the animals were safe on the other side, I smiled when Rambo tried to get their attention by barking. The deer glanced at us feeling their own safety at a distance then resumed consuming their breakfast. Rambo yapped a few more innocuous barks, but the deer simply ignored him.

Feeling a bit chilled I fluffed my damp hair in the breeze, separated into thirds to braid it into a single braid. All dried off, I got dressed. The breaking of camp had me warmed up in moments. The final step in moving on was donning the backpack, not seeming any lighter each day that I strapped it on.

After we packed up, I felt the joy in my step while we followed the current down stream. Spring sprung up everywhere in glorious shades of green from the sprouting new growth in lime green to the dark green of the forest, with swaying grass abutting burgeoning bushes. Wild flowers floated along in the gentle breezes among the sea of grasses.

"You will go out in joy and be led forth in peace. Isaiah 55 verse 12." I heard Gran's voice as I remembered our early morning walks, Our hands clasped together, swinging between us, we sauntered down the dirt road beside her ranch. I talked to the sheep on our way. Near enough to pat some of them through the fence, I remembered the soft feel of their wool. That thought reminded me of the big horn sheep that all but rescued us the day before.

I watched the clouds drift by overhead. "I miss you Gran."

A sense of peace settled around me as we continued along the picture perfect river.

"Sorry Ram, we'll just have to finish off the last fish for lunch. Of course, if you're hungry enough, you can catch whatever you like."

Not being particularly fond of fish, I had to admit that the ones we caught were quite good. *Maybe I was just starving. Anything would taste good.*

144

"I hope we can find something else soon if…when." I shook my head. *We'll be rescued soon.*

Mm! Sweet grass! I plucked several blades. While I chewed on the ends, Rambo surprised me by tearing up some of the short green blades. Maybe animals sense when they are missing some nutrient. I hustled him on. The last time he ate a bunch of grass he threw up. "Can't have that again, buddy."

About an hour into our hike after lunch, I heard something.

We stopped.

I looked at Rambo, but it wasn't him. The sound hummed, soft in a higher pitch than Rambo's. After a few more steps, I heard it again. What was it? The noise sounded like a baby. When it grew a little louder, I knew wasn't human. *But what could it be?*

When I crept toward a copse of trees, the twittering of the birds had ceased. The silence spread around me like fear. The hairs on my neck bristled.

I stood perfectly still.

Then I saw it.

Chapter 37
The Unexpected

Under a large leafy bush, nestled in the soft grasses, I connected with the large, limpid, set of brown eyes belonging to a very small puppy. It looked like a miniature Rambo though all fluffy with the most endearing pair of golden brown eyes.

Rambo barked.

"Don't scare it, Rambo. See. The poor thing is trembling."

Rambo sniffed it.

"Aren't you the most adorable?" I sat on my haunches wondering. *Should I touch it?* Taking a 360 degree view of my surroundings, I didn't see any movement, or any animal to which this pup must belong.

"What will happen to you, sweet baby, if I leave you here alone?"

No. Its mother must be around. I must leave it be.

"Where is your mommy?"

I sniffed. About the same time, Rambo let out a shrill howl followed by vicious growling. It filled the silence of space around us with alarm.

"No Rambo. Let's leave this baby to his nap. Don't hurt it."

I picked up a large fallen branch, about six feet long with leafed limbs still attached. I could use it to help hide the pup.

"Listen!" That wasn't a purr that I heard.

It sounded a lot like Rambo—only stronger, savage, deadly and huge.

Then I saw what had upset Rambo. He didn't bark at the baby.

I backed away slowly, clenching my teeth.

The cougar was crouched atop a flat rock about 20 feet away from me. With his front paws braced, his body hunched above his haunches, the cougar's perch just above me provided the perfect spot for a leaping attack.

It crossed my mind that it might be the same cougar that took down the buffalo who would be plenty hungry by this time.

A low slow guttural sound rolled in his throat followed by malevolent hiss.

Neither Rambo nor I could take on this huge beast. Together, the two of us, didn't seem any better odds. Being closer to this animal, I realized how large a cougar was. He outweighed me by a hundred pounds I speculated.

I took another slow motion step backward.

Rambo didn't budge.

Would this cat attack me? Maybe he would wait for Ram and me to leave. After all I bet he had been after the baby, hadn't he?

I couldn't count on that. *I'm a much bigger meal.*

To ward off an attack, I had no chance for me to cover my arm as I had done with the wolf. If I put my arm up to cover my throat, it would snap like twig. I could almost feel his sharp teeth digging into my flesh.

The branch still clutched tightly in my hand, I stared at the beast. He stared back.

His lips curled open with a roar baring his enormous set of canines.

I grabbed my hatchet.

Rambo growled. In a flash, Rambo leaped forward at the same moment that I flung the hatchet.

The cougar was faster. My hatchet clanked against the rock just as the cougar flew in the air over the top of Rambo. He landed a few feet in from of me then charged.

It must have been instinct, because I had no remembrance of thinking through my move before I executed it. I seized the branch I still gripped with both hands. Holding it like a baseball bat, I swung as hard as I could. I battered the cougar across its body. This blow knocked him off to the side. After a roll, he sprang back to his feet.

"Ahh!" I swung again. A loud crack rattled through the air. He paused stunned for a moment. Another direct hit, but this time, I connected with his skull. A loud smack echoed out. He lay sprawled on his side. He must've also smashed his head against the rock. After a twitch of his massive paw, he didn't move.

Ram braced, growling and snarling.

From the rise and fall of the cougar's breathing, I knew he wasn't dead.

How long until he came to? Minutes? Seconds?

Fear kept me from going close enough to kill him with my knife. *If only we could get far enough away...*

I heard the growling behind me.

"It's okay Rambo, let's get out of here."

Not wanting to leave this cute little helpless pup for the cougar when he awoke, I scooped up the whimpering baby and turned to run.

When I spun around, I could see that it wasn't just Rambo growling.

I stood as still as a log.

Fear hung around me in every direction.

I had no escape. I was trapped between two inimitable forces.

Chapter 38
And More to Go

Was I breathing?

About 15 feet in front of us, stood a huge wolf. We eyed each other. *Would the wolf leave me alone if I set the pup down in front of her? Would she leap at me even if her babe were wrapped in my arms?* She bared her teeth with her threatening growls raising the hairs on my neck.

Analyze. I had her most treasured belonging. On the ground behind us, lay a cougar. Even me—I am not only a threat to her and especially to the babe. Attacking me might mean the demise of the baby. If the cougar got into the fray, the whole scene could be lethal for more than one of us.

That was a lot to process for the defensive mom. *Are such creatures endowed with that ability?*

My mind twisted in knots thinking of alternatives, as the seconds seemed like minutes ticking away. *I could throw the pup at her the run the other way. But I might hurt it. Then wouldn't that mean the mother would really be mad. Surely she wouldn't go after me leaving the babe alone with the cougar.*

I tried to make sense of my situation. That's when I noticed the white cross, etched in white fur across the wolf's forehead. *Could this be the same wolf—the very same wolf that I previously fought off? If so would that fact make her even more bent on my destruction? Or could she be a bit afraid of me since I drove her off before? Could she be beholden to me for not killing her when I could have?*

This time I had Rambo beside me. That fact emboldened me.

She snarled, bared her teeth and then growled.

Would the cougar awake while we have this stand off? How much time did I have to make this decision?

The mother leapt toward me with teeth bared.

She stopped just short of me, assuming a threatening stance.

Just a few feet in front of me, she stood close enough to smell her scent.

A shudder ran up my spine. I remained so still I wasn't sure my heart still beat. *Had this wolf witnessed the whole scene with the cougar? Did she understand that I'd rescued her pup? That I just tried to keep it safe?*

She eyed her pup then me.

Tension kept me motionless.

I let out the breath I held.

I trembled along with the pup.

Rambo's low growl, just audible continued.

My voice dropped to a soothing whisper. "It's okay wolf mama. I'm not going to hurt your baby." I held out the pup. "See. Everything is okay. I'll just give you back your cub."

Taking a small step forward, I leaned over. The mother whined.

Without taking my eyes off the wolf, I laid the tiny fur ball in front of her creating a barrier between her and me. "There mama, I'm just going to be on my way."

I inched backward.

Rambo still emitted a low threatening roll in his throat as we sidestepped the worried mom.

Mother wolf gave a little yelp, looked me in the eye, and picked up the pup by the scruff of its neck. When she took off vanishing into the woods I exhaled. "Come on Rambo. Let's go." I gave his collar a tug with my still trembling hand.

Should I run or just keep walking backwards?

I paused taking it all in. The cougar lay still passed out on its side.

Now what for me? I remembered. My hatchet! I knew it still lay on the flat rock, on the other side of the cougar. Only a few minutes had elapsed, though it felt like an hour.

If I tried to go past the cougar for my hatchet. . .would I have time to retrieve the hatchet and get away? I thought about a cougar attack. I had watched a cougar dash for his prey once. He sped fast as a flash of lightening. I envisioned his over-sized canines tearing off hunks of flesh from my body like that poor bison calf.

No. I would have to leave my hatchet. I paused to think it through.

150

I have survived so far without using the hatchet as a weapon, though gathering firewood is going to be a lot harder. Will my knife plus my slingshot provide me with enough protection?

I didn't have a choice.

I saw the jerk of the cougar's paw and the decision was made for me. He wasn't going to stay that way for long.

"C'mon Rambo. Let's get out of here." We raced off with a glance over my shoulder at short intervals. The cougar didn't follow behind me. I stepped up my pace until my side ached.

After a pause, I continued to move as fast as I could to put myself out of the cougar's sight.

How could I be sure the cougar wasn't tracking me?

I just had to get back to the river.

When could I count on it being safe enough to camp? The loss of my two best weapons made me sure I would never feel safe until someone found me.

After a short traipse through the wooded area, I returned to the river to following what I could be sure of—sooner or later there would be people. I slogged along in the water hoping to kill my scent in case the cougar wasn't far behind.

When the river took a turn, I felt safer. Before that change of direction, even if the cougar couldn't smell me, he might've seen me.

Shortly before dusk, I stopped for a drink where the river swirled out creating a small pond. I contemplated a swim with a bath but decided that I need to stay clothed, shod, mobile and ready to dash if the cougar showed up for a rematch.

Rambo had no such reticence. He charged into the water for his drink and then a quick swim.

He has a special whimper when he wants something from me and there it was, his high-pitched whine melted down the scale. *"Please come swim with me."*

"Not now Ram. I want to make sure there's no cougar coming to dinner tonight. Maybe in the morning I'll take a swim."

Pausing for a moment I listened. I checked around for signs of the cougar. A piece of driftwood lay by feet. "Nice bat, huh, Ram?"

I took off I my pack and dipped down, hands cupped to take several long slurps of the cool fresh water.

I heard the honks of geese flying north.

High in the clouds, their V formation dotted the picturesque sky. Thoughts of my lost rifle reminded me that we would not be having BBQ goose for dinner.

After I found my washcloth, I washed away the fear from my neck, face and armpits. There is a different scent that builds when fear sweats from your pores, different than the odor of honest hard-exercising sweat.

"Silly!" Rambo played tug-a-war with my washcloth.

As I leaned down for another rinse of water on my washcloth, I notice a slight movement at the water's edge.

I turned for a better view.

"Don't move Rambo."

I put a finger to my lips. "Shh."

Ram stood still, ankle deep in the water with his nose pointed right where I was aiming.

"Stay still."

Chapter 39
Gourmet Tonight

With my washcloth stretched out in both hands, like a flash I spread the cloth around a nice sized, plump bullfrog that struggled inside the cloth. I squeezed my fingers around him not allowing him to slither through.

"Dinner my boy, dinner!" Though I didn't feel like this one frog would do us both for dinner.

Rambo didn't seem to appreciate my catch. He glimpsed my frog then padded off. Rambo had his own idea for the menu because he waded out deeper into the water in his fishing stance. It wasn't long before he caught himself a wriggling fish. With that one safely on shore he went back for seconds.

While I prepared to clean the frog, Rambo trotted out of the water. With much gusto he consumed the second fish he caught.

His dessert was the left overs from me cleaning the frog and my fish. He gobbled them down in great haste.

After I built the fire, I set up camp in a clearing near the edge of the river so no animals could approach from behind. I stacked some rocks at the front of the tent that I could throw. Then I collected some pebbles for my slingshot ammo.

Watercress usually meant that water was clean so I was pleased to see some. I gathered the cress at the edges of a small stream flowing into the larger one. I closed my eyes with visions passing through my brain. I loved to eat watercress dipped in mayonnaise, though I would have to just enjoy the nip of my watercress salad without the benefit of mayo. Mayonnaise, cheese, bread and butter were the first foods I really missed. I tasted it. "Mm, way better than dandelion greens."

Rambo splashed out of the water with another fish hanging out of his mouth by its tail, resembling a long silver tongue.

He stepped on shore not releasing the fish. He shook himself.

The fish wagged in his mouth.

Laughing, I patted his head. "Could you bring two more for breakfast and lunch tomorrow?" Pointing toward the river, I didn't actually expect him to go back. He dropped the fish he had just caught and trotted back into his *fishing hole*. "You are one smart pooch!"

Gathering wood for the fire was definitely more difficult without the use of my hatchet. The fire would consist of smaller limbs that I could trim into shorter branches. That would mean I had to gather more to keep the fire going. Fortunately there were several branches, dry driftwood that had washed up on the shore.

While I fired up the two fish with my *Poisson de jour et les cuisses de grenousilles al la Gabi* in my skillet, Ram sauntered over by my side. He promptly consumed his latest catch.

Though I gnawed on my frog legs poised in my fingers, I used a fork to attack the smallest of the three fish.

"Ah. . .Chez Gabi's combination plate of the evening—fish of the day plus frogs legs. Not like Mama used to make. However hunger is the spice that seasons these fruits of the river."

As Rambo settled into a snooze, snout on my toes, I ran my hand down his back before I set the other two fish on spits to smoke for tomorrow's fare.

It was a while until I could swallow the fear that the cougar would return to exact his revenge from my besting him let alone stealing his baby wolf.

With my arms wrapped around my knees, I rocked back and forth, listening to an inner melody. Rascal Flat's words played in my mind. . .*I will stand by you, I will help you through, I will hold you tight and I won't let go*. . .thank you, God.

The deepest twilight blue melted into the inky night sky, bespeckled with the pinpricks of twinkling stars.

"Beautiful isn't it, Ram?"

I studied the almost full moon.

Sometimes it took me a few minutes to find the man in the moon that Papa always told me stories about. As a child, I remembered sitting outside in the back yard, toasty under a blanket with Papa's arm around me. We'd drink hot cocoa while he pointed out the star formations accompanied by his made-up stories.

"Right there! That's the big dipper."

I kissed my fingers and threw him a kiss. Wherever he was, I imagined he would actually feel it tickle his cheek. Then he would know that I'm okay.

One night after doing our star gazing, I woke abruptly with a cold chill. Being scared, I slipped downstairs. There was Papa sitting in front of the fire still as a star in the sky. I hadn't seen him cry but the one time after the funeral in the cemetery. The firelight glinted off the tears rolling down his cheek. I ran to him.

When I hugged him tight, he rocked me in his arms. "We miss her so." I must have fallen asleep in the warmth of his embrace because I woke the next morning tucked in my own bed.

As I now sat by my campfire, my face was wet. I wondered if my tears were shining on my face because that remembrance had touched my heart.

In the breeze, I drew in a deep breath experiencing the smell of the moist plants joining the fresh pine scent from the nearby forest. *I wish I could take this fragrance back home in case I needed aromatherapy.*

A sense of contentment settled through me as the silver glaze gently rippled on the surface of the river.

Soon my eyelids were drooping. When I moved to the tent, Ram followed me. After I pushed my legs into my sleeping bag, Rambo nestled next to me. His warmth filled me with a sense of safety. Accompanied by only a fleeting thought of fear, it wasn't long before sleep rescued me from the remembrance of the day's peril.

Chapter 40
Delirium

"Wil! It's me, Wil. I'm back! I'm home!"

He stood with his back toward me, dark, silhouetted as he filled the doorway. I ran toward him. He caught me up in his arms. He swung me round and round. I closed my eyes in a delirious thrill of his touch.

Tilting my face up, I anticipated the softness of his lips against mine. My adrenaline coursed as I drew in his intoxicating scent. The kiss was electric. I opened my eyes waiting to fill my senses with the freckled handsome face of Wil. I froze. It wasn't Wil. A smile beamed. It wasn't Wil's.

His features coalesced. Stunned, I recognized him. "Greg?" It was the air marshal.

The blue of his eyes touched mine with such gentleness, I felt the heat in my cheeks while I swallowed the question in my mind, "Where is Wil?"

I woke feeling dizzy. Sitting up with great difficulty, I propped myself on my elbows. I opened my eyes forgetting where I was. Everything went blurry. Chills engulfed my body and the next moment I felt hotter than a baking oven. My world spun in a murky haze around me. *Where am I?* Burning hot I touched my forehead with the back of my hand wiping aside my wet bangs.

Rambo whined. *Oh yes, I know where I am. But what's happening?* I shook all over.

Weakness kept me from rising again or turning over. *Had I accidently finished off Buck's whiskey? Could I be drunk?* My head ached. The spinning continued. My stomach churned. *Queasy!* Bile rose. I held it back. *What's wrong! I'm spinning, Everything is spinning.*

My stomach churned.

I crawled away from my sleeping bag.

Outside of the tent, I raised myself to my hands and knees and crawled as far as I could before everything in my system hurled from my stomach into the bushes.

I closed my eyes to stop the spinning before I collapsed backward, immobile on my spine like an upturned turtle.

I'm so hot. Flames! I blocked my face. Heat! Flames! Water! Everything was bathed in flaming shades of blazing red.

Faces appeared like clouds nearing me. I trembled. Then the faces withdrew in a swirl, vanishing like a tendril of smoke.

My stomach tightened. The sweat of fear engulfed me.

"They're after me!" I screamed.

"Help me!" I am out of breath. I can't run any more. They're gaining on me. A wolf! A pack of wolves. Then one leaped. His huge canine teeth were at my throat.

I shaded my eyes against the glaring bright lights. Reaching for my snarled hair, I slashed it out of my eyes. "Help Mama!" Faces with white masks covering their mouths leaned over me. I couldn't speak. Papa's face, I reached for him. Oh Papa, something's happened to Mama. Help her, Papa!"

I thrashed my arms trying to tear out the tubes poked in my arms. "Papa, is Mama is. . .is she dead?" Words careened through my head. They floated like snakes of sentences around me. Is this a hospital? Papa, stop this spinning I want to get off! I kicked. I screamed trying to get out of the hole I was in. Let me out of here!

Stop it! The voices...I clamped my hands over my ears but they wouldn't shut up, loud, mumbling all speaking at once. "What do you want?

My head thudded like I was hooked to boom box speaker. The pain throbbed with each beat. Covering my ears made no difference.

The trees moved, closing in on me and spreading their branches out over me, attacking like tentacles. Then as they neared my face, they disappeared like vaporous whiffs.

I can't breathe.

A cocoon of fog enveloped me in the trees. "Yea though I walk through the shadow of death. . ."

I'm so hot.

"I will feel no evil." Whose arms closed around me? Papa?

My throat rasped. My eyelids were swollen and encrusted. The world no longer spun when I finally opened my eyes.

Rambo had his snout resting on my shoulder emitting small puffs of breath. He whined. He lifted his head when he felt me move. I didn't know how I got back into my sleeping bag after I threw up. Nor did I know if I became sick more than once. When I tried to sit I puddled back to my sleeping bag. I rubbed my eyes. I pushed aside the flap of the tent. From the deep tone of the shadows outside I could tell it was late afternoon.

What had happened? I know it had been night when I went to sleep. But which night? How long had I slept?

I wiped my sweaty forehead. I still felt feverish and engulfed in dizziness. I lay there until the tent finished spinning. My ears rang.

Shivering with chills, I touched Ram's fur.

"I must have caught a germ. Let it just be a 24 hour one."

"Did the frog legs make me sick?" The thought of them cramped my innards. My mouth felt dry as cardboard. The canteen lay by the edge of the tent, just outside the flap. I couldn't reach it. The effort to do so left me breathless.

Ram watched me in my struggle.

"C'mon Rambo. Push it here."

I stretched for it again staring as I pointed in the direction of the canteen, imitating him when he wanted something. He eyed me. He eyed the canteen then me again.

"You can do it. C'mon, Rambo."

He pawed the canteen and shoved it with his snout until I could reach it.

"Good boy, Ram. What would we do without each other?"

It felt like the cap was welded to the top of the canteen. It took all my effort to unscrew it. Weakness! I couldn't even sit up without my tiny world in a spin. Trembling, I raised the canteen above my mouth. I almost choked trying not to drown myself. Finally I dribbled the water into my parched mouth. I slumped back down. My heavy lids closed.

Where am I? High. I rose into the sky. Flying, I'm flying. Below, my camp spread from the river to the stand of trees. Then I hovered over myself in the tent. Clearly I was watching me, studying my own self while I tossed and thrashed in the sleeping bag.

"Get up Gabi. The wild animals are coming." I could see their wild eyes. Wild grimaces bared their teeth.

"You're not safe . . ." Suddenly, engulfed in a bright light, my *Mother's face appeared, "Wake up Gabi."* She wiped my brow. *"It's not time."*

I wove in and out of sleep for how long I wasn't sure, but I woke early in the morning feeling fully conscious. I felt my head.

Although no longer feverish, my clothes were damp clear through. I had one of my legs hooked out of my sleeping bag. My head felt like I'd used it for a battering ram.

I didn't feel like moving. I felt paralyzed. *Was I?* Just as though I was a doctor, I examined myself. I tried moving my fingers then my toes. The effort to lift my limbs I likened to lifting weights. Everything seemed to be working though in slow motion.

Meanwhile Rambo couldn't sit still. He thumped his tail wildly. He circled around me in the tight quarters of the tent.

I lay there for a long time content to be a layer on the land like a geological addition. Rambo was not. He scooted the canteen closer to my hand, alternately pointing to it and looking at me.

"Okay, Doctor Ram. You're right. I need to drink. I am very thirsty. I am probably very dehydrated, too."

This time I raised myself caught in a dizzy awareness of how frail I felt. Tilting my head back, I drained the last of the water from the canteen tasting that peculiar container taste that almost turned my stomach. If I wanted any more water I would have to retrieve it myself.

I lay back down trying to remember my dreams. My mother and the accident often found themselves inflicting the nightmares of that night, though this was the first time I remembered Mama speaking to me.

I ran my fingers through my damp, matted hair. "It must be time to get up, Ram. I'm thinking of how I look. "Can't get rescued looking like this." My hand caught in a tangle of my sticky mass of hair.

I'm sure I resembled a sloth as I drug myself up. I crawled out of the tent. *Feeble—is this what it must feel like to be really old?*

Looking around, I squinted trying to adjust my bleary eyes to the brightness of the day.

I truly had no idea how long I had been ill. One day? Two? I didn't think any more time than that had elapsed.

Disoriented, I sat again.

Rambo raced around in circles, beyond being excited. On his hind legs, he jumped like when we did our jumping jacks. "No Ram, I'm not going to do exercises today."

While I found my primping kit, brushed my teeth and carefully combed the mats out of my hair and braided it into a single thick braid. Rambo stood in his fishing spot with his muzzle pointed. His eyes followed the circling fish.

When he brought his catch out, he flopped it in front of me. I almost gagged. "I turned my head away. The mere thought of fish turned my stomach in waves of nausea.

Rambo pushed the fish toward me as he tried to make me look at his present.

My eyes suddenly scrinched shut.

"I know. I am hungry but fish. . .ew! No, Rambo!" I patted his head.

Chapter 41
Recovering
Day 10?

Fighting light-headedness, I managed to fill the water bottle by dragging myself to the water's edge. I drank water most of the morning while I did little more than lay still. If I sat up, I stared straight ahead. Ram fished several times during the day, but there was no way I could eat the fish he dropped in front of me. My stomach refused to consider it. Rambo didn't let any go to waste, however. He gobbled them down as soon as I refused them.

I ate a little watercress, which I could barely swallow. I napped a bit off and on. After dozing a while, I woke. Not surprisingly I had dreamed of sitting at a table at Fresh Harvest ready to dig into a plate of waffles, crispy bacon with a mound of scrambled eggs. The imagined aroma seemed so real I wrinkled my nose. Though I woke before I could take a bite. That dream had my stomach growling. Without food I became weaker. A good sign though—I was hungry, really hungry.

While I put on my boots I noticed my blisters were much improved going a couple of days without being bound up. *Still better Band-Aid them.* While I had focused on my feet I hadn't noticed Rambo.

Checking the area, I couldn't see Rambo. He was gone. "Rambo? Where are you?"

Suddenly I cringed in fear. I hugged myself feeling as cold as ice. I was alone.

Standing, my head swam. I teetered a bit until the dizziness subsided. I adjusted belt that slung down. I felt my ribs. I could've counted them if I hadn't scared myself with how much weight I'd lost. I tightened my belt a notch. Touching my knife, I warded off the fear I felt being alone. Too weak to hunt for Rambo, I couldn't even think of hunting for food.

I plunked down on my bony rear.

Before I could really worry about Rambo, he trotted out of the woods.

"What have you got there, boy?"

As he padded along, a mouth full of twigs bounced in the grip of his jaws. "Where did you get this?" I took the twigs out of his mouth. "It's a bird's nest!" Four small eggs lay tucked in the bottom of a beautifully formed bird's nest. "Good boy. Scrambled eggs! Yeah! Did you read my mind?"

I summoned enough energy to start a small fire with a few of the pieces of wood I had gathered before the illness attacked.

"Okay let's see whether I'm lucky enough to have an omelet or fried embryos." That thought made me wonder. *Could I be that lucky twice? Could I eat them if they were embryonic?*

"Only one way to find out." Rambo sat watching me like my nurse, *"Eat your food now. Get better."* His wagging tail slapped the ground as he watched me.

I shook an egg. Nothing bounced around inside. The egg cracked. It's yoke slid into the cup. "Yeah!" I giggled. Real eggs even if they were small.

Fire started, I gathered some dandelions and watercress for my omelet. After I whipped up the eggs in a cup, I poured them in the skillet and sprinkled in the veggies. Thank goodness. With a roll, I flipped the eggs into a roll about the size of a regular one-egg omelet.

Rambo must've sensed there wasn't enough for two of us as he trotted out of the river sporting his catch flopping out the edges of his mouth.

Amazing. I felt much better having eaten. Even the fresh mountain water tasted good. I made some dandelion tea. Its warmth spread though my body. I lay back to rest for a while.

Noticing how grungy I felt, sticky with hair greased down. I knew I must have felt better to even notice. I stripped out of my clothes. "C'mon Rambo, Let's take a swim." I grabbed a washcloth and the soap on my way to the stream.

I stood in the shallows shivering. After the initial shock of cold water against my skin, I enjoyed the pure luxury. Finished sudsing up, I threw my soap back to shore. Too bad it didn't float. But I did. Buoyant, we glided around playing in the water.

Afterward I washed my clothes. Using the bushes as a clothesline, I draped the wet wash to dry.

The effort at living totally exhausted me.

Both of us napped for a while. When I woke, I almost felt normal, healthy and clean. My meager gourmet omelet was wearing off. I felt genuinely hungry for anything we could find, though fish still remained the last thing that sounded tasty.

I heard a sound in the woods behind us. Something small moved. Rambo pointed. I saw what he had spotted. A squirrel rustled out of the bushes. It dashed up a tree. Perched motionless on an outstretched branch, he pretended to be invisible.

I tried not to think how cute squirrels are.

So I focused on my hunger. I remember reading one of Granny's Scottish storybooks where the hunter had said a prayer before he killed his prey.

"Thank you, Lord, for this food I am about to receive. And bless this spirit as it returns to your care."

Moving about very slowly, I found my belt. I unsnapped my slingshot. Rambo remained absolutely still while I selected a pebble, loaded and drew my slingshot back. I took aim. The stone snapped forth with a, "Zap!" The squirrel fell from the tree with a thump and rustle of the brush. Rambo hit the ground running. He scooped the squirrel up into his jaws and gave it a good shaking.

I had never eaten squirrel. Feeling a little queasy, I cleaned our prey. Ram, always a good housekeeper, eliminated the innards with the spare parts. I turned away so I wouldn't have to see them and gag.

By the time I skewered the squirrel and roasted it, I would have eaten anything.

Gran raised rabbits in the hutch behind her house. I never wanted to fall in love with them because she often served rabbit for dinner or she sold them. In either case, having a relationship or getting close meant heartbreak. Though I really wanted to take them out to cuddle up next to their soft furry bodies. I kept myself away from the hutch and those adorable rabbits. As it was I could barely take a bite when they were served up for Sunday dinner.

The smell of the meat roasting practically made me drool, and drool enough to bypass my reluctance.

It did taste pretty good. I suppose the squirrel's flavor was pretty similar to rabbit.

Cooked or not, Ram didn't seem to care.

He gobbled everything at the same rate of speed. I savored mine, though I filled up rather quickly.

Even after all the sleep I'd had during the last couple of days, I dozed as I sat by the fire just staring. A bob of my head woke me.

I left Ram sprawled out by the fire while I tucked myself in the sleeping bag. I had wasted time being sick.

"After a good night's sleep I should feel strong enough to go on."

The worst just had to be over.

"Strength, Lord, please."

Chapter 42
Moving on
Day 11

Waking early, I set about cleaning up camp so I could pack. For breakfast, we ate a small portion of squirrel meat. As soon as we finished our meager breakfast, we were off.

As we ambled along side of the river, I whistled making up little melodies. My sickness had taken its toll, as I needed to sit down to rest every so often.

How did my 25-pound pack become 100 pounds? The longer we trekked, the heavier it became. What a great relief when I exhaled a hefty breath and set my backpack aside to rest. While I took out lunch, Ram thoroughly sniffed the area. As he examined the ground, he circled, re-sniffed all the while snorting.

"Hey boy, what are you so excited about? What do you smell? Come over here. Let's eat."

When I took out one of my last Ziplocs filled with our leftovers, Ram's nose took a new interest in our repast. Lunch consisted of finishing off the squirrel with a side of watercress. As I collected the watercress, I had surveyed the crystal clear water and saw that fish were still plentiful. I suppose that we would have to catch fish for dinner. By then I hoped I'd feel more amenable to fruits of the river. *Maybe I ate a poisonous toad instead of frog*—one thing for sure— no more frog legs.

I took out my sketchpad. Rambo snoozing in the grass among the wild flowers with the water and rocks behind him, made ideal subject matter for a sketch. "You're a great model, Ram, lounging so still, with just a twitch now and then."

I stretched. "Maybe I'll take a little siesta too, boy." I slid down. Resting my head next to his, I let my heavy lids have their way.

Panic overtook me. I whipped around trying to get my bearings.
Tears rolled down my face. As I wiped them away, I heard a voice.
"What's wrong?"
"I'm lost. I can't find my way.
"That's okay. I'm here. I'll take you home."
Eyes all blurry, I studied the face leaning down. The sun blinded
me.
"Who are you?"
His arm closed around me, "Don't be afraid."
"But who are you?"

When I woke, the gentle sound of the river shushing by left a peacefulness settling over me.

From the angle of the sun, I noted we still had a couple hours left to continue on, even if it would be on half speed. As I sat up I rested my weight down on my right arm, spreading out my hand to catch my weight.

"Eeeew…" Immediately, like touching a plate full of worms, I snatched up my fingers.

Rambo's head snapped up at my squeal with his nose twitching at the source of my displeasure. The goosh, the texture with the pungent odor gave me no desire to bring it any closer to my nose. I had no doubt as to what I had leaned into.

Scat. With my nose askew, I examined the sample. Judging by the circumference of the circular set of droppings, it had been left by a pretty large animal.

I twisted around checking my surroundings for the creature that occupied this space before we arrived. Outside of the sounds of some insects, bird chatter accompanying the slushing of the river, I saw or heard nothing that would suggest that the culprit hadn't moved on. Since I had been sleeping for around an hour, not surprisingly, the pile of doo was no longer warm. With its consistency still squishy, I knew that it had not been left there a great deal of time before we arrived.

Remembering my home back in Oregon, around a forested area, we could see bears roaming through our yard. Similar excrement had been left by our black bears that were known to be mostly passive. Those bears had become accustomed to living in close proximity to humans. With an occasional sighting, there hadn't been incidents of bear attacks other than breaking into houses for food.

Only my present location was grizzly country. Grizzlies were not known to be very agreeable beasts.

Hopefully our little snooze gave our grizzly time enough to mosey on his way and be at a safe distance from us.

My nose askew, I held my hand out in front of me. I followed it to the stream. Scrubbing, I thoroughly washed away any traces of my fecal faux pas. "That feels better." I snapped fingers full of water at Rambo, who shook himself at my attack.

I appreciated being near the river for hunting our meals, as all animals had the need to find water. This being true, I might meet a variety of them if I stayed on this path. It would mean that that I would also need to stay alert for some thirsty creatures that would not take kindly to finding us. That might change my dinner plans.

I whisked a strand of hair out of my eyes as the wind whispered a chill, so I slipped on my Pendleton.

"C'mon Ram." I swung my backpack over my shoulders. "This backpack is putting on weight." I adjusted the straps.
"Let's hope we don't run into Mama or Papa Bear."

Rambo skipped ahead of me, He looked over his shoulder as if to say, *"Are you coming."*

"Yeah, Ram, but I'm not in any hurry to catch up with the bear family."

Chapter 43
It's good to have friends.

Ram and I drifted along our pathway beside the stream. Now and then we'd have to scramble across some rocks. Various trills of water drizzled from small rivulets or streams that emptied into the river flowing along side of us. While it burgeoned wider and deeper, I didn't have any reluctance to call it a river. I became aware that the defined space between the walls of rock where we hiked became narrower. The narrower the space became, the river tapered, rushing faster, deeper, churning rougher and appeared to be much more dangerous.

The sound gradually rose from a murmur, a rippling, a sloshing and splashing over the rocks until I couldn't hear the birds over the ruckus of the seething water.

Moisture filled the air from the spatter and slosh to the splash and mist as the water burst forward and bashed against the rocks. I felt chilled, so I unhooked my down jacket from my backpack, off-loaded the pack and stretched a bit. I donned my jacket before slinging the backpack in place.

Soon the roar filled my ears and the space along the edge of the river became nonexistent.

I checked my options. I could go back and try to climb out of this abyss, though the sides were pretty steep. I had to consider Rambo. Any plan I made would have to be viable for the both of us. I would never leave him. It would be a long way back to open forest.

Could I cross to the other side? Stones protruding from the roiling water were pretty far apart. One misstep on the slippery rocks…I didn't want to think of smashing my head and being drawn under the churning river.

The other side of the river seemed to have more shore. *Could I swim across? Could I jump in, swim or float and hope the river would once again widen so I could swim to the shore?*

168

The current racing along kicked up white caps. Swimming across to the other side seemed to be dangerous. *Was that shore much wider than my side anyway?*

With the next few yards, I realized what was next. I could hear it. Water rushed, cascaded over rapids or a waterfall.

Twirling around taking an assessment of my surroundings didn't help my decision.

Was it possible to get through this pass? Was it too dangerous? Should we go back? How far back would I go back before I'd find a pathway into the forest? Then where would we go? Leaving the river meant having to hunt again. We have limited hunting equipment with the loss of the rifle then my hatchet.

The other way to feed us would be to trap. That would mean staying somewhere longer to wait for a trap to snap. Then could we find our way back to water again? Hunger and thirst ruled everything. We could wait by the river expecting to be rescued. That expectation had no basis in reality.

No one would find us here. We had to find someone.

Up to this point I could always see a solution.

My heart began thumping in my chest. A sweat broke out across my neck. A breeze caused me to shake uncontrollably. I bent over and grabbed my knees. *Breathe Gabi. Breathe.*

Rambo pawed my leg.

I took several deep breaths. *Don't Panic. You have come a long way to give up now.* I looked up.

You are not alone.

Chapter 44
Beyond

Just what awaits us over the edge? I couldn't find a solution until I found out what we were facing. I had to get close enough to the edge of this cascade to judge how we could or should continue.

"Stay here, Ram. I'll just have a little look."

He sat on the shore whining.

"Good boy. Stay right there." I stretched out a flat-handed stop signal toward him.

Tensely he observed my careful progress as I crawled ahead.

I turned away from him while I proceeded. On hands and knees I inched my way out on a slippery rock perched on the brink. As I crawled, my heart sped up until I could feel it pound in my ears. Though I couldn't hear much over the roar of water.

At the precipice, a wall of water surged over with such force I inhaled a moist breath in shear awe at the view of the valley below. The vista showed me what is meant by *breathtaking*. I felt like an eagle soaring in the sky.

The mist generated by the rushing water sent chills that rippled across my body but also laid a slick dampness on the rocks.

Holding tight I leaned forward to peek at the river's progress.

I wasn't sure whether one would technically call this roaring cascade, waterfall, rapids or what. Captured by its beauty, I paused. It was incredible the way the river flowed over the rocks and plunged into a wider area below where part of the river swirled into a quiet pond. The main flow continued downstream. The grassy area below spread out through a wider expanse than where we were currently located. Edged by a sparse forest of aspens backed with pine, a space of shore, which left plenty of room to hike along side.

The only question—how can we get down there?

It didn't take much time to find out the answer to that question.

Over my shoulder I saw a fish leap out of the water. Startled by its appearance, I didn't notice Rambo.

He splashed into the water.

"Stay Rambo!" Antsy he perched next to me poised, ready to leap. I prayed there wouldn't be another fish. Even closer, a silvery fish wriggled into the air. I knew Rambo couldn't resist.

"No Rambo!" I tried to grab him.

By the time I reacted it was too late. As Ram vaulted, his outstretched legs flew by. He caught the fish midair. The two of them dropped into the flow, surfaced for a moment then they were swept over the brink. Buried in a rope of roiling water, they completely disappeared. I gasped. "No!"

I could've done nothing in my tenuous position. As I had lunged forward to catch Ram, I teetered with my backpack shifting to the side. Unbalanced I desperately grasped for a handhold. My hands slipped across the rock tearing at my fingernails as I raked the crag before I slid into the water.

My head bobbed out of the river long enough to catch a mouthful of air. I took a quick peek at the boiling river that sucked me under down into an abyss.

Chapter 45
Which Way is Up

The force of the raging water pummeled me over the rocks then down to the depths. Thrust to the surface for brief moments, I grabbed as much air as I could before being dragged under again. I cracked my head against something. I kicked against rocks though unable to tell which way was up. I imagined myself tumbling, flipping summersaults under water with rocks being thrown at me. I panicked. My lungs felt ready to burst. With every mouth full of air came water as well. Each time I thought I wouldn't to get to the surface. I flapped and kicked fighting to find my way up.

My boots together with my backpack acted as weights dragging me under. I struggled to free myself, but no, the more I struggled, the more I failed. My clothes hampered the movement of my arms and legs. I had no control. It felt like the undertow at the beach.

For a moment a bright light beamed. Then down I went.

A malaise engulfed me. I wasn't sure I cared anymore. Too exhausted to fight I floated free. Beauty surrounded me: blues and greens swirled on all sides of me. My hair billowed and flowed in heavenly patterns soft, swirling like watching a kaleidoscope. The rustle of water lulled me limp. I rolled with the current.

I quit my struggle as I gave in to the surging water, ready to waft away in a sublime drift.

My mother reached out toward me.

"You are not alone." I heard it clearly, Mama's soft voice reassured me. "Mama!" I took her hand.

Abruptly I shot to the surface. I coughed. I sputtered before I breathed in a lung full of blessed air.

When I opened my eyes I saw Rambo ahead of me. The sight of him with the luxury of finding air in my lungs renewed my spirit.

Just barely capable of keeping my head above the angry water, I fought the weight of my backpack, pawed desperately, swimming to catch up with him.

The rushing water caught my pack, which plunged me under.

When I rose to the top, I determined that the current was definitely too strong for me try for the edge. I tried to free myself of my backpack, however that hindered me from swimming, which kept me afloat.

Nearly together with Rambo, I quit struggling to let the slipstream move us ahead. We drifted down stream until the river began to spread out. The only effort I expended was keeping my head above the surface and staying with Ram. As it became shallower, I could kick against the bottom whenever the weight of my burden pulled me under.

We fought through another small set of rapids. It was then that I began to notice the pains spreading around my body parts where I banged against the rocks.

Finally the river gave up its anger. It smoothed out giving us a chance to challenge the current. Heading for the shore, I kicked and swam as hard as I could, but I bobbed along in the grip of the river. That's when Rambo took a mouth full of my jacket and started for shore. "Okay Rambo." With a renewed burst of energy, I flapped, kicked and swam.

It seemed like it took an hour before my feet touched the bottom as we fought our way onto shore. It felt like someone drug me along by the back of my jacket as I took my final steps.

Once on shore I stumbled and fell down like a felled tree. I lay face down with my forearm under my cheek. My feet were still in the water.

Panting, I rolled over on my side. Gasping for air, my chest heaved.

I know I had never been that spent before.

Breathing caused my lungs to ache.

Rambo shook himself then sat next to me, he panted as if it was just another day, with another regular activity he chanced upon.

I finally sat up breathing deeply, appreciating every molecule of air. "You're amazing Ram. I couldn't figure out how to get down here but you sure did."

After such a desperate struggle I marveled that the world around us was so calm, tranquil and picturesque. Bright blue skies melted into the beauty of the wilderness. The stand of aspen trees stood with their branches and leaves aflutter in the soft breeze. The backdrop of majestic firs framed a perfect picture. It was hard to imagine that moments ago a terrifying struggle for life had just played out.

Motionless I took it all in until my heartbeat calmed.

"Thank you Lord for the safety of your arms. And thank you Mama for being with me."

"You, too, Rambo. Thank you." I rubbed his damp head, which sprinkled me with a fine spray. "I will never again take breathing for granted. How about you?"

With a small whimper, he dropped a paw on my leg.

When I stroked Rambo, I noticed my wrists hurt from the fall. I swiveled them around. "Good. Not broken." My fingernails were another issue, no wonder they were sore. I remembered a couple of nails had been ground to the quick when I grabbed for the rocks, before I plunged into the falls.

I released the straps on my backpack. The soggy pack plunked on dry land. I let out my breath. "Thank goodness I hadn't been able to release this pack, or we'd be in serious trouble!" I sat quietly watching it drip until at least a calm had settled in my bones.

Checking for injures I rotated my shoulders, bent my knees and stretched my arms. *Where wasn't I sore?* But it didn't feel like I had done any serious damage.

My wet clothes clung to me as I stripped them off. Standing in my underwear, I checked the multiple bruises appearing on my legs and arms. I wiped away the blood from a few minor cuts.

I spread my wet things around on some bushes.

That's when I touched my face and came away with blood on my fingers. In my backpack I searched for my mirror as I pulled out damp items. Then I remembered where I zipped the mirror into my jacket. After I located my mirror, I wrung out my coat.

I focused in on my forehead. A small gash shaped like an eye welled with blood. I wasted a moment worried that I might have an ugly scar. Then I smiled thinking about what a great I story I'd have to tell if anyone asked me about it.

A few more small cuts weren't deep. I looked like I had been fighting an alligator. I should have been glad it wasn't worse, though I felt a little like 'poor me'. Then I realized—*How grateful I am to be here with Rambo and not washing down the river somewhere.*

I made it! Woo! Hoo!"

Rambo reached up his paw. We shook. "Congratulations, Rambo! We won!"

Buck's thermos rattled. When I unscrewed the lid, the inside glass liner had shattered. My shoulders slumped.

"I guess we're not having cocktails tonight, Ram."

Careful not to collect any glass shards, I dabbed my shirttail in the whiskey to pat on my cuts and scratches. The first aid tin had remained airtight. Thus I had a dry Band-Aid for the cut on my forehead.

"Okay Ram. Nurse DiCarlo on the job."

Awkwardly I checked the cut.

I drew the cut's edges together and tapped it closed. Maybe it needed stitches but I couldn't get at it close enough in the right angle even if I had the guts to sew it closed.

"I'll have something to talk about if anyone asks about my scar." I scratched Rambo's ears. Besides my hair will cover it.

After finishing my hospital treatment, I checked my hair. It lay matted to my head, half in the elastic, the other half out. I loosened the elastic and pulled out the limited hairs that were still attached to it. So as not to lose my rubber band, I slipped it down onto my wrist. I ran my fingers through my hair trying to rake out the snarls.

When I lay down next to Rambo, I spread out my mane to dry. Resting, I absorbed the sun on my body, breathing deeply and enjoying the fresh air with a normality I would never take for granted again. As soon as I closed my eyes, sleep came.

I spun under the water—swirling, twirling while I swam around. I dove to the bottom like a mermaid. Mounds of my hair swayed around like seaweed in the current.

Fish cruised by, big-eyed looking with wonder at their new friend. A tail—I smiled as I reached for my tail to see. Is this real? When I touched it, it disappeared and suddenly I couldn't breathe. I fought for the surface. Rambo pushed me up...up...up.

I woke coughing and gasping for air. Rambo lifted his head and stared at me as much as if to say, *"Not another dream!"*

He shook himself off.

"Thanks, for waking me. I'd be burnt to a crisp!"

As I sat up my stomach rumbled. "Okay, Rambo it's been a long time since lunch. We'll start a fire and lay out all the stuff to dry while we fish."

175

I gathered some driftwood, branches, twigs and dried grass. Laughing as I probed the pocket of my shirt, I removed the soggy grass I had placed there to start a fire.

I forgot about my matches. *They would probably be wet. Maybe the lighter would work—if the water hadn't killed it.* When I found the little metal match container, I twisted the lid open! I pulled out the last three matches with the lighter. "Dry! Whoopee!" *Now the only problem would be wasting one of them. I need to careful.*

I made a pile of small dried grasses for tinder. After I added some sticks, I blocked the breeze, struck the match and torched the grass. I smiled when the tiny blaze grew. The flames curled around the pile of wood.

Next I prepared our shelter. I couldn't use stakes since I didn't have my hatchet to pound in stakes. In the stand of trees I found two saplings close enough to suspend the bungee cord between them. I tried a tent peg to see if I could pound it into the ground with my heel enough to hold the tarp out. I smiled when I succeeded.

I hooked the bungee cord up. The drop cloth I used for my tent got soaked but dried pretty quickly. I threw the cloth over and finished pegging it.

"Voila!" Rambo lolled as I worked under his watchful eye. "Hey, Ram. Are you my boss overseeing my work?"

I draped my clothes around the fire. After removing the shoestrings from my boots, I staked them near the fire. Maybe some things would be dry soon. I hung my sleeping bag over some bushes near the fire. *No way for it to be dry enough to sleep in tonight—just be dry by the morning.* In a short time all my belongings were spread about to dry. And my campsite looked like tent city.

As I emptied my drenched backpack, I felt lucky not to have lost my precious tools. I fitted a stick about three feet long with my fishing gear. "This should suffice as a fishing pole. Though I can usually expect you to get us a fish or two, I can't depend on it."

I shivered.

By now I was so cold the water felt almost warm until I waded out into the icy depths that chilled my thighs. Rambo followed me in and took up his fishing stance. My delicate feet felt each of the pebbles beneath them. Soon they could feel almost nothing. *Turning blue* isn't just a saying. Evening dropped its curtain as the skies darkened. With its beauty came the temperature cooling.

Everything I owned lay about waterlogged or still damp. By the time I caught a fish, I was content to feed my growling stomach half a fish rather than stand again in the icy water. Not exactly like Gran's comfy, cozy quilt, I wrapped my thermal blanket around me and tamed my quaking and teeth chattering, with nothing left of my chill except a mere suit of goose flesh.

While I cleaned my fish, Rambo snatched a nice plump fish out of the water. Hungry, he wolfed his down then finished cleaning up my fish residue. He padded back to the water.

"Good boy. Maybe we'll smoke some for lunch tomorrow if you catch another one." He caught two more—breakfast and lunch.

As soon as we finished dinner, I coaxed Ram into the tent with me. The fire had kept us almost warm. Inside the tent, I shivered against him. We had nothing but each other under a small thermal blanket to keep us warm.

For a few moments I worried about having another nightmare, but exhaustion—what a great sleeping pill.

I wrapped an arm around Rambo. Soon after his first snore I was gone too.

Chapter 46
Every Day's A New Day
Day 12

The morning sun greeted us glowing into our tent. I woke after sleeping like bear in the winter and with nary a nightmare to interrupt my rest. "Must be a good omen, Ram." I wrestled him to the ground "Want a rub down, old boy?"

After that I crawled out of the tent with a big stretch. Before I did my exercises, I perused the area. "Wow this place looks like ground zero after a scud missile." Everything I owned lay strewn about or hanging from shrubbery. The wind had tossed some of them into lumps.

"Hey boy, since much of this is nearly dry maybe if we hang around a bit, the sun will have a chance to finish its work. Let's not hurry." I flipped the sleeping bag inside out.

Even being stiff and achy, I managed some exercises. Then I surprised myself. I had forgiven the river for testing me. I grabbed my soap. "How about a scrub down?" The icy water jolted me awake as I dove in, shaking my hair as I surfaced. Ram barked then scampered in after me. The shampoo felt fantastic. There was still a strong current so we didn't dare venture past where I could walk or stand comfortably. We played around a little. A stick just right for Rambo to retrieve floated by. I plucked it up and tossed it on shore. Sure enough he chased it.

Shivering, I came out of the water. Rambo dropped the stick in front of me. "Hey, somebody taught you well." I threw it again.

"Just a minute. Let me get some underwear and dry clothes on." I plucked up some of my laundry. "Yeah! My silk underwear is dry! My long-johns too!" I pulled them on.

"Hey Ram, heads up!" I threw the stick to the far end of our camp and off he scurried, skidded to a stop, picked up the stick and raced back to me. I ran, threw the stick and played tug-of-war with

Rambo. That's how I warmed myself.

I luxuriated at finally being warm.

I felt my cheeks. Were they hot from my stick play? I could be already suffering the effects of brilliant sun on my fair skin.

I splashed some water on my face.

Along with my sunglasses, my baseball cap had disappeared on my dive over the falls. I would burn if I didn't protect my skin.

So I hung my little mirror over a limb. I rubbed makeup on my face then smeared the tops of my ears. After I brushed some mascara on my lashes, I finished off with lipstick. Posing, I checked out myself.

I brushed my hair then swept it into a ponytail that I braided. "Today would be a good day to be rescued." I kissed the mirror and patted my hair. "I'm lookin' pretty good."

Ram sighed a small noise. "You're almost humanoid the way you roll your eyes, Ram."

By the time we had finished makeup time, breakfast and I'd brushed my teeth, most of my things were dry.

After I folded, I stuffed things into my backpack and I noticed my small drawing pad. "Yes this could work."

When I opened my drawing pad I thumbed through the pages. All the ink sketches and watercolors bled. They were nothing but smears on the pages. After I ripped out the pages, I zipped them back into the backpack. "Kindling!" I studied the small rectangle of cardboard of the cover. "Hmm…" I looked around. "I could weave or braid some grasses for ties. Then I'll have a visor." With my knife I twisted two holes in the ends of the cardboard, then trimmed the corners with my Swiss Army Knife's scissors. After I braided the grasses to make a strap, I tied on my fashion statement. After I checked myself out in the mirror, I strutted around like a high fashion model wearing the latest French chapeau. "Not bad, huh Rambo?"

When we finished our exercises, I packed up. I devised a way to drape some of the damp things over my backpack until they dried as we continued on toward civilization. Maybe it would be today that we'd find someone to help us get home.

All loaded, I imagined myself to be able to stand aside and view my appearance. My get-up reminded me of those guys hitching a ride along highway 101. They looked as though they were carrying everything they owned as they walked along with their dog. I stuck out my thumb. Like someone would stop to pick us up. "Take us to your nearest Holiday Inn!" I thrust my arm in the air and we were off.

Rambo yipped as he trotted along side of me on an easy-going day. I adjusted to my reality, like getting used to ignoring all my achy muscles. I couldn't remember when I wasn't sore someplace.

Noticing the birds twittering, I whistled along with them as we walked, and enjoyed the comforting feeling of safety. As I thought of lunch, I watched the tiny birds flitting about overhead. "Too small, huh, Rambo. I guess we'll have to have fish again for dinner."

I hummed John Denver's *"Take Me Home Country Roads"*, blurting the words here and there as I remembered them. I hummed the rest. "I should have been home yesterday, yesterday, take me home…" Rambo offered his own accompaniment. *Home—What I wouldn't give to be home in Papa's beautiful little craftsman styled house, sitting on the front porch rocking in those big old rockers while I regale him with all my adventures.*

When Rambo and I were silent, except for his breathy panting once in a while, I listened rather than let my mind worry about what would happen next. I really listened. We were part of God's symphony, the sounds of nature. Birds filled the air with their song. The wind rustled through the trees and rippled the leaves. The water lapped the shore, rumbled over rocks and gurgled in swirls. A bee buzzed past on its way to a wild flower. Rambo and I left our footprints as we waded through the grasses in harmony, like snare drums tapping, or like one of those wire brushes, swishing across the drum's taut surface.

The scene took me back. Wil and I went on one of our first hikes together. We'd taken the trail along Sweet Creek to the falls. We hiked along feeling a similar serenity where the moist air and fresh aroma of the foliage peaked one's senses. He'd taken my hand. Our smooth palms clasped together. With my thumb caressing the soft hairs on the back of his hand with sudden awareness of the mini pleasures that make a big impact. That sensation made me feel as though that was the first time I'd ever held hands.

All the damp clothes that I had draped over and hung from my backpack were dry, so I stopped and stowed them away. Then we continued on.

Songs rolled though my head as I hummed to the inner music.

Becoming so relaxed in the beauty of this place, I didn't pay attention to the fact that I hadn't heard the birds for a while.

I stopped suddenly. I detected movement ahead.

We were not alone.

Chapter 47
Beary Nice

Rambo and I moved ahead slowly. I inched forward when I thought I saw another movement.

After we rounded an outcropping of flat rocks, we ambled back to the water's edge.

My eyes darted this way and that.

Something moved. I had no doubt.

Rambo's antsy behavior alerted me. He circled, his sniffer in high gear.

I stood perfectly still.

About the same time as Rambo, I saw it too. There it sat. We must have been down wind. The bear cub hadn't noticed us. I gasped.

I put my hand down to stop Rambo. "Shh!"

Rambo's bark sounded vicious.

Small, round and furry, the bear cub sat splashing in the water much like a human baby enjoying a bath in the tub.

Mom couldn't be far away.

But where was she? I checked both ways down the river and behind us, though it didn't seem as though we could've passed a mother grizzly bear without noticing.

Among the trees another cub grabbed at tree branches while he tried to climb.

Rambo pointed his nose at the first cub. Head down, he started forward.

I grabbed his collar.

Rambo bared his teeth, a snarl rolling in his throat, then he let loose. Rambo's growling and barking would surely bring the mother around.

"Shh! Rambo."

I clamped my hand around his snout.

While I backed away moving in the direction we had come, every muscle in my face contracted as I clenched my teeth.

Rambo strained against my grip on his collar though he continued to bark.

Maybe we could wait out the bear family outing if we could backtrack and hide behind the boulders we had just passed.

After a few steps into our retreat, I realized it was too late.

From the water just behind another pile of rocks, fish in her mouth, she fixed her angry stare at Rambo and me.

I gulped.

She dropped the fish back into the river.

From all fours the grizzly reared up on two legs. The way she snarled and roared she made Rambo's efforts sound puny. He stood braced with his head jutting forward. A vicious growl rolled in his throat. I held Rambo's collar. *What if he charged the bear?*

The beast was huge.

I cowered with her shadow looming toward me.

What did I remember about the ranger's visit to our school so many years ago? Black bears lived almost in harmony with the citizens of Florence. However if you threatened them or their cubs, look out. My mind raced.

Think, Gabi. Make a lot of noise? Clap my hands? Scream? That's what we did at home. Wouldn't that ruckus just seem to be more threatening because the cubs were so close to us. Spread my arms out to make myself big? However big I made myself, she dwarfed me. Rearing upright would mean letting go of Rambo's collar. Would Rambo lunge at the creature and try to defend me? That would be deadly for him. If he did, maybe I could escape. No! I would not use Rambo to save myself. I couldn't. "Whatever we do, we do together."

Help me Lord.

The tears welled in my eyes. How many seconds, minutes passed as I thought through my choices?

I had only three weapons. With my Swiss Army Knife, I would have to be very close to that massive beast.

I felt feverish at that thought.

I took the snake rattle from my pocket and shook. The rattle created only a momentary reaction. The bear paused then roared.

I could throw my hunting knife. Could I throw it hard enough to penetrate the bear's thick fur and skin? Probably not. Even if the knife did penetrate, one paltry stick would surely not stop a charging bear. She'd just be infuriated. My slingshot? How accurate could I be? The stone would have to hit the bear's nose or eye. Those were pretty small targets. A miss at one of those vulnerable spots, she'd hardly notice the ping of a puny pebble. However, that's my only option, my only chance.

Trembling, I sucked in a huge breath.

I glanced down and unsnapped my knife with a quick prayer that I wouldn't need it. Then I drew out my slingshot. At the same time, I released my hold on Rambo. I extracted a rock from my pocket and loaded the stone.

Every beat of my heart played a drum solo in my ears.

Rambo growled

The bear roared.

Rambo shot forward.

So did the bear.

I screamed.

184

Chapter 48
How Now Grizzly Bear?

In that split second I raised the slingshot. The bear swung a massive paw at Rambo. The dog sidestepped but not fast enough. The claws raked across Rambo's rear, swatting Rambo aside as though he were a stuffed toy. Rambo flew side ways. I shrieked, took aim and released the stone.

Rambo's painful yelps penetrated the air and my heart.

Almost one frame at a time, simultaneously I observed Rambo land with a thud. The stone flew straight at the bear's face. It struck the grizzly's right eye. A high-pitched bear shriek joined Rambo's pained utterances.

Instantly she reacted grabbing her face. When she touched her eye, she was obviously stunned. She stood like a monolith on two hind legs blasting out a thunderous roar.

I shuddered.

Had I just angered her or had I perhaps blinded her? How long would my attack keep her immobile?

A second later, I rushed forward. I roused Rambo. He shook himself upright.

"C'mon Rambo."

He hesitated. "C'mon, boy." I pulled his collar.

One last glance at the bear noted that she stood still dazed from her injury. She held her paw over her eye. Roaring her anger, she remained right there on shore.

I tore away from the scene as though I bounded across hot coals. Rambo limped but he kept up with me. My backpack shifted from side to side often throwing me off balance, wind-milling my arms sometimes to keep my balance. Other times I bounced off a tree.

Even if her eye didn't receive a severe injury, it probably incapacitated her momentarily.

It didn't appear we were being followed into the forest.

I thought it more likely the mother would stay near her cubs. Were she to follow, her cubs wouldn't be safe.

I found myself hoping that the mother bear would be okay. If not those adorable cubs were in serious trouble.

When I finally slowed, I bent with my arm across my aching side, I noticed. "Blood!"

Rambo whimpered. He sat down trying to lick his back haunch.

I raised my hand up to see. It dripped blood but I was not injured.

"Ram, come here, boy."

He just whined pitifully. The plaintive whimpering pulled on my heartstrings.

I bent down to inspect his backside. Gashes created by the bear's claws, slashed across his back hip. I rolled Rambo on his good side. That's when I recalled what happened to Buck's whiskey. I hoped I could find some disinfectant in the emergency kit. Infection could be Ram's bigger enemy.

Before I off loaded my backpack, I checked to make sure the bear hadn't followed us. I let out a breath when I didn't see her behind us.

The thick forest stood as still as a library.

I stared into his eyes. "You're okay, Ram." The tears rolled down my face feeling unsure of my prognosis.

I located the first aid kit.

Using one of the gauze bandages to wipe away the blood, I washed the wound by pouring water from my canteen then blotted it dry. Two of the wounds were just surface scratches. However the other two-inch slit looked deeper with the blood oozing out over my hand. "Why are you so hairy, boy? A dressing isn't going stick to all that fur."

The blood continued to flow. Rambo whimpered.

I pressed a gauze pad against the laceration. "Okay Doctor DiCarlo, what are we going to do?"

Assessing the situation, I could see no way to bind it up that would keep the wound closed. I would have to sew it together. *Could I do this? Would my flimsy sewing kit be adequate to accomplish this operation? Am I capable?*

"I'm sorry Ram." I hugged my arms around his neck. I stroked him. "I love you, boy. I don't mean to hurt you, but I have to do this.

186

First I spread out a thermal blanket and lifted Rambo on top. "You have to stay still. Can you do that boy?"

I pawed through my backpack's pockets until I found the small sewing kit. Then I opened my Swiss Army Knife. With the scissor blades I cut away some of the fur next to the wound. I ran my finger across the scissors blades. They were pretty sharp but the task took more time than I though it might.

Meanwhile, Rambo continued to bleed slowing my work as I mopped away the blood to see the wound. He jerked up periodically. "Stay, Ram."

As gentle as I could be, Rambo wasn't happy lying still while I operated on the wound.

He kicked in an effort to sit up. "No boy," I soothed him back down, patted his head and finished with a soothing stroke down his back. "Stay still my little boy," I whispered. He whimpered.

I finished cutting away the fur. That gave me a better view of what I needed to stitch. Then I smoothed on some disinfectant from the small tube I found in the kit.

"How sharp is this needle?" I had no idea how tough his skin would be. I had assembled my sewing kit myself from some of my mother's supplies in her sewing machine. I had included several sized needles but only regular size thread. I selected the strongest, sharpest looking needle. "What color thread? I had red, blue, black or white. "Red will be easy to see when the stitches needed to be cut out of your fur."

I lit my last match to sterilize the needle then rubbed it with disinfectant. The needle shook in my fingers as I tried to guide the skinny thread through the eye.

"Dear Lord, guide my hand."

Whispering, I rubbed his ears. "Oh Rambo, I love you. I'm sorry this may hurt but you have to stay still. Okay."

After a brief glance upward, I approached my task. My stomach quivered.

I hesitated another moment then pushed the needle into the bottom end of wound. Rambo twitched. I held him down. "Stay still honey." I kept murmuring sweet nothings, making gentle sounds as I stitched the length of the gash. Alternately, I issued a soft push to keep him down.

Each time I thrust the needle, I felt his pain when he responded with pathetic whimpers. He cried until I thought my heart would burst. "Just be still. Just a couple more, boy." With only a few of kicks, Rambo made a pretty good patient. It seemed like this operation took hours though I'm sure not.

"You did good, boy." I kissed his head. Did he actually know that this pain is what would make him better?

"Okay. Now what? Should I try to bandage this up? It might heal faster if I leave it open to the air. All you have to do is stay quiet. So don't get it dirty."

I took out some supplies to make camp.

"Just stay there on that blanket."

He lay his head back down while I worked.

Rambo snored while I built the tent over him. Was he just sleeping or had he passed out. I leaned down. "Are you okay, Ram?" I decided that it would do him good to sleep. This way, no dirt would get into the wound.

My stomach growled while I set things up. We had skipped lunch due to our rendezvous with the grizzly. In my haste to get away from the bear, we had been driven away from the river. Since we couldn't fish, I appreciated the fact that we still had a portion of fish we hadn't eaten.

As soon as I took out our dinner, his nose twitched. He pawed the dirt next to him.

"Oh Rambo, I could never hide food from you." His nose quivered as he sniffed.

When he stood, he shook himself in a way that appeared as though he regretted he did that. He wobbled back down.

"Good to see you up and moving, but you need to be careful."

Then something happened I hadn't planned for. He leaned around. As he licked his wound, he bit at the stitches.

"No Rambo!" I rushed over to him. "What am I going to do with you?" I pushed his head away as he tried again. "No licking!"

I would have to bandage him up somehow, but how?

Chapter 49
Grateful
Day 13

"Where's the duct tape?" I searched through some zipper compartments until I found it. I wish I didn't have to do this buddy because it won't be easy to get this duct tape off when the cuts are healed."

After I washed and dried the wound thoroughly, I disinfected it again.

"We only have two more of these gauze bandages so you have to be a good boy. No biting. No licking. No scratching."

With the dressing on, I wrapped a couple of rounds of duct tape securing it all around his leg.

He whined.

"And no more whining. It breaks my heart."

Ram tried to bite at the tape. "No!" I held up my hand flat. That's how I told my dog at home to stop. I grabbed his head and pulled it away.

He tried to bite the bandage.

"NO!" I held him tight. "NO!"

He gave it one last try, "NO!" Finally accepting his fate, he lay down next to me.

"It's gonna make you better, boy."

He wasn't much interested in food after a couple of bites. So I hand fed him until he refused to take any more. When we finished the last of our dinner, I slumped in exhaustion. Almost immediately Ram fell asleep. I settled back in the tight quarters, I slept restlessly. I thought I'd hurt Rambo if I rolled over. *Could infection set in? Would Rambo be worse when morning came?* Whines intermittently during the night caused my throat to lump up.

Rambo licked my face as he lay next to me, my morning wake up call. "Oh Rambo, you're okay. You're awake. You're gonna make it." I hugged him gently.

When I got up he lay still. He whimpered up at me like, *"I don't feel like getting up right now."*

The tears rolled down my face.

"It's okay, just rest."

"Thank you, dear Lord. Thank you for watching over me and especially Rambo. He needs you. Over all our misery, stress and danger, you've been there for us. Give Rambo strength. Take us home, dear Lord."

My stomach rumbled. It had been a long time since we'd eaten. We'd missed a meal the day before. We had nothing to eat for breakfast.

With a quick camp check, I didn't see or hear any birds.

While we hiked next to the river, I hadn't filled our spare water bottles. When I picked up the canteen sloshing it around, I wasn't surprised. "You hear that boy? The canteen is nearly empty. That means we have to hike today. No food. No water. We have to get back to the river. Can you do it, boy?" I patted down his back. "I'll take it slow and we'll rest."

He stood slowly with a whimper. He teetered unsteadily.

He tipped his head to the side as if to say, *"What did you do to me?"* Rambo tried several contortions trying get the tape off.

"NO!" I held him tight so he couldn't struggle with it. With several reprimands like that, he gave up. "That's a boy. Just leave it alone so it will heal."

He lay back down.

Looking around, I wondered how far into the forest I had run when escaping that bear. How far back it would be to get to the river? Then I found myself feeling guilty that I had injured the mama bear.

"Dear Lord help that mama grizzly heal so she can take care of her babies. Oh, and send her away from the river, okay?"

I poured out a cup of water for Ram. Then I took one for myself. It sloshed around in my stomach much the way it had in the near empty canteen. I had to hold Rambo up to drink his.

I packed up.

Rambo rested just watching me with my tasks.

We started off with Rambo limping slowly behind me. After a couple of steps I realized this wasn't working. "You can't break the stitches open. Let's wait."

Immediately he fell down.

"Okay Ram." Maybe you need to take a ride."

I took out the blanket to fashion a makeshift stretcher. When I finished, I attached it around my waist and shoulders then dragged it behind me.

"You're heavier than I thought, Ram."

I slogged along. There were some broken branches and smashed-down grasses that we had flattened on the run from mama bear. We followed along that same path. I assumed that the bears would be gone by the time we returned to the river.

After a period of slow going, I was getting weak too. We hadn't gotten far before I sat down. I leaned against the tree. "Whew!" My blisters were acting up. I checked the first aid kit and unwrapped the Band-Aids. I saved the wrappers for a fire starter.

"Hey Ram I hope we get home soon before my feet fall off. Only six Band-Aids left." I pulled off the old ones and saw that the blisters had popped. That meant that infection could be a real threat or else they would heal better. Healing better might mean I should stop for a while. "When we get to the river. . ."

I squeezed on some disinfectant from the tube. There wasn't much left. I added an extra gauze pad and taped it down.

"We both better heal quick! Or be rescued! C'mon boy."

Chapter 50
What's next?

Dragging Rambo behind me proved a bit tricky. I tried to be careful to avoid rocks or bumps in our pathway, but I didn't follow a well-beaten path. When we hit a root bulging up in our path, Rambo yelped. "Sorry, boy."

I needed to stop often. "You know, you're getting heavier by the minute, Rambo." I took off my cardboard visor and wiped my forehead.

We hadn't gone too far when the forest became sparse and I could feel the moisture from the river. "Must be close now, Ram."

I kept a watch for signs of any animals. When I finally hit the shore, I plopped down. Shedding my burdens. I let out a huge breath. "Finally."

I slogged to the water for a drink. When I glanced back over my shoulder, Rambo hadn't moved. "Oh Buddy. You're not feeling so good, huh?"

I filled my canteen and a cup of water for Rambo. He rose very painfully. As he strained to get up to take his drink, I helped him by lifting his rear end. After a few laps of water, he sank back down.

"I'm pretty hungry. How about you?"

I got a small fire going then I searched through my backpack for the fishing line. Then I set about making a pole. Hunger captured my attention while I finished those tasks.

"I don't suppose you're going to be fishing with me?" I looked over at him lying with his snout on his paws. He answered me with a whimper. I hoped not. Replacing his dressing would be a chore.

"Okay, I'll get us brunch." I waded into the river, avoiding the strong current. Rearing back I cast my line. Maybe the fish weren't as plentiful here as back where we came from.

I could see the fish swimming past me. I think they were trying to tease me because my hungry stomach was growling.

It seemed like forever I had been standing and casting. My toes against the rocky bottom turned to ice cubes before I finally snagged a fish. I held it up. "Sorry it's so small. There's no fishing police, so I'm going to keep it."

I brought my catch over to Ram, but he didn't seem interested in eating. He lifted his head, sniffed then lay back down. "Maybe you want yours cooked huh, Ram. I'll catch another one."

Following another lengthy wait, I did catch a pretty good-sized fish. "Now that's more like it." After I subdued it, I showed Ram.

I worried as I cleaned the two fish. Ram showed not even a little interest in scarfing down the entrails with his usual voracious appetite.

I rubbed behind his ears.

"Okay, I'm going to cook these guys and maybe the smell will excite your taste buds." I flopped the fish in the skillet and placed them over the fire. I tried wafting the smell toward Rambo. I thought I saw him twitch his nose a little, however, he just closed his eyes.

Rambo snoozed a bit while I cooked the fish. When they were done, I sat next to him while he sprawled on his stretcher. I tore off a piece for Ram. He sniffed for a long moment then took the bite. "Good boy. Not your usual gusto, but you ate it." After a few bites for me, I fed Ram a few bites.

When I brought over a cup of water he rose. With my help, he drank a small lap or two. Lying back he exposed his tummy. "Good sign, Ram. I think you're getting better with a little food in your belly and expecting a tummy rub." I smiled as I gave him a complete massage, being very careful with his injury.

Overhead the sky clouded up, reflecting the sadness in my heart.

I cleaned up the food mess washing the entrails and the pan in the river. I didn't usually have those leftovers with Rambo scarfing them up, but their smell might just draw some animal to have me for dinner. "You're making more work for me boy. So you better get better!"

Already wet, I decided to take a bath. I stripped down and washed my clothes before I did me. Morose, I swam around for a few minutes remembering that only a short while ago we played chase the stick. *Is that ever going to happen again?*

193

I splashed out then hung my outfit on bushes to dry. I spread out for a suntan, just watching the cloud formations drift by.

When a large bird flew over like a kite, I thought of Papa. We'd sprint along the beach, flying kites every summer. Mama sat on shore all bundled up because we only flew kites on some of those cold windy days. She'd wave on our way by as we raced across the sand with the kite soaring higher in the sky.

"Are you watching over me now? Are you remembering with me?"

Knowing the birds would be too far away I didn't race for my slingshot. *I guess I should always keep it beside me. Never know when I might need it.*

I thought about my drawing pad with all the ink and watercolor sketches I had made. I had hoped to make a little memory book when I got home. This would have been a great spot to sketch. But alas, when I took my waterfall dunking, I used those dried out, runny, ruined pages for kindling. Not to mention that I made my ever-so-stylish visor out of the cover.

I glanced over at Rambo who softly snored. He continued to snooze while I took my time setting up camp.

I fished again for dinner. *Fishing alone—what a melancholy task.* I didn't stand long enough in the icy water to get fish for the next day.

Usually a song or two lifted my spirits. When Rambo woke I sang a few songs. He listened but didn't feel the need to accompany me. And that made me begin to sing sad songs, ones in minor keys.

When he ate a little more fish, I felt relieved but couldn't tell if he was on the mend or just hanging on. I just kept poking in little bits of fish until Rambo refused any more. I had tried all day to get water into him, but he only took a few laps each time.

I carried him over to the tent where I settled him next to me. The small feeble sounds he emitted raked my heart.

After I lay down next to him, I stroked his head and held his paw. "I love you Ram." I kissed his head. "You just have to get better."

The lump in my throat swelled.

For the longest moment, I patted him, hoping my strong love would transfer my strength to him. His breathing seemed labored, which filled my mind with the worst thoughts.

Facing the darkness staring straight up, I remembered Gran, her voice soft in my ear. "Psalms 18 verses 6 and 7. I called upon the Lord and cried out to my God for help. He heard my voice from his heavenly dwelling, my cry of anguish came to his ear."

"Please dear Lord. I cry out in anguish. Please send your healing power to my Rambo."

The tears flowed and I didn't try to stop them. My chest heaved.

"Please Rambo, get well."

I snuzzled into his fur.

Chapter 51
Will it be today?
Day 14

When my eyes opened that morning, I looked around for Rambo. He wasn't in the tent.

"Rambo." I crawled out of my sleeping bag and slashed aside the flap.

"Rambo. There you are." In slow motion, he teetered a few steps then took care of business. I was never so glad to see anything, as when Rambo lifted his other leg. "You're better."

He limped over to me. I knelt down and wrapped my arms around him. "We're gonna make it."

We needed to start up a fire right away, if we were to have a hot breakfast. My matches were gone, but I still had the lighter. It had been in a watertight container with the matches so I hoped that after our forced water plunge, it still operated. I assembled some kindling then gathered some driftwood with dry branches. I flipped open the lighter and snapped the small wheel. Nothing. Again I snapped it. A spark! After several more futile and frustrating tries the lighter decided to work. I hadn't realized I had been holding my breath, but the ember liked the stream of air I breathed on it. Up it flared.

A couple of birds flew over. I grappled with my belt, however by the time I grabbed my slingshot they had soared away.

I had to fish if we were to have any kind of breakfast.

Ram lay down again just watching me from his prone position.

"No Ram!" But it was too late. Rambo already waded into the water up to his bandage. "What am I to do with you? At least you're better. "

Very fortunately Ram caught a fish almost right away. So did I. "Good, breakfast and lunch are caught. You must be hungry!"

196

I set the fish to smoking.

"Come here Ram." I spread out the blanket. "Down." I patted it.

He hobbled over. I gave him a slight push. Rambo seemed to know I wanted him on his side. He kicked a few times then settled down. "No more stitches Ram, just changing the dressing.

I checked Ram's wound. I assessed the bandage situation. If I just cut away the Band-Aid part but didn't rip off the duct tape, it would be less painful. Then I could re-bandage by simply duct taping on top of the old tape so he would experience one tape-yanking when all was healed.

On the blanket, I positioned Ram. I carefully used my Swiss Army scissors to snip away the large square Band-Aid, taking a little fur with it. Rambo yipped when I pulled it off. "Oh now don't you whimp out on me. Take it like a macho canine. A wet dressing is worse than no bandage."

I paused a minute, a little afraid of what the wound would look like. Then I carefully removed the gauze pad. "Maybe your swim helped." The gauze didn't stick as I gently pulled it away from the wound. "Thank goodness."

I didn't know what the laceration should look like though it wasn't pussy or swollen. It did look like the skin scabbed back together.

I patted it dry with a clean sock.

Ram tried to get up. "No Ram. I'm not finished." I pressed him back down. "Now stay!"

When I had rolled down the tube of disinfectant, I squeezed it along the stitches. "Not much left of the tube." I rolled and pressed it close to the stem. "Well maybe we can do this one more time, then what?" I patted his head. "Maybe it'll be healed."

I smoothed on the large Band-Aid patch and finished it off with duct tape.

Rambo sniffed his new dressing then gave it a lick.

"No!" I pushed his head away from his target. "And don't look so pathetic."

After bandaging his wound, the little hospital session reminded me to look at my blisters. I hadn't had my boots or the Band-Aids on for almost two days. The exposure to the air had helped. My blisters were almost gone. Good thing since I could use duct tape, but that was dwindling too and I only two small Band-Aids left. Waiting until we assumed our trek to put my boots on I wouldn't waste the

Band-Aids.

I wiggled my toes.

Ram rolled his sorrowful eyes as he lay back down on the blanket. Soon his soft snores eased my worry. I shook my head. *Maybe it's better. He needs to rest. We'll have dinner. Maybe he'll gain some strength if he eats.*

"Okay. Ram. I'll take a little swim, bathe and do my laundry while you rest."

I checked my belt as I added another notch. "Today marks the two week mark, Rambo and we're still here!"

After I caught a couple more fish, I went for a swim. We enjoyed a sunbath in the warmth of the sun. I didn't dare fall asleep or I'd be burned like a lobster. While it wasn't that hot, lying down in the sun felt quite warm.

A few minutes later, I sat up. I fluffed my hair in the breeze before braiding it. Rambo lay sprawled out beside me. "I think you exhausted yourself." I let him snooze.

I remembered before I left Florence, I had read in the Register Guard that a man had been lost in the mountains while he hunted. They finally rescued him on the fourteenth day. He had been able to hunt to feed himself. "Just like us, huh Ram? Maybe today, maybe today they'll find us. It is day 14. Two weeks."

As Rambo raised his head, I noticed his tail slowly thumping on the rock. I laughed. "That's the first time I've seen your tail wag in days! Does your rear end still hurt?" I gave him a small rubdown then patted his side. "There you go."

Ram seemed better though he was very lethargic and still moving painfully, if he moved at all.

"You're amazing Ram. You know that? But how much better are you?"

I had to decide to go or stay.

Rambo was better but could he travel yet?

Chapter 52
Not Today
Day 15

By afternoon, I finally came to my decision, after I watched Rambo limp, not taking more than a couple steps at a once and sleeping most of the time. He glanced up at me with sorrowful eyes displaying not even a smidgen of a tail wag. I messaged his ears and raked down his back. "It's okay boy. Let's stay here for another night."

When not traveling during the daytime, I didn't have much to do. More than once I wished I had brought along a book. It was great to have eBooks but there's nothing like settling back with a real book in your hands, feeling the paper in your fingers when you turn the page. When your phone quits, all your eBooks are spread out in cyber space.

The area around the campsite—what an eyesore! My clothes lay about draped around bushes. Some of them sprouted out of my backpack. It reminded me of my messy old room. I heard my Mother's voice, "Why don't you clean your room?" When I couldn't find anything to do as a kid, Mama knew just what to say. Her question sent me off doing something, anything but clean my room. *Today, though, that is a perfectly good notion. Thanks, Mom.*

After I gathered my laundry off the bushes, I took everything out of my backpack. For the last few days I had just stuffed things in when I packed up. While I repacked I found a deck of cards I had forgotten about.

When my things were neatly folded, all back in and zipped up, I took the cards to a place out of the breeze. I sat down then smoothed a flat space in the dirt. As I dealt out the cards left-handed for solitaire, I laughed. I remembered how my brother had taught me how to play cards. Leo was left-handed, so while he showed me the way to deal, I became a left-handed dealer.

We'd play poker for coins. Most weeks, half my allowance went to Leo. I just loved solitaire. It was even more fun when I played double solitaire with him, and sometimes, triple solitaire when Papa joined us.

I smiled. "I'm coming home, Papa. I'm coming Leo. If not today then soon."

Left-handed, I dealt out the row of cards in front of me. While I played with the cards, I realized how many things my brother had taught me, in between teasing me unmercifully. *I bet the way I shoot my slingshot is left-handed too.* After I had played a few hands of solitaire, a breeze came up. The wind tried to play cards with me, taking the cards and flipping them over. A gust ran off with a few cards that I had to chase while they cartwheeled toward the river. After I chased them, I zipped them into my backpack.

When I lay back down I tucked my arms behind my head. Swift moving dark clouds rolled across the sky. With them, poetic words floated through my brain.

During my repacking, along with a pen, I found a scrap of paper that I planned to use for kindling next fire. Since I couldn't stop a poem floating in my head, I decided to write it down:

clouds
> swift as a bird on the wing
> soft as a morning kiss
> fluffy as cotton candy
> gentle as a mother cuddling her babe
> ethereal as breath in the cool night wind
> threatening like a snarling cougar
> stormy with the fury of a mother bear
> heavenly with bursting sunrays like God's blessing
> vivid as a colorful canvas in the setting sun

clouds

As I wrote the last lines, that's exactly what I saw as the sun hid behind some dark clouds. *Was rain coming?*

I tiptoed past Rambo as he lay stretched out on his side, a soft snore decorating the air with his middrift rising and falling in a regular rhythm. The last thing I needed—my expert fisher dog following me. Getting his dressing all wet again wouldn't be good. Without waking him, I bungeed him to a tree.

It took a while before the fish were bitting. Though after I snagged a couple of pretty good-sized fish, I tiptoed trying not make a noisey splash. Just out of the river, Rambo woke. Since it took him a while to rise, I manged to clear the water before he could strain himself against his tether, so he just flopped back down when I sat next to him.

This time the fish interested him. His nose twitched. He snorted like a pig in a sty. "Yeah! Your appetitie's returning!" He lay next to me while I cleaned my catch. I smiled. He was back to scarfing up the inards. "That's my boy. Bet you are pretty hungry by now. Now I don't have to clean up this mess!" He paid no attention as I raked my fingers through his fur, like, *"Leave me alone. I'm eating!"*

My face hurt from smiling as I watched this disgusting act. At least I wouldn't have to dispose of that refuse. Though he quit eating and I did have to dispose of some of the left overs.

He got up and slowly padded over to the river. He lapped up a long sloppy a drink.

Pretty sure I'd be traveling the next day, I wanted to get my latest catch smoked so we would have food for tomorrow when we took off.

After worrying so much about Ram, I had a chance to relax because I heard nothing but Ram's soft snores uninterrupted by whimpering.

At first light, I woke to Rambo barking. I sat up when I heard him howling.

"Okay, okay, Rambo." He continued quick sharp yaps. I patted his head as I eased out of the tent. By the time I had pulled on my pants and laced my boots, I discovered that we had something new to be in a frenzy about. As usual, his snout pointed where he wanted me to look. As I surveyed the problem, my heart sped up keeping pace with Rambo's barks.

Chapter 53
Where There's Smoke…

"Fire!"

What I saw the night before the sun set were some dark clouds with the sun beaming behind. What covered the sky that morning were deep dark clouds laden with the heavy smell of smoke.

Fire? The ridge above us glowed. Verifying my assessment, little white ashes swirled and flitted through the air.

From the breadth of black sky, this fire was close.

With the sudden realization that we were in the midst of a forest fire, my heart pounded in my chest.

I took a couple deep breaths. The air filled with the taste and smell of smoke.

Think! Don't panic! We are already at one of the safest places we could be. The river could be our best friend.

I set about gathering up our stuff rapid fire like fast fowarding a TV show. I split our breakfast fish in half. Ram felt much better. He wolfed down his share before I could take my second bite. I imitated Rambo by stuffing mine down as fast as I could.

Meanwhile the ridge glowed an eerie halo.

The fire definitely headed our way.

Ram snoozed again. "Don't get too comfy, boy. We can't stay here."

I glanced around. *What about my pack? We might have to get into the water to save ourselves.* I shuddered thinking of the last time we had to fight the currents of that river. My backpack and boots drug me down like an evil sea monster.

Yes, my backpack needs to come with us. I need take some essentials. Though there are some supplies I could leave. If we make it through the fire, we will need certain things to survive. Do I have enough time to decide what I could leave?

I swept my eyes across the sky. The scene had not changed since I last checked. I would have a bit of time.

At my pack, I unzipped pockets like crazy. I yanked everything out. *So glad I just repacked all this yesterday! At least I know where everything is. Some I can just leave packed.*

The art stuff went first, but not before I wrote a quick note on the back of my poem. "Goodbye Dad and Leo. I love you," I dated it so they'd know how long I had survived. I stuffed the poem note into a small Ziplock and slid it into a pocket.

My phone? It's never going to work again after swimming down the falls with me. I reared back and hurled it into the river.

I folded one pair of bikinis, 2 pair of socks, and my jacket. The rest of the clothes I jetisoned. *Silverware, plates, pans? I can use spits or skewers to cook or eat.* They clattered as I threw them aside. *The canteen is too heavy. One water bottle. One cup for Rambo. Tent, Tarp?Bungee? Yes.* I folded them. I slid them back in with the firstaid kit, fishing gear and my precious lighter. I thought twice about my makeup. *How vain! Sunscreen only!*

Cards? I stood up with the deck in my hands, spread them out then tossed them in the wind. *That may be the last frivolous thing you do, Gabi.*

Rambo became antsy, nose on super speed. He wore an expression like, *"Hurry up!"* He didn't react to the cards I flung about. Re remained poised on the ground, yiping.

I set my sleeping bag aside. *Could I do with out it? Yes, I can use the thermal blanket. It weighs less.*

I filled a couple of water bottles then drenched myself by dumping several bottles over my head. I poured bottles of water on Rambo trying not to wet his bandage. I tore up a shirt and made two masks, in case we need to cover our faces and noses.

After I strapped myself into my backpack, I grabbed the regular blanket. *If the fire comes closer I can wet it. If absolutely necessary we can get into the river and I can dump this blanket.* I rolled it over my backpack. I did notice a difference in the weight as I strapped it all back on.

Fires move fast creating their own wind, and it was picking up. They engulf everything in their way.

I didn't want to be in the way. *Which way should I go? Move down wind?Up wind?*

I checked the wind direction then looked heavenward. "Which way Lord?"

Feeling a pull, I decided. "Okay, Ram, let's stay close to the river. We'll follow it as far as possible. We just have to keep moving as long as you are able. We'll be okay."

Sounding so sure wasn't exactly how I felt inside.

The air filled with the smell of smoke as the ashes danced. When I didn't see any flying embers, I thanked God.

Chapter 54
Help!

Would Rambo instinctively know that the river meant safety or would he panic and speed away from the danger into the forest? He could be overcome with the smoke, or worse—head right in the path of the fire or become surrounded? Is it possible that animals have an instinct that tells them how to escape this danger? Should I let him loose so that I follow him? Is that even fair? Should I let him take the lead? Maybe he could escape if he were free. Should I hook him to me?

I vacillated before I hooked the bungee cord into Ram's collar. "Stay with me. Whatever we do, we do it together."

The clothes I tore for face covers, I stuffed into into my pocket. It might not be long before we would need them. I could already feel the burning in my eyes and throat.

When Ram tried to clear his windpipe, I winced watching his discomfort. As we trudged along at Rambo's painfully slow pace, I wondered if anyone had reported this fire. *Were they fighting it right now? Would they see us?*

My eyes darted around checking for flames or floating embers which could rapidly change our course. Small fragments flitted in the ever increasing wind.

The first indicator of a change in the status of the fire were the flames that now danced across the rise. The flames were still a ways off, however, the blaze definitely threatened us. It certainly headed toward the river.

Next the black clouds covered most of the sky as they ballooned in the wind.

My eyes watered and my throat burned.

The roaring of the fire provoked Rambo to bark back as if this were a beast he could challenge.

The temperature rose.

The wind picked up.

Sweat dripped down my face. When I wiped my brow I felt the grit of ashes. Taking my hand away showed that my skin had collected a layer of dark soot.

When Rambo slurped at the edge of the river, I stopped. After I scooped up some water, I slopped some on the two of us. A drink soothed a little bit.

The speed of the rampaging fire picked up.

I tied the masks around Ram first then myself.

Rambo wrestled with his restraint. "No! Rambo you have to keep it on.

My options seemed limited.

If we keep moving in the direction we are going, the fire is racing toward the river aiming at us. It would probably stop at the edge. Though where does that leave us? The last fuel to be caught up in flames? Sometime soon we will need to get into the river. How fast is the current? Is there another waterfall or rapids anywhere near? Caught in the current—could I survive again?

I eyed the flow of the river before I stepped into the shallow water. I slogged along. *My wet boots! If I need to swim they will drag me down.*

I sat at the edge on a flat stone to take off the boots. I tied their shoelaces together then found a place to tie them onto my backpack. Whiney, Rambo became antsy. "If we move past the fire, we won't get far in my bare feet, so just sit here a minute." I patted the ground. He sat while I finished securing my boots. He kept a watchful eye, rotating his head each time an object in the path of the fire exploded or flamed up.

The flames licked the trees near the shore. It reminded me of watching dominoes fall. One after another caught and torched in seconds. Embers flew and connected, dotting the hillside with mini fires. I marveled at the speed it traveled. Remembrances of how painful small burns I'd gotten from cooking had been, tinged my fear. I cringed at the idea of being burned to death.

Even with my face covered, my throat rasped. I hacked. Rambo whined and coughed as he tried to clear his windpipe. That action knocked his mask askew.

Along with the flames, the winds picked up intensifying the heat like a blast furnace.

When I pictured my hair catching on fire, I stopped, braided it and pinned it on top of my head.

Either barefooted or with boots, trekking along in the water across the pebbled bottom made slow going. We weren't heading away from the fire, just parallel with its edge.

I ventured a little deeper into the river as I resisted the strong current. This path at the shoreline did not seem like the answer to our problems, nor did the possibility of swimming to the other side where the fire hadn't jumped the river.

When an ember caught on an aspen just to the side of us. the tree burst into flames. I gasped. Soon it became a ball of fire that quickened my heart rate while the wind blasted me like a blow torch.

The air burned with smoke.

I coughed.

"Oh Lord, show me the way!"

Chapter 55
A Better Way

Just about the time I decided to change my plan, I looked behind me. A fairly sizeable log flowed along on the swift moving current. *Would the log smash into us if I didn't move? If I could catch the log. . .could I stop it or would it just plow me under? If I did catch it could we hang on? Would it be possible to climb on top of it and ride it?*

"It's worth a try, Rambo. I don't see any other options."

My heart hammered. I struggled with each breath getting harder and harder to inhale.

"Don't panic, Ram."

Who am I talking to, now?

Rambo stayed still while I waded a few more steps toward the middle. Since he stood shorter, I didn't doubt that deeper wasn't something he would or could handle, especially with his weak leg. *What if I lost my balance in the current? I could be swept away!*

As the log neared our location, I noticed there were a couple of branch stubs sticking out on the top and side near the front end of the log.

"Okay, God. I need you to help me."

As soon as the log came past, I grabbed two stubs. It jerked me for a moment but I jerked back.

The forward motion of the current plus my sideways yank turned and pushed the log with me closer to shore.

Breathing in a superficial breath of smoky air, I tugged the log into the shallow water where the current slowed. Struggling, I held the log steady as the front of it dug into ground by the shore.

Think, Gabi.

I had watched loggers showing off by trying to walk on logs. The logs seemed to have a mind of their own. When they rolled and sent the logger scrambling into the water.

Did I dare straddle the log? Would it heave me off? What about Rambo? Could we both get on this log and use it as a canoe to float down river and escape the fire? Except we wouldn't have any oars to steer. Would Rambo slip off while we jiggle the log to get on? What if he did slide off? I have to bungee us together so we won't get separated. Could I drag him along and keep his head up out of the water? Would he pull me off too if he couldn't balance?

The fire raced our way becoming a wall of flames closer and closer. With that advance, breathing became more difficult. The hairs on my arms rose.

Both of us coughed, hacked and my throat burned. Only seconds remained when there would be no choice. I knew without the log we would risk drowning in the current. If we stayed on shore we would flame up and be burned to death.

My mind was swimming as my eyes blurred.

Use the log?

Chapter 56
Where to Now?

The blanket hindered rather than helped us. I detached it. It drifted away with the flow. As the log bobbed, I grabbed Rambo. "Help me boy." I dragged him over to the log. He clawed and splashed. We struggled until I realized he was trying to do what I wanted him to. He pulled himself up with his front paws while I lifted his hind end. Finally he sat on the front of the log and he arranged himself, with my help. He braced his front paws against the two branch stubs.

"Smart boy!"

I gave a quick push off. I lobbed my leg over so I straddled the log. It pitched. It lurched like a bronco trying to dislodge it riders. When I just about balanced, the current caught us, jostling us this way and that.

I countered the pull of my backpack as its weight shifted by grabbing onto one of the stubs. A lucky bob of the log forced my arm to whip around Rambo. I stretched and tried to grab the other stub. I screamed. With a roll in the opposite direction, my arm flew up. Finally I worked my fingers around the stub. When I got a firm hold of both stumps I braced Rambo against me between my arms.

I imagined watching this whole maneuver from grandstand seats. The popping of the crackling fire offered its applause.

Would the log stop rolling? At any second, as we bobbed back and forth, one or both of us could have been washed off.

Somehow we weren't.

I balanced at last.

We stayed perched on the log like a bike rider with Rambo sitting on the handlebars as our 'bike' traversed an off-road trail plagued with rocks, dips and bumps. I squeezed my elbows in as I held Rambo as tight as I could. His strength surprised me because his brace against the stubs kept us from flying forward. My grasp of the stubs held us from falling backward. I have no idea what held us from flying off sidewise as my backpack shifted.

The whole experience reminded me of taking the log ride on Splash Mountain at Disneyland. This ride however became quite exciting though definitely not fun. Every move was a life and death struggle.

I had been so busy planning this escape, managing the log, and being scared of drowning that I almost forgot about the fire.

I glanced back. "Look at that, Ram. We just escaped in time."

The flames touched the shore right where we had been standing. Ashes swirled in the air. Red embers flew about like fireflies torching off every bush and tree in its path.

"Thank you Lord. Keep us in your arms. Bring us safely through this fire. Please keep those embers from reaching the other side of the river." Before I could say Amen. A slipstream caught us pushing us sideways. I needed a whole different grip to keep us mounted.

"Hang on Ram!"

By the time we figured out how to stay put riding sideways, the log flipped around backwards.

When we finally faced forward, the current relaxed. I let out my breath while I hung on like an octopus.

It wasn't as if I could steer us to the side where the shore was not burning. Though I did find that there were certain ways to shift our weight that gave me some minor degree of control over our runaway raft.

Finally I relaxed my clenching teeth.

That's when I heard it.

211

Chapter 57
This Hadn't Occurred to Me

Barely above the roar of the fire I heard something. I found it hard to concentrate on anything other than lifting my feet so they wouldn't get smashed against rocks or floating branches.

Was it an engine?

I checked the sky. My pulse quickened. I hadn't thought about the fire being my means of contacting help. But there it was, blades whirring. The chopper overhead dumped retardant or water on the fire. I watched the bucket swing from the rope hanging below the helicopter then splash its contents on the flames with very little affect.

Letting loose from the log handles always proved a challenge. By the time I realized where the noise came from, looped an arm around Ram and got ready to signal, the chopper completed his dump. He headed away from us.

Could he have seen us? Maybe he will come back. Only he's probably paying more attention to his task than perusing the outer areas of the fire. Maybe he dunks the bucket in the river. Therefore he will be back even if he didn't see us this time.

"We have a chance, Ram!"

Hope is an amazing thing. My mood changed from how can I do this another minute, to yes you can hang on until someone sees us, no matter how long it takes. My knees ached from pressing them into the log. However, I began imagining my rescue rather than worrying about my plight.

Meanwhile we rushed along clutching each other with a death grip on the log. I grabbed a couple of deep breaths, as the fire took a different path than where we were headed. Also the fire hadn't reached the river at our location yet so the visibility increased. The air seemed a little cleaner.

"See God's helping us with clean air!"

Finally I felt comfortable taking a deep breath, which hurt a little. I began to relax a little.

I adjusted Ram with myself so we remained balanced.

Just as I unclenched my teeth and eased my elbows, I saw the boulder jutting out into the river. It loomed directly in our path. *If I don't do something the log will probably smash right into it. Even if we don't crash into it, we might skim it with my leg hanging over the edge of the log. My leg could be crushed between the log and the boulder. My feet were bare. Could I kick off from it before it smashed my leg? If I tried that maneuver, would Rambo or I fall off? Would leaning to one side or the other help?*

I tried leaning to my left.

Big mistake.

That effort caused us to turn around backwards. I sucked in a muffled scream. Assessing my last move, I leaned again. The flow turned us back forward. *If I was learning to steer this thing my learning curve had better be swift. Help me Lord!*

A small limb floated a short ways ahead of us. *Could I use it like an oar?* I swooped my arm out and grabbed it. Rambo leaned the other direction. That countered my thrust. A rolling wobble resulted which caught me flailing. It almost knocked me off. Then I caught Ram just teetering the other way off the log.

By the time we were stabilized, the rock rose directly ahead of us like rugged teeth. As we rushed toward the menacing boulder, I used the limb to push against the rock. That action thrust us back out in the middle of the river. Ram's howl punctuated my scream as we swirled about.

Even though we narrowly missed the rock formation, we were still in trouble. Next I used the branch like an oar to straighten our pathway. I grabbed for Ram. My fingers gripped him by the scruff of his neck just as his paws splashed into the water. Lurching this way and that, I tugged with some inner strength I didn't know I possessed. Ultimately, I settled Ram back into position. He braced against the stubs. "Good Boy!"

Breathing hard I spoke to Ram in spurts. "That. . . was no easy trick. . .keeping us both. . .aboard keep us heading the right direction." I secured my hands on the stubs with an extra squeeze for Rambo. "You'd think. . .I'd be used to being scared. . .huh, Ram?"

The branch may have been helpful in steering but retaining it for such a use—I couldn't hang on to the log, the branch, and Ram, so I threw it aside while I struggled. Besides, I didn't really know how to use an oar properly. Practicing on this river with this "boat" didn't seem like a viable option.

"I've got you Ram." I hugged in.

A few moments later, I gasp at what we were facing next.

Chapter 58
A Rough Ride

Ahead of us the water roiled and splashed. I couldn't tell how deep the water was but something was clear. We fast approached a new set of rapids.

I should have kept the branch! Everywhere rocks!

Involuntarily, I shrieked as we pitched over the edge. The log shot down the rapids, hurled sideways then pointed straight into a rocky landing.

I pictured my feet or my ankles being crushed between the protruding rocks. I sucked my knees up as close as I could while I hugged closer to Rambo. However that didn't stop the rocks from attacking my feet and ankles. I winced. My shrieking as we rolled on through caused Rambo to yelp.

We had no choice but to let the flow take us where it would. I pushed away from protruding rocks and floating debris with my raw hands or feet. My scuffed ankles were bleeding, but still we angled our way through together.

When the log rolled one way, we countered the other way. We started out facing front then the river took control of our vessel. Our positions varied from side to side rolls, to 180 degree turns, even sideways trajectory before we finally spun around facing down river where the cascade ended.

One good thing, the smoke billowed at our back. We had left the fire behind us.

Between our floundering maneuvers, I shot a glance toward shore. Firefighter crews hacked with axes, dug trenches and cut back brush using power saws.

"Help! Help! Help me! Look up please!"

I was so busy avoiding the treachery of the rocks that I couldn't see if the men had even glanced up.

The noise of their power saws still buzzed in my ears.

How could they hear me with all that buzzing, plus men yelling orders? Then there's the roar from the rapids.

If I could have slumped, I would have. As the situation dictated, I didn't dare unclench a single muscle.

As I clung to the log, I ached everywhere, especially my hands and knees.

How long could I hold on before my grip gave way?

A cloud of dust blasted up from the bank. In the midst of traveling along with the blanket of flying dirt, a white pick up truck raced beside the river. A dirt road apparently paralleled the river then veered away between the trees before returning to the shore.

When the dust bomb passed, it pulled ahead of us. I was sure all that cloud must've obscured the driver's visibility. When I couldn't see the car or the dust anymore, I was positive. "No one saw us Ram."

My tears disappeared in the spray of water that continually spattered my face.

Chapter 59
A Face From the past

The river widened out a bit. I began wondering if I could drop off the log. *Maybe I could swim ashore.* The crystal clear water flowed by, swift enough and churning so that I couldn't see the bottom.

Was drowning still a possibility? Not yet. Stay put.

"I know you are with me Lord, please. . .Help us get to shore."

I couldn't see around the bend in the river's pathway.

When we rounded the curve, I saw it.

The dust cloud reappeared.

Was someone coming for us?

Ahead in a swirl of dust, the white pickup truck barreled up right next to the river where it fishtailed to a stop. A man, appearing small in the distance, got out of the truck. He stood on shore with waving arms.

He sees us! That man is definitely waving! He sees us!

A huge smile spread across my face. I let loose for a minute to wave, to let him know I saw him.

"Hello!" My loudest scream blasted the air. With a roll of the log, I didn't dare wave back.

My heart raced faster than my log sped along.

"Hey Ram. See that man. He's gonna help us."

"Hello!" He waved again though this wave looked different.

"Hello!"

A Lasso? Was he trying to throw a rope to us? Yes! This is cowboy country. Why am I surprised?

The rope swirled around over his head like he was separating a dogie from the herd.

I swallowed hard.

We were too far away? Oh please don't let us speed past him...

The lasso soared through the air. It dropped into the water just short of us. I stretched out trying to catch the rope.

When I missed, I think my heart stopped, until the jostling of the log forced my attention back to hanging on. I had to keep Ram from falling off.

The man pulled in the rope then gathered it up.

Soon we were right adjacent to the roper.

Swirling once more above his head, the rope flew toward us.

I let loose of the log and stretched out for it.

Quick as a lick of flame, we flew past him. The rope fell behind us.

I didn't dare stretch back for it. It floated away too far even though the rush of the river carried the rope along behind us.

My pulse quickened.

Don't give up on us! Please. . .

A quick glimpse over my shoulder caught the dust rising again.

"He's going to follow us Ram! It's going to be okay." This time I believed myself!

When the flying dirt cloud disappeared, I shuddered. *How long would it take him to find us again? Or would he need to send help? I can hang on. I can. Help me Lord. I can.*

I think I can, I think I can.

The child's storybook about a little train engine making it over the mountain put a limp smile on my face.

I think I can. I think I can.

Chapter 60
Hang in There

We pitched and rolled along with no help in sight. I held on even tighter. I checked the sky and scanned the shore for someone, anyone. There wasn't another human being in sight.

He wouldn't leave us. He'll come back. I had to keep reassuring myself as the time stretched from minutes into what seemed like an hour before I heard the chopper blades slicing through the air.

I squinted up as the sun blinded me. There was something hanging from the copter.

At first I thought the helicopter was headed for the fire with another water drop.

But no! It hovered overhead. "It's following us!"

My neck craned. The wind whipped against my face as the chopper blades agitated the water around us, splashing waves and spattering us like being inside a washing machine. This made it nearly impossible to hang on.

A man dropped out of the copter suspended from a rope.

"Hang on Rambo. He's coming for us."

The rope descended, dangling as the chopper aimed the man toward us. He pointed at the belted rope he attempted to hand me.

I screamed, "I can't let go of my dog!" With the roar of the engine plus the whir of the blades, I didn't think he heard me.

Indicating my reluctance to go without my dog, I hugged an arm around Ram as I leaned in against him.

The man signaled.

The chopper lifted away.

I sucked in a breath. *Going away again?* "Don't leave me!"

Without much time to worry if he was returning or not, the chopper circled back around. It approached from the rear.

Directly behind me, I saw the man dangling.

With a swooping jolt, he collided against me. Suddenly he engulfed me in his arms. I clutched Rambo against me.

"Let go of the log!" the man screamed in my ear.

The mere thought of hanging loose without the security of the log made me pause. However the pull of the copter persuaded me.

Slowly I unclenched my knees. When I let loose of the log, my legs swung loose sending the log lurching down the river. As I hugged Rambo tighter he became heavier and heavier.

My stomach flipped over.

I felt each beat as my heart pounded.

Before I knew what was happening, all three of us dangled over the river. We swung imitating a clock's pendulum.

I watched the log streaming away. The bird's eye view reminded me of the view over the falls. That thought ran shivers through me. *What if he dropped us? Could we survive again churning in the river?*

The man clamped his legs around both Ram and me.

"It's okay. I've got you. It's going to be all right. You're safe now." I will probably always remember that moment, a moment when his manly scent blended with the wet dog smell. The man's kind voice spoke soothing and gentle. It settled around me like Gran's quilt.

I've been scared before, however this thrilling moment became a wave of relief that spread over me.

We're gonna make it!

I might have been squeezing poor Rambo too tight, but I just couldn't let up for fear that I might drop him.

I had no idea what would happen next.

Would we be raised up into the craft?

The three us swung in a spin.

Wafting in the air for a few lengthy moments, the helicopter rose causing us to dangle while swaying until we stabilized.

The gusts of wind prompted me to tighten every muscle even tighter.

My jaws ached from clenching.

The copter pitched. I felt the man's legs ease their grip first then let loose. My weight must've jerked against his arm hold around me.

Suddenly I hit the water like torpedo, plunged below the water while Rambo slipped from my arms.

I couldn't see what happened to the man but saw and felt another plunge next to me. *The Man? Rambo?*

I bobbed to the surface where I saw Ram. The current sucked me under again.

Instantaneously I saw red with flashes like stars twinkling. That was the last thing I remembered.

Chapter 61
Where Am I?

My first sensation was the warmth of my hand. I held my eyes closed as I absorbed its comfort. Someone held my hand. I gripped tight. "I can't let go or I'll drown!"

"Gabi?. . .Nurse she's awake."

When I opened my eyes, lights over me blurred. Not clearly, but I could make out a man standing next to a woman.

As things began to clear up, I surveyed my surroundings. Machines of all kinds blipped and beeped. Blinking, I tried to focus on the woman. I could see her silhouette. Her grayish hair was drawn on top of her head in a bun. She smiled a kindly smile.

"Where am I?"

"You are in the hospital, young lady. Looks like you've had quite a time of it. I think you're going to be okay now."

I touched my achy, bandaged head. "What happened?" The last thing I remembered I had dropped into the river.

"A concussion that knocked you out. My name is Sophie. I am your nurse. I have to make some rounds. I'll let the doctor know you're awake. Your savior can tell you. Oh, be careful of that ankle. It's broken."

I reared up. "Wait!" I grabbed at her arm but missed. "Where's my dog? Where's Rambo?"

She stepped away leaving the man who stood at the railing. He touched my cheek as he took my hand. Just that act soothed my worry. "Rambo is fine."

"Where is he?"

"A friend of mine is a vet. She's taking care of him at her office."

I fixed my stare on his sapphire blue eyes.

"Is he okay?"

"Yes. He'll be fine. She said his stitches were a life-saver."

"So glad to hear that. I thought I might have lost him."

An attractive doctor came in. He eyed my chart. He reminded me of Papa the way he ran he ran his fingers through his dark wavy hair. He sanitized his hands and instructed me to do the usual breathing intakes as his stethoscope moved from my chest to my back. "How does that deep breath feel?"

"A little sore. So's my throat."

"I think you're a very lucky young lady, emerging from that forest fire. I don't see that you have any symptoms that won't go away in a day or two, except the broken ankle."

I smiled.

"I'd like to keep you an extra day to keep check on that head injury. Maybe we can fatten you up a little." He had the kind of smile that was infectious. He pointed at the black boot on the bench at the end of my bed. "Have Sophie help you on with that boot before you walk on your ankle. You have a sleeping boot on right now."

The doctor patted my shoulder. "I'll be back later to check on you."

As I lay back against the pillows, I refocused on the man that stood behind the doctor. He had his back to me, staring out the window. Somehow the tilt of his head, his broad shoulders seemed familiar.

As he turned to face me my eyes began to clear. "Greg? What? How did you get here?"

"You remember you were in a fire?"

"Oh Yes!"

He touched my hand and held it. "I just happened to be with the crew. I'm a volunteer firefighter. After I saw you floating by on a log, I tried to catch up to you in my pick-up. When I tried to rope you in, I missed."

"Were you the one that dangled from the helicopter, snatched me off the log then dropped me?"

"Er, yeah sorry about that. . .but I did pull you out. . .gave you CPR and. . ."

I touched my chest, "That's why my chest aches."

"Sorry…"

"Don't be sorry. . .I mean. . .How can I ever thank you?"

"You can have dinner with me when you get out of here."

"Uh. . .?" He released my hand as I raised it and spread my fingers. I paused for a moment feeling a loss as he let go. "Didn't you see my. . ." I held up fingers for a second look. "Where is it?"

"What?"

"My ring? My engagement ring."

"I didn't see one when I plucked you from the water. I would have noticed."

"Oh? Do you think the nurses took it off? I could have lost it in the river? Or. . .Well it could disappeared in any one of my. . . experiences." I could feel my brow furrow.

"I can ask the EMT's. Maybe they can check their rig. I kind of know one of them."

"Thanks, I'd appreciate that." I looked up at him. "Do you happen to know what happened to my backpack?"

His dimples deepened in a smirk. He walked over to a cabinet on the wall next to my gurney. With great flourish, he pulled the door open. He swung out his arm. "Voila, Mademoiselle."

"I left half my stuff on shore before we escaped the fire. But I am glad you rescued what I have left. I see my coat is there too."

"Your backpack is why I dropped you. The load shifted, the chopper rotated, and I lost my leg grip around you, not that I'm trying to excuse myself from the blame."

"Doesn't seem to matter. I'm here now, am I not?"

"I bet your parents are glad of that."

"My father. That reminds me—I threw away my phone. I have to call my papa and my fiancé. Do. . ."

"I hope you don't mind I washed and dried the few things that needed it. They were all wet and musty." He took out his cell from his pocket before I could ask. "Here, I already called."

"How? I mean how did you know who I was? Who to call? I didn't have my ID."

"I checked with the airlines. The only girl on the plane with a name close to Gabi was someone named Gabriella Di Carlo. That is you?"

"And if not?" I smirked right back at him.

"Then someone else's dad is probably on that plane."

"Oh thank you! Since you didn't know about my engagement, I don't suppose you called Wil?"

"Wil? He crossed his arms across his chest. "I'm not sure if I knew about Wil whether I would have called or not." He scratched his head. "Then I suppose dinner's a no go?"

"Well. . ."

"It's okay. I understand. When someone loses, someone else wins."

I smiled, though I did feel a sting of disappointment. Dinner would have been nice.

"However, I do think I deserve to hear the story behind the log ride, all those experiences where you might have lost your ring." He sat down in the armchair next to my gurney, crossed his legs with one hand resting on his knee. "Well?"

"I suppose you do deserve an explanation. First though what's going on with that fire?"

"Well it started with a car fire. The owner called the authorities immediately. Since it occurred close to a road, they dispatched fire vehicles. The crews got there pretty quickly. The river was the fire's nemesis. It worked as a firebreak. The blaze is about 90% contained. I think we lost somewhere around 350 acres so far. They should have it out pretty soon. Some of the evacuated ranchers are already returning to their homes. . . Okay, your turn."

"Not before I get a drink. I am so thirsty."

After he handed me a glass, he filled it from the pitcher on my tray. "Don't drink too much, too fast and make yourself sick."

I just savored the long cool drink.

"You can't believe how good water tastes unless you haven't had any for a while. Well. . .shall I start with my plane ride?"

Chapter 62
I'm Big News

When I'd finished explaining my adventure, Greg handed me the morning's newspaper. "You're famous." Big, bold headlines— MISSING TWO WEEKS WOMAN RESCUED stared up at me. The accompanying photograph, an aerial view, captured a picture of me on the log, with the dog, floating down the river, against the backdrop of the fire and puffs of black smoke.

I learned that my search and rescue began the moment they knew the plane went missing without letting up. Helicopters scoured the Wyoming wilderness from Yellowstone into parts of Idaho, Montana, Utah, with crews working as far east as Rapid City. They decreased the intensity of the search after a week, with forays continuing until they found me.

After reading the story, I looked at Greg. "You're pretty famous too. My hero!"

"Aw shucks!"

"Hey don't minimize what you did. If they told half the truth in this article, they talk about my rescue as nothing short of a miracle."

I didn't think a macho man like Greg could blush, but he did.

"Do they know about Buck?"

"Not sure, but I can let the authorities know. When you're better, you can elaborate."

"Thanks."

Next Greg gave me his phone along with the vet's business card. As I called the vet, I wondered what Wil knew about me yet.

"Rambo's doing fine."

"Did my stitches. . .?"

"Not fancy but they worked. Now we're fighting the infection. He should be ready to be picked up in a day or so. We will take care of him until whenever you are released."

"That's the best news yet. I am very grateful, but I miss him so."

I held up the phone to Greg. "Do you mind?"

He gave a nod with a swish of his hand.

I thought for a few moments. All the numbers you store in your cell are not as easily remembered as you might think. Papa's number came to my mind first, so I punched in his number.

"Ciao, Papa!"

"Hey! Gabi! Ciao tesoro, come stai? Che cosa hanno fatto i medici?"

"The nurse said I had a concussion. Oh, also a broken ankle."

"I am so glad to hear your voice. Are you really okay?"

"Nothing gets me down anymore, Papa." *Not after what I've experienced in the last two weeks.* "Especially not a slight concussion and a little broken ankle."

"Look, my plane just got in and I'm on my way. I rented a car so I'm driving there right now. I'm going to be at the hospital pretty soon."

"I don't want you to get a ticket for talking on the phone. I'll just be here waiting for you."

"I called Wil. He should be there too."

"Thanks, Papa. Love you."

"See you soon and I love you too—more than the stars in the sky."

"Bigger than the moon." I smiled at the childhood expressions we used to exchange as we studied the night sky.

Wonder why Wil isn't here already?

When Sophie returned, she removed all my cords and needles so I no longer felt like a dartboard. " The doctor said it would be good if you got up. Take a little walk. Maybe Greg here will take you for a cruise down the hall."

I looked down at my hospital gown and recalled how most of those fashionable gowns usually gaped down the back.

"Well. . .?"

"Maybe you could use this." As if he'd read my mind, he handed me a box wrapped in shiny pink paper and tied with a fluffy white bow. "Here."

"What's this?"

"Just open it."

I pulled off the bow and unwrapped it.

"Don't tell me you're going to save the wrapping paper."

"Okay I won't tell you."

I folded the paper and set it aside with the ribbon on top. "Wow, this is lovely" I held up the luxurious deep purple robe. "It's so soft." I nestled it against my cheek.

"From the color of your jacket, I figured you like purple."

I eased my legs over the edge. My ankles and legs were bandaged here and there with minor cuts scabbed over. Sophie helped me on with my walking boot. Securely strapped, she gave me some walking instructions.

"Here let me." As I got out of bed, Greg helped me slip my arms into the sleeves of my new robe without exposing my derriere.

I cuddled the plushness up around my neck then tied the ties around my waist. "I feel like a queen. What a nice thing to do."

"I just remembered what kind of garments are hospital issue. Although I'm sure the male nurses would appreciate the rear view."

Greg took my arm. I thought it not necessary but I did feel a little wobbly. As we started down the hallway, I hugged his arm.

Greg had me laughing at everything we passed in the hall, making outrageous claims about the uses of all the devices, machines and gauges we passed by. On the way back he made up stories about the patients as we passed their rooms.

"Oh, I almost forgot. After we landed, I ran a check on those scruffy men that hassled you on the plane. I think that you were right in your assessment of them when you ran into them in the forest. One just got off parole for armed robbery and assault. The other one has been arrested several times for domestic violence. Not exactly the heroes who might have rescued you."

Chapter 63
I Am Becoming Famous

When we returned to my room, Greg handed me his phone. "I suppose you'll want to make another call? To that Wil guy?"

Before I could reach Wil, an army of reporters swarmed into my room. Flashes went off, cameras and mikes were pointed at me.

"Hi, Star Tribune here."

An attractive blonde reporter leaned in. "KCWY"

A young man pointed a mike at me. "Tell us about your experience."

"Survival Quarterly. Tell me. . ."

Questions, like machine gun bullets exploded at me. Most of them overlapped each other so it felt as though I were having a bad dream.

"Is it true you survived an airplane crash?"

"How did you survive?"

"Was anyone with you?"

"Where is the dog now?"

"What did you find for food?"

"What about wild animals?"

At first I tried to answer all the queries. However, the questions went on and on 'ad nauseum', often repeating the ones I thought I had answered.

"Did you ever give up hope you'd be rescued?"

" 'And thou shalt be secure, because there is hope.' Job 11 verse 18.' God—don't leave home without him."

Without a square inch of space in my room, I had never felt claustrophobic before. I assume that's what I felt, all those overlapping voices and wall-to-wall bodies. The air felt thick with aftershave, perfume and body odor. *Is this what high blood pressure feels like?*

I peered around the room.

"Greg?" When I tried to defer more questions to Greg, I didn't see him among the choir of faces.

"Greg?"

He was gone.

Suddenly, I felt his loss deep in my chest.

I announced, "Hey everyone, I'm very tired. Please go."

Sophie came to my rescue. "Okay, everybody out. She needs to rest."

Disappointed faces tried for more questions, though I just raised a flat hand. I refused to answer as they fired off the last volley of their questions.

Sophie almost physically shoveled the last reporters from my room.

She checked me over with all her gadgets and pronounced, "Well, you're no worse than you were before. If you can survive what you did, I'm sure you'll survive our media hype. You're big news in a small town. You feel okay?"

"I guess I must be feeling better because now I will have my face spread across a variety of media and the only thing I'm worried about is my appearance."

"You look fine." She patted my shoulder.

"Any chance I could get a mirror and maybe a brush?" My sticky mouth tasted like I'd eaten too much broccoli. "And a tooth brush?"

Quickly I realized I really did feel exhausted. Not long after their departure, before the nurse came back with my beauty tools, sleep crept over me.

Chapter 64
My Men

Papa's face came into view when I opened my eyes. "Papa!"

Behind him the sky filling the window seemed like late afternoon.

Pop rushed over. "Cara mia." He kissed my forehead and tapped my nose. "I need to fix you some pasta. How much weight did you lose?"

"I don't know but I had to cinch my belt up a few times despite the fact that during my adventure I enjoyed a gourmet diet of fish, poultry, eggs, BBQ buffalo, dandelion or watercress greens plus more fish! What I want now is a hamburger and fries."

"Wow! How you acquired those gastronomic delights is probably a pretty interesting part of what happened in the last two weeks. Gonna tell me?"

Meanwhile, Wil came through the door holding two cardboard cups of coffee. After I finished reciting my hiking menu, he offered one cup to Papa and he came over to the side of my gurney. He took my hand then gave me a coffee tasting kiss with a back up tickle of his beard.

"Mm, coffee flavored mustache." The ceiling lamp overhead highlighted the auburn growth on his upper lip and chin—grown enough to already be curly. When did you start growing that?"

He rubbed his chin. "I started it graduation day. I never grew one before so I didn't know how fast it would grow. Like it?"

I thought of those idiots on the plane. "Depends. You gonna trim it or let it grow like the Duck Dynasty group?"

"Want some coffee?"

"No, I'd rather have a chocolate milkshake and a hamburger."

"You mean to tell me they are not feeding you that kind of food?"

"Yeah, sure." I rolled my eyes.

I rubbed my chin as I squinted at him. "And you changed the subject pretty fast, mountain man."

"Your dad has a point. Want to tell us about surviving all alone?"

"I wasn't alone, you know."

"Oh?" Papa raised his eyebrows."

"I had Rambo."

"Who?" Papa asked.

"I'll explain Rambo, my dog, during my account. However, you were both with me—so was Mama and Gran. Remember how Gran always quoted the bible, chapter and verse? "

Papa nodded.

"I could hear her voice as clear as the blue skies of Wyoming quoting the scriptures and telling me just what I needed to hear when I needed to hear it. 'Be strong and courageous. Do not be afraid; do not be discouraged; for the Lord your God will be with you wherever you go. Joshua 1 verse 9.' He traveled with me wherever I went. How do you think I could survive that long by myself, or even by myself with Rambo?"

"You tell me."

"Well. . ."

Wil seemed distracted as if something caught his attention. He eyed the cute little curly-haired aide that swished by with a tray for my dinner. Between bites of meatloaf drowned in gravy, and mashed potatoes that I smooshed together with peas and carrots, I told them my story. I began to think of it like an adventure as I told it.

They were rapt as I told them about the crash and Rambo. I thought they'd fall asleep as I recounted the story, because I don't think I left out a single thing, not even the singing around the campfire with Rambo, together with a description of the beautiful places I rested. But they didn't snooze. Wil chuckled at my tree climbing and missing his voice during our fireside recital. Papa sat up a few times wincing as I told about the wolf, the rattlesnake strike and the buffalo stampede. They both grimaced at my blood cocktail. I kept rattling on. My hero, Rambo dominated much of my story.

Papa shook his head. "Wow. I think you should write a book about that adventure." He patted my hand.

"It'd be hard to believe if it hadn't actually happened. Always knew you were amazing. I am so proud of you."

"Me too, woman! What are you gonna need me for on our next hike?"

As I thought about that, I too, wondered. *I am a different person now. I am confident that I can do anything, anything I need to. I can take care of myself.* "See that paper over there? I guess I'm sort of famous."

"I did see it. Who is this guy that rescued you?" Wil scratched his head.

"Remember I talked about the Delta plane I was on? And those obnoxious men? It just so happens that the air marshal who rescued me from those men, is a volunteer firefighter. Kind of ironic he was the one there just at the right moment to rescue me from the river. I think he was heaven sent."

A smile curled on my lips at the thought of Greg. I hoped I would see him again.

Chapter 65
A Goodbye

The next morning they re-bandaged my head with a smaller patch rather than the turban dressing I wore the day before. I helped the nurse as she gave me a sponge bath. As I scrubbed down, sticking my ankle out of the way, I wondered if they gave me a sponge bath to remove all that soot, because the last I remembered, soot covered me from my head down. Sophie did some kind of shampoo. Afterward I brushed my hair then checked myself in the mirror. "Now why aren't the reporters here today snapping their photos?" I addressed the mirror. I donned my new robe and luxuriated in its softness.

The smiling curly-headed girl brought in my breakfast. Eating my scrambled eggs, I remembered my last meal of eggs. I fixed a far away stare out the window.

Then I glanced at the doorway. "How long have you been watching me?"

Greg stood leaning his shoulder against the doorjamb, hands in his Levi pockets, smiling. "You probably wouldn't believe how angelic you look with the sunshine lighting up your hair like a halo. Or maybe you would—considering you may have achieved that status once or twice during your survival."

"You have a lot of nerve escaping yesterday and leaving me alone to face the piranhas of the media." I worked up the poutiest face I could muster.

"Well, if you survived two weeks of hell, you can handle a few obnoxious reporters." He took a rolled up newspaper out of the back pocket of his worn jeans. "Looks like you're the star of your own story." He flopped it open in my lap.

I frowned while I stared at my photo on the front page of the Star Tribune.

"You look a lot better today."

"Gee thanks. Seriously though, I'm not sure I really thanked you properly for being my hero."

"Properly?" He strode over to my bedside. Before I knew what was happening, he held me in his arms. He kissed me ever so softly. Then he released me.

When I opened my eyes, he stood across the room.

"Properly enough?" He scuffed his cowboy boots then locked his blue eyes with mine.

I couldn't speak, however I was very aware of every heartbeat.

"Anyway I just dropped by to pick up my phone I left here yesterday. Also I wanted to say good bye."

I pointed. "I put your phone over there."

At that moment, the doorway filled with giant of a man. "Hi, I'm Jeremy your physical therapist."

As Greg retrieved his phone, the therapist proceeded to instruct me on walking.

"This will help you learn to navigate stairs using your new boot." Jeremy dragged over a small set of stairs. He stepped over and dropped the rails at my bedside. "I'm going to get you ready to get around." He helped me up as if I weighed 90 pounds. *Hmm. Wonder if I do?* I certainly did weigh a lot less than my normal weight.

While I listened to my instructions and practiced using the stairway he brought with him, I didn't notice.

Greg was gone.

Even on my trek through Wyoming, I hadn't felt so alone.

Chapter 66
I'm Getting Out

After lunch, Sophie came in. "Good news. You're going home this afternoon."

That news should have buoyed my spirits but it didn't

I'd been told they cut off my wet clothes. I sat there wondering if I would have to wear Greg's robe out because I didn't have any clothes. I hobbled over to the wall of cupboards and kept opening until I found the one with my backpack. That's where they had hung my robe, draped over my backpack. As I pulled aside the softer than soft purple sleeve, a denim skirt and a white tee shirt, still with the price tags on them, sat on top of my backpack. *Pretty sharp whoever had left them. Jeans or pants would have been hard to get over my ankle.*

I smiled. "How thoughtful." When I checked the tags again, the store name matched the tag on the robe. *Greg, you're a pretty nice guy for someone I'll probably never see again.*

I picked up the clothes and found a pair of white lacey bikini underwear. *Well aren't you thorough, Mr. Greg. I wonder if you blushed when you bought these? No bra? Am I so thin it doesn't look like I need one?*

"How did you know what size I wear?" I said as I tried on my new outfit. I admired myself in the mirror. The Tee said, 'Welcome to Wyoming." *And Wyoming has given me a very interesting welcome to say nothing of its initiation.*

After I primped a little, I waited around to be checked out. I sat down in the chair and read the newspaper story about me. Holding up the paper, I scowled at my appearance. After folding my two newspapers to save, I thumbed through several magazines someone had left. It was hard concentrating and I couldn't tell you even what kind of magazine I had in my hand.

I balled my fists at not being in charge of my world.

For the last two weeks I had taken care of every aspect of my existence. Now I became dependent on outside forces and other people. It wasn't something I liked.

Luckily Papa came in. "Ciao, Il mio bambino. How are you today?" He rescued me from my self-pity.

"Great! I'm up walking around." I got up and modeled my new clothes plus my big black walking boot. I gracefully bowed. With the flourish of a professional model, I pointed at my boot. I showed him my sleeping boot. "I guess I'll be wearing these for six to eight weeks."

"I ran into the doctor down the hall and he says you are doing remarkably well. That's why they're releasing you today."

"I know. I just don't know what's next, though."

"I talked to Wil this morning."

"Is he coming by?"

"I told him I would take you out to his parents' ranch. They've invited me to stay there too, so they can get to know us."

"That'll be nice. It's always good to have my papa around. I've missed you."

"Since I didn't know when this all would happen, I need to go check out of my hotel. You know what a cheapskate I am. I wouldn't want to pay for another day! Then I'll be back to pick you up. Okay?"

"What about my dog?"

"Don't worry. We can pick him up after you check out."

"Now that's something that really excites me."

"Do you know where he is?"

"My friend Greg left me the vet's card. Here." I picked up the card off my tray.

"I'll check MapQuest and find out how to get there." He threw me a kiss then waved as he exited the room.

"Ciao, Papa."

It seems like everything is falling in place. So why am I feeling like a limp flower?

Chapter 67
A Real Reunion

As we passed a Walmart on the way to the vet's, I sat up. "Stop, Papa!" I always yelled just like that when I wanted to snap a photo—something Pop became used to. "How about an early birthday present, Papa? I don't have any clothes, and. . ." I looked sheepish. "My phone died going over the falls."

"Having you safe is worth every dollar." He spun the wheel to aim for the parking lot.

With help from the spikey-haired young clerk who pointed us down a long aisle to women's wear, I didn't take too much time to pick out some underwear, a mini shift in pale blue plus white sandals. Though I could only wear one of them, the sandal looked a lot better than my well-traveled hiking boot that had made it through my rescue. Because the evenings were still cold in June, the perky girl next to me suggested a navy blue sweater she thought would go with everything.

The tech section had a smart phone just like my old one. "You mind, Papa?"

On the way out, I noticed some lip-gloss and mascara on the make up aisle. "It's going to take most of my savings to pay you back for all this stuff."

He shook his head. "Let's not worry about that now."

The curly haired check out clerk recognized me. I didn't mean to cut her short with her questions about my rescue, but I was so eager to see Rambo.

Back out on the road, Pop veered into McDonald's.

We sat across the table munching our Big Macs. "Oh, Papa. I love you!" I poked in a mouthful of fries.

"As much as you love that Big Mac."

"Ask me after I'm finished!"

As we drove up to the vet's office, I barely waited for the car to stop at the curb. I tore into the waiting room painted pale blue. I'd read that was a soothing color. It wasn't working for me at that moment.

I stood at the counter. "Just a moment." The dark-haired woman behind the desk pushed a curly strand of dark hair behind her ear.

I teetered from one foot to the other noticing the wall mural of all kinds of pets plus farm animals. I wondered where the horses and the cows entered for their treatment, certainly not through the waiting room where I stood fidgeting.

She finished whatever captured her attention on the computer then glanced over her half glasses. " Sorry. I needed to finish this prescription." She removed a page from the printer and handed it to the lady behind me. "May I help you?"

"I'm here for my dog Rambo. Greg uh. . .brought him in a couple of days ago." I blushed. I didn't know Greg's last name. *I have to make a point of noticing that info in my news article.*

The receptionist stood. "Have a seat. I'll see if the doctor can see you."

"Wait!" I followed her.

She paused. "Why don't you take a seat out in the waiting room? I'll bring him out." She swished into a long hallway.

"Oh. Okay. I'm just so excited to see him. . ." Just then I heard a bevy of yelps and whimpers that most certainly came from Ram.

"But. . ." Ram must have heard my voice.

She pointed toward the front desk.

Papa had parked the car and stood at the front desk when I returned to the foyer.

"I just thought of something. I don't have any money to pay the vet bill, either."

"Isn't that what fathers are for?"

I hugged him.

When I heard Rambo's excited yips, I spun around. He strained against the leash held by the attendant. His tail wagged his whole rear end as I rushed toward him.

I dropped to the floor and hugged him.

When he jumped with his paws on my shoulders, down I went flat on my back with Rambo washing my face. His thick tail thumped against the wall. We tussled on the shiny floor with me crying. "Oh Rambo! You're better!"

"Sorry," I looked up at the attendant as she stood over me laughing. "No doubt about whose dog he is."

Rambo's whimpers, yips and whines—what sweet music to accompany my heartbeat!

When I sat up I realized that I couldn't get off the floor. Number one, Rambo was all over me. Number two my ankle clothed in the bulky black boot wouldn't accommodate me. The way it felt, if I did try to get up I would re-break my ankle or I'd have to crawl over to a chair to hoist myself up.

Thank goodness Papa came to my rescue. Behind me, he reached under my armpits and boosted me up. It reminded me of being a little girl when I danced on his toes.

The doctor came out of an examining room laughing at the scene on her office floor. She scratched her thick mane of steel gray hair. "Well, somebody's glad to see you!"

"Thank you so much for taking care of Ram. How is he?"

Well, as you can see, he's looking pretty good. I took care of the wound. He still has an infection going on."

I eyed Ram's scruffy fur where I assumed the duct tape had been snipped away. Rambo scanned me with his big brown eyes while he talked to me with little whimpers. "I see you have better bandages than my duct tape. Hope is wasn't too hard to take off." I patted his head.

"If you hadn't stitched the wound, he probably would have lost too much blood. He could have died before I got to see him." She handed me a pill container. "These are antibiotics to fight his infection. Directions are on the bottle."

"Any other things I should know?"

"He'll need to have those stitches out next week. Though one thing I'd like to know—How did he get those slashes?"

"We were attacked by a grizzly bear. Rambo leaped up to protect me. The bear just swatted Ram aside like swatting a fly."

"And you? How did you escape the grizzly?"

"A lucky strike with my sling shot. My stone caught the beast in the eye."

"Oh yes, I remember reading your story in the paper. You had quite a. . ."

"An adventure. Yes I did."

Papa stepped up. "How much do we owe you?"

240

"Not a thing. Greg took care of the bill this morning."

Learning that information, I'm sure I could have caught flies in my gapping mouth. "Pretty special guy, huh?"

"I'd say so. Always been that way. I've known him since he was a kid. His mom and I have been friends since high school."

"Thanks again. If you see Greg, please tell him I am very grateful for his kindness."

"Will do."

Once outside Rambo took care of business. I could hardly contain him on the way to the car. "Mind if I sit in the backseat with him, Papa? Papa scratched the back of his head. "I think if you didn't, he'd be trying to leap in front to be with you. Guess you two bonded."

"Neither of us would be here without the other."

Pop bent down to give Rambo a good back rub and a hug. "Thanks, boy, for taking care of my little girl."

Chapter 68
At the Ranch

After being lost in the forests of northwestern Wyoming, the austere beauty of Casper and Douglas lay out in stark contrast. I had to be thankful that I wasn't lost in this country, for I don't think I would have survived. Small rolling mounds covered in prairie brush and grasses spread for miles in front of us. Snow still capped the distant mountains. With a hand out the window, I could tell it felt much warmer here. The scenery was beautiful in its own stark way, but I found myself missing the green timber of Oregon.

In the backseat I cuddled up with Rambo. After a good reacquainting with him, I called my best friend, Deanne. We were both very excited to speak to each other. Of course, I retold my story in detail. When I finished, I asked her to send me everyone's cell number. As much I wanted to be connected again, I have to admit that two weeks off line really was way less painful than I thought it would be. Too busy living to miss it, I guess. After my call to Deanne, I soon fell asleep cuddling with Rambo.

I woke to the gravel kicking up from the tires as we traversed the long entry road into Wil's ranch. We passed through the sculpted metal arch bearing the name, Wild Warren Ranch. A combination of those three initials made up the brand's design.

I sat up with Rambo rolling his eyes up at me from my lap. I ran my hand down his back and out his tail. "Good boy." He sat up panting.

I'm sure our approach had not been a secret as the dust flew around our car and in its wake. I don't know what I expected for Wil's ranch. I knew it covered a number of acres. We made our way to the sprawling ranch house perched on a rise. The massive log house with rugged stone pillars framing the entryway made an awesome impression. It looked nothing like *the little log cabin* Wil described.

Maybe I expected someone would come out to greet us, namely Wil. Then we would race toward each other like I had dreamed, but no. Papa and I climbed the broad stairway up to the porch that stretched the full length of the house with nothing but some beautiful empty rustic rockers.

"Wow, Papa. Some ranch! Huh?"

"You done good, girl. You picked a winner."

"Oh. . .maybe better than a doctor you always wanted me to marry?"

Considering this rustic opulence, I should quit panicking about losing my engagement ring.

We rang the bell then knocked with the giant brass knocker that hung in the middle of a stunning, carved, wooden door. We waited a bit before an elegant woman opened the door. Her auburn hair streaked with gray swirled up into a chignon. So I could see where Wil got his rusty hair.

She touched the collar of her peach silk shirt with her French manicured nails. "Oh my dear Gabriella." With an arm around me, she gave me half a hug then kissed the air next to my cheek.

"So good to meet you, Mrs. Warren." As I addressed her, I had hoped she would say something like, "Oh call me..." but she didn't. I realized I didn't know her name. Wil always referred to her as Mom.

She smoothed her hand down her doe-colored straight skirt.

"Vito." Papa shook her outstretched hand, "Beautiful place you have here."

"Come in, won't you?"

She looked askance at Rambo. I held his leash near his collar. I hoped she didn't hear his small rolling growl.

I surveyed the high-beamed ceiling and the massive fieldstone fireplace that rose all the way up to the beamed ceiling, but I didn't see Wil.

"Is Wil here?"

"Oh. Yes he's out in the barn. He should be back by now. He's with his dad. They went for a ride. Let me have Rocky show you. Rocky?"

Rocky came through the doorway, nearly filling it like John Wayne.

"Rocky, this is Vito and Gabriella DiCarlo."

I smiled up at him.

"They'll be staying with us for a few days."

She turned toward us. "Rocky will take your bags upstairs. Then he can park your car around back if that's okay."

My eyes followed the unique wooden stairway wind up to the second floor. Each newel was a twisting branch and totally different than the one next to it.

"Sure." My dad dropped the keys in Rocky's open palm. "Gabi's clothes are in the shopping bags along with the backpack."

"Very good, sir."

"Maybe I might just slip round the back of the house to surprise Wil in the barn?"

Her face stiffened. "Well, I suppose you could. Just follow the porch around to your left."

As I stepped back outside, a breeze refreshed me from the atmosphere that imitated a posh hotel. The meeting had made feel totally misplaced.

"Come on Ram. Let's go see Wil." I quickened my step to a jog.

A bit further out than I thought it might be, the large red barn with white trim looked just like a magazine picture.

As I came closer, I heard yelling. I paused for a moment. "Wil?" The yelling stopped.

"Wil?"

Rambo growled. "Be good, Ram. It's Wil."

As he sauntered out of the barn, Wil wiped his hands on his jeans. He greeted me with a broad grin. The sun lit his russet side burns as he tilted his cowboy hat back. "Gabi!" He swung me around.

His strong male smell couldn't eclipse my favorite aftershave.

"Mm." I squeezed him back.

"When I saw your car coming, we hustled the horses back from our ride. "Hey Dad." He yelled into the barn. "Gabi's here."

A large man approached his hands outstretched. I could see where Wil got his smile.

His hug seemed more genuine than his wife's.

As we walked toward the house, Wil smiled big and drew me aside.

After he kissed me, I wiped my cheek. "You tickle." I wasn't sure about that beard. I missed seeing his dimples and his cleft.

Rambo barred his teeth. "No Rambo!"

Wil reached toward Ram but quickly withdrew his hand when Rambo barked.

"Okay, we'll give it some time." I patted Rambo's head.

His father continued on so I asked Wil. "What was that yelling I heard coming from the barn?"

"Oh that. He can't do anything right. I think we should fire him. Not much of a ranch hand. Nothing to worry about."

Chapter 69
Reacquainted?

Slowed by my gimp, we fell further behind his dad. I expressed interest in the rangeland, the animals, and my surprise at its magnitude. "It's very impressive."

He explained how they sectioned the land, the herds and their breeding. As we held hands, he raised them as though he was looking for my engagement ring.

A breeze blew. I cleared the strands of hair from my face. "I have a confession." My stomach tightened.

"Oh?" His raised his eyebrows.

"I don't know what happened to that beautiful ring you gave me. . .I lost a lot of weight. Somewhere in or out of the river, it must have slid off. I am so sorry."

He paused. "Don't you worry, I'm just glad you didn't lose more than that. Anyway I had it insured."

"Whew. I feel better."

"You'll want to freshen up before dinner. Let me show you your room."

In the room, I unpacked my meager belongings and put them in the empty drawer of a natural wood dresser that looked hand-hewn. The room was spacious like a suite. Dominating the room stood a rustic king size bed where tall tree trunks were polished posters. The bed had been turned down with the pale green linens that complemented the striped woven Indian blanket. *Was there a mint under the pillow?*

The whole affect had me imagining a uniformed attendant might knock to announce, "Room service."

After drawing the drapes open I stood for a moment taking in the vastness that spread toward the snow capped mountains. Visible in the distance about a dozen horses grazed in a nearby pasture.

The early evening sky framed the scene like a painting.

With this tranquil setting why is it that I somehow feel unsettled?

As I undressed, the full-length mirror reflected my thin body from a different angle than just looking down at it. I smiled. *At least I won't have to worry about what I eat. Mm, hamburgers, steaks, fries, cookies, pies and ice cream!*

Luxuriating in the strong spray of warm water, I spent a long time showering and washing my hair. Fortunately a hair drier sat on the sink board. I tamed my hair then braided the front across to the side and left the back flowing down my shoulders.

After that I smeared on my lip-gloss and rolled on mascara. I stared into the mirror, patted my hair and kissed the air. *Not too bad, wild woman.*

Rocky said he would take Rambo to the stable where the other dogs stayed. I missed him. *When I'm in my own place I'll have my dog inside.*

I prepared to descend the massive circular staircase. I had to think about the steps considering what the therapist said about using stairs. Slowly I reached for the rail to steady myself, experiencing the ultra smooth finish to the gnarled wood banister.

The sound of crying captured my attention. I listened. Still at the top of the stairs, I glanced down to the entryway. I paused, a bit ashamed I was eavesdropping on the scene below.

Wil stood near the open doorway with his arms wrapped around a dark haired girl. They rocked together for a moment.

"We thought she died. We didn't know. We should have waited."

I ducked when she gazed up at him, red-nosed and tear-stained. "Wasn't what we felt real?"

"Sure, but . . ."

"Are you going to tell her?"

"The situation is complicated."

"We have a lot of history. It's as simple as you and me the way it's always been until you went away to school—or it's not."

"Well she's here now and. . ."

"And you have to tell her, or I will."

"All right. I'll talk to her. Go home now. I'll call you later."

"Promise?" She grabbed behind his neck, pulling him down to her and kissed him.

Chapter 70
Decision Time

After some time passed, though I don't know how long I sat there, I rose. With my arms crossed, I stood in front of the window. The scene had changed. A deep blue sky hosted a million stars as the moon provided enough light to see the silhouettes of the horses still out enjoying a beautiful summer night.

Was I just surprised at this revelation of Wil with someone else? Hurt? Sad? Was I jealous? Did I feel relieved? Am I annoyed I could lose to another woman? Was he being kissed or did he kiss back? It's not as if you didn't kiss some one else, Gabi. And did you kiss him back? Even if I didn't kiss Greg back, I felt something more than just, "Gee thanks."

I knew I needed to analyze my true feelings before Wil and I talked.

Wondering if Pop had already gone down for dinner, I limped down the hallway to his room. I knocked. "Hey Papa, Are you there? Could we talk?"

"Just a minute."

"Okay."

I felt so relieved when he answered the door that I threw my arms around his neck, immediately awash in the fresh smell of his aftershave.

"Cara mia, what's wrong?"

I sputtered out what I witnessed in the foyer and also my feelings for Greg.

"Come sit down. He sat on the edge of the bed and patted the space next to him.

After I sat, I couldn't look at him. I just sat, head bent, wiping my eyes, or watching my hands curl together. All of my explaining just confused me more. "What should I do, Papa?" I sniffed.

"Well. . .Only you know what's in your heart."

He hugged me close. "Maybe just ask yourself a couple of questions like, "Do I want to spend the rest of my life with Wil and never see Greg again?"

"I'll think about that. For now, I suppose we should go downstairs for dinner."

"C'mon." Papa wrapped his arm around my waist. " You'll know what to do. Let's go."

I pushed myself off the edge of the bed like I weighed a ton.

"There, now." He handed me a Kleenex. "Something wonderful about being young and having the rest of your life with all those possibilities in your own hands."

Suddenly I felt empowered.

Chapter 71
Dinner Date with Destiny

I knew dinner would be hard for me—probably difficult for Wil as well. Wil held out my chair as we sat next to each other. Were we trying to avoid eye contact? I forced a smile as I sat down.

The atmosphere around the table seemed strained, or was it just me? Had Wil also consulted with his parents?

Conversation started slowly. I suppose to assume Wil's family would be interested in me, interested in my amazing two weeks is a bit self-centered. They did ask a question or two. When I began to expand the answers they changed the subject to the livestock auctions or the upcoming rodeo. I guess they had read the papers and heard Wil's rendition so my version wouldn't add much.

His parents all but ignored my papa. It occurred to me that his parents already knew something between Wil and I wasn't right. Perhaps they just tried to sidestep any family bonding until everything was settled.

Nothing would, however, stop me from enjoying the big fat steak that I heaped on my plate as the platter came to me. Butter and sour cream on my baked potato had me drooling. Everyone eating eased the tension around the table. It seemed like a very long time since I had so enjoyed a meal. I ate until I almost burst my new sundress.

Afterwards, I helped Mrs. Warren serve the three tiered chocolate cake topped with vanilla ice cream.

"Coffee anyone?"

"Not for me, Mom."

Pop raised his hand. "Sure, black, please."

"No thanks. I am stuffed. Couldn't have been more delicious." I patted my stomach.

"Well, why don't you kids go on then?"

"I could help with the dishes."

"That's okay. Maria will take care of them."

I faced toward Wil. "I'd love to go sit on that beautiful porch."

As we stepped out into the fresh air I took in a deep breath and let it out. That helped ease the tension I felt. "What a beautiful night."

"Yeah, it is."

Once outside, we strolled, or rather he strolled. I hobbled, to the end of the porch and back to the rocking chairs without saying another word. I sat in one of the chairs, folded my hands in my lap and rocked for a moment. Then he eased into the rocker next to me.

When we both started to speak at once, I asserted myself. "It isn't necessary to tell me about this afternoon in the foyer or what happened in the past two weeks."

"Were you spying on me?"

"Not exactly." I looked off in the distance wishing I were anywhere else but on this porch. "After I left my room, I started down the stairs." I paused, "Because with this," I pointed to my boot. "I don't move very fast. I couldn't help hearing the crying plus a little bit of your conversation. So I stood still. I guess I should have gone back up stairs, but I was glued to the spot."

He crossed his legs, resting one hand on a knee, stilling his rocker as he stared out into the open space. He scratched his beard.

I don't know what I expected in his explanation, but I remained silent and waited until he spoke.

"Lily and I were together for years, all through elementary school then high school. We were king and queen at the senior prom."

"So if you didn't feel something for her, I'd be surprised."

"I don't know what it is, but when I thought you were dead. . ."

"If there are doubts about us in your mind then you'll understand that. . .that I have doubts, too."

His head snapped up from peering out to the landscape. He stared my way, eyebrows pinched and his mouth slightly ajar. "You do?"

"After those. . .perilous experiences on my adventure, I became a different person. I started out as a naïve girl afraid to even fly. I came back a very self- sufficient woman."

He nodded his head. "I can see how that might happen."

"It's not that I don't love you. I do. How much, I don't know."

252

I fiddled with my sweater. "We were best friends." I looked over at him. "What I would like to see is where my new persona is going."

Could that be an expression of relief I saw on his face?

I flipped my hair over my shoulder. "So what I'm saying is that we both have to re-evaluate what's next." When our eyes connected, I saw it all clearly. "I think I want to go back to Oregon."

Did I just want to zap him back for his relationship with Lily? I sat for a moment to think through telling him about Greg—how I felt when I am with him. Then I decided, no. It's more about me doubting that Wil is the one.

"Are you sure?" He scratched his nose.

"What are you feeling?"

He leaned forward with his elbows on his knees. "I am feeling okay."

"I think you need to explore what's here for you." I stood up. "I think Pop and I will be going tomorrow."

He leaned back, rocking for a minute or two. "Okay."

"See you in the morning?"

"Yeah."

Just as I opened the front door, I glanced back at Wil.

When I saw him reach for his cell, I realized I made the right decision, not just for me but also for him.

As I walked inside, clunking my boot across the wide planks in the entryway, I envisioned a very big grin on the face of a dark-haired girl named Lily.

A smile inched across my face.

Chapter 72
So?

Breakfast seemed a little stilted but still cordial.

Rocky stowed our luggage in the trunk of our car while Wil and I stood on the porch, facing each other with not much else to say.

Standing on my tiptoes, I kissed Wil's cheek. "Bye." I swallowed a lump in my throat. This meant I was probably losing a good friend, my best friend, and that I might never see him again. I wiped my eyes as I descended the stairs and made my way to the car.

Papa suggested that I sit in back with Rambo. "There." I opened the door and tossled the fur on Ram's neck. He hopped in with me right after him.

"Ready?" Papa started up the car.

"Yup. Let's go."

As we drove off, Wil remained on the front porch with his hands in his pockets. When I waved he answered with a tip of his Stetson.

Pop and I talked about driving back to Oregon together. It would have been a great bonding experience though Papa had to get back. If we did drive, it'd have to be a push to get back in a short time, not a leisurely drive. His crew was ready to go out fishing again. It wasn't so much that Pop needed the money, though he had spent a lot on this trip to Wyoming. Pop's crew did need the money. The tides were right. Anyway, I was anxious to get home. It seemed like a year since I'd been there. Flying meant that Rambo would have to be crated. "It's a short flight, Ram."

I felt a little guilty when they took Rambo's crate to board. Once on the plane, we stowed our gear overhead. I sat back in my window seat and let out a deep, breath.

Pop took my hand as it rested on the arm of the seat. "You okay, dolce cuore?"

"I am, Papa. I'm just fine."

I leaned back and relaxed as the plane rose in the air.

I recalled the last time I boarded an airplane. I was filled with great angst at the thought my first flight. In my mind, I'd rehashed all the dangers of flying. Now I just found the thrust of take off like a ride at Disneyland. I smiled. "Imagine being me afraid of flying, Papa? When I boarded that airplane in Portland only three weeks ago, I gripped the armrests with white knuckles."

He squeezed my hand.

"And now what's a little thing like being thousands of feet in the air, buckled into the seat of a heavy metal contraption that resembles a bird to those on the ground?"

I stared out the window enjoying the clouds floating in the sapphire blue sky. I thought about my adventure when Gran's voice spoke to me. So I turned to Papa and recited, "Straight from Gran. 'Thou wilt show me the path of my life, in thy presence is fullness in joy and at thy right hand there are pleasures for evermore.' Psalms 16 verse 11."

As I smiled at Papa, I heard a familiar voice emanating from the aisle. "Excuse me ma'am. Is there anything I can do for you?"

My pulse quickened as I beamed up at the handsome man with sparkling blue eyes grinning at me.

"Greg?"

"I hope you don't mind that I switched my assignment to be on your flight."

Everyone told me I should write a book about my Wyoming adventure. So I did.

Visual Mysteries abound in the workings of an author's mind, especially when the author is an artist. Karen Nichols relocated to Oregon from Southern California where she was a teacher. Beside Elementary school, Karen has given workshops in drawing and writing. She wrote and illustrated a number of children's books. Her artwork appears in books, in logos, and on book covers. Her fine art paintings, sculptures, novels and poetry books are currently shown in Backstreet Gallery, Florence, OR.

She has written articles for the Siuslaw News, for Backstreet Gallery as their Marketing Manager and was the managing editor for Carapace Scrawlers' Writer's Journal containing stories by the Coastal Writers Group. She is a board member of Florence Regional Arts Alliance and also The Florence Festival of Books.

After taking a class, "Drawing on the Right Side of the Brain", she emerged with an adult book swirling through her mind. Thornton House, a spellbinding mystery, with a dynamite ending, is her first novel. Completed next, The Unexpected Gift is an inspirational novel where a Marine reclaims purpose and trust through redemption and the love of a childhood friend plus a very special dog. Inspired by real people, Second Chance Heart is a stirring love story between a man, a woman and a child during their struggle to reclaim joy while learning to trust. This latest novel, Triumph over Fear, takes an Oregonian girl to the wilds of Wyoming, alone with her dog Rambo, on a journey of death-defying adventures and back again. All her novels have ties to the Oregon Coast and include a subplot involving dogs.

Find them on Amazon.com under Karen D. Nichols or -

http://www.amazon.com/s/ref=nb_sb_noss?url=searchalias%3Dstripbooks&fieldk eywords=Karen+D.+Nichols++

She lives in Oregon with her husband, Ralph, and Buddy, her King Charles Cavalier Spaniel, who always noses into her novels.

Bibliography

The Bible: King James Version

"You'll never Walk Alone"
Music by Richard Rogers
Lyrics by Oscar Hammerstein II
Show Tune from Rodgers and Hammerstein musical, Carousel
1945

"Take Me Home, Country Roads"
Music by Bill Danoff and Taffy Nivert
John Denver's Album "Poems Prayers, and Promises"
1971

Piper, Watty (pen name of Arnold Munk)
The Little Engine that Could
Published by Platt & Munk
New York, New York 1930